The Mortician's Clue

Miss Hayward and the Detective series

By Helen Goltz

Atlas Productions

The Mortician's Clue
First published in 2022
Copyright © Helen Goltz 2022

Atlas Productions
Greenslopes QLD 4102
Web: www.atlasproductions.com.au
This book is a work of fiction. Names, characters, places and incidents are either the product of the author's imagination or are used fictitiously. Any resemblance to actual persons, living or dead, or to actual events or locales is entirely coincidental. Any medical experiments or results cited in this novel have been fictionalised and any slight of specific people, experiments, research or organisations is unintentional.

Proofread by: Penny Clarkson, https://ariadneproofing.wixsite.com/ariadneproofreading
Cover images: Victorian woman by KathySG, Shutterstock; Woman's head by Ironika, Shutterstock; Grave by Rudy and Peter Skitterians, Pixabay; Graveyard background by Gaby Stein, Pixabay; Angel by Emsalgado, Pixabay.
Cover design by Atlas Productions.

NATIONAL
LIBRARY
OF AUSTRALIA

A catalogue record for this book is available from the National Library of Australia

Dedicated to my eccentric, trail-blazing, great aunts:

'Pip' (Frances Maud) Goggins

'Connie' (Annie Constance) Goggins.

Author's note:

I have taken a few historical liberties in relation to the death industry in this novel which is set in 1889. While the word "mort" has been around for centuries, the term *mortician* was believed to have been first used in 1895 when *The Embalmers' Monthly* magazine suggested the industry needed a new name that was less confronting than undertaker. Hence mort plus physician became mortician. I have introduced it six years earlier.

Also, it was not until late in the 19th century and early 20th century that the undertakers/funeral directors prepared the deceased on their premises, removing the death scene from the home. There were exceptions to this. For example, the hospitals paid undertakers to remove and bury a body if a patient died in the hospital and had no one to claim them, and on occasion, a bachelor's estate paid for the undertaker to do the duties normally performed by the family. For the purposes of our story and characters, we are a little ahead of our time.

For those fascinated by this era, there is more detail and my references at the end of the novel.

Chapter 1

Miss Matilda Hayward braced as she turned the page of her book; it was a particularly ghastly crime mystery and Matilda was pleased she was reading it in the daylight and not alone in bed at night. She was not one for sitting idle and reading, but sometimes the twilight demanded it – that brief time between the light of the day fading and the dark of the evening – calling for relaxation. Although, admittedly there was a purpose to her reading. Seeing her brother, Daniel, bound up the path of the family home in Highgate Hill, Matilda put her bookmark between the pages and closed her book.

'Early mark?' he asked, dropping beside her, shrugging off his jacket at the same time. 'This infernal heat.' He took a handkerchief from his coat pocket and mopped his brow.

Matilda flicked open her large, ornate fan and fanned them both. 'It's almost over, autumn is knocking.' She waved a book at him. 'And no, I did not get an early mark. I am working. I've been assigned two books to review for the next issue of the *Women's Journal*. Mrs Lawson likes to choose a different writer every month to do the reviews, so the perspective is always fresh. She's amazing,' Matilda said, thinking of her editor, of whom she was in awe. The three days a week she spent in the company of Mrs Dora Lawson and the ladies of the journal was the highlight of her week, and she was learning so much.

'That's not by a female author though,' Daniel read the book's spine and stated the obvious.

'No. There are no new books for the next issue by female writers, sadly,' she sighed. 'But this is very good. There's just been a most intriguing murder. It is a little scary though.'

'Give Thomas the heads-up and see if he can solve it before you reach the end,' Daniel joked, referring to his closest friend since childhood and now Matilda's beau, Detective Thomas Ashdown. He nudged her: 'Only a few months until the wedding, and then he'll be on hand every night to protect you if you are frightened.'

Matilda smirked at the brother she was closest to of the four; she was well used to his teasing. 'I don't frighten that easily.'

No sooner had Daniel mentioned Thomas, than a hansom cab pulled up out the front of the Hayward household and he alighted. He said something to the driver who remained to wait for him.

'He's not staying,' Matilda said, rising to greet him as Thomas opened the gate and made his way up the long path to the front veranda to the waiting pair. She brushed down her pale blue dress and hoped her hair was still presentable.

'Matilda, Daniel!' He took Matilda's hand and pressed a kiss to it. She smiled at him with affection.

'You look particularly handsome today,' she teased.

'I can't help it,' he said and laughed at her wry expression. 'You look beautiful as you do every day.' He held her gaze and then, remembering Daniel was there, Thomas cleared his throat and looked at him. 'Ah, Daniel. You're looking well too,' he joked. 'Interesting day in court, wasn't it?'

'Indeed,' Daniel grinned. Like his brothers, Daniel still found it peculiar to watch Thomas and Matilda courting, having all grown up together as friends.

'Why? What happened?' Matilda asked keenly.

'I was illustrating an intriguing court case today,' Daniel said, 'a man accused of murdering his wife was on the stand, and in she walked.'

'No!' Matilda exclaimed. 'That's a good thing, is it not?'

'For him it was,' Thomas agreed, 'he gets to return to his home and own bed tonight instead of the jail cell. I am sorry, but I have to run,' he said with a glance behind to make sure the cab was still waiting. 'I just called to apologise that I could not stop by tonight.'

'That makes sense,' Daniel said, hovering around them, to Matilda's dismay.

'I'm sorry,' Thomas said again, hoping it would not upset Matilda. With a recent spate of crime in the city, he had been a most unreliable date of late.

'I understand. What's happened?' she asked, always keen for a story.

He grimaced. 'Just police business.'

'You know I will find out, Thomas, so do save me the time, please,' she begged. 'Even just a morsel of information, given you have to choose crime over me?'

He groaned, and she smiled, knowing too well after years of competing against her brothers and Thomas as children, how to get to Thomas's soft underbelly.

He relented. 'I won't know until I get to the scene of the crime, but I believe a body has been found – my second one today,' he added with a glance at Daniel. 'Only this one is a young lady wearing her pyjamas.'

'Oh my, how extraordinary. Where?' Matilda asked.

Again, his lips thinned before declaring, 'On the steps of the Catholic Church near the river in South Brisbane.'

'Not the church we go to, then?' she asked.

Thomas shook his head and muttered an oath about the heat, which Daniel agreed with while Matilda continued to pry.

'I can't tell you anymore as I don't know myself,' he assured her. 'Please don't go there,' he said hurriedly, knowing she might show up on the guise of writing for the newspaper. 'Promise me?'

'No,' she said.

Daniel laughed and then sobered at seeing his friend's expression. 'At least she's honest.'

Thomas rolled his eyes. 'Promise me you won't go there unaccompanied?'

'Of course not,' she assured him, which seemed to satisfy Thomas. 'Promise me you will be careful?' Matilda added.

'Yes.' Tipping his hat, he bid them farewell, and with

another glance at Matilda, he was off again, down the path and to his waiting ride. Matilda studied him most intensely as he walked away.

'What is it?' Daniel asked. 'He'll be alright, Harry will meet him there for sure,' he assured his sister of Thomas's long-term police partner's involvement.

'It's not that.' She watched as he departed in the cab with a wave. She turned to Daniel. 'The lady in her pyjamas, dead on the church steps… that's the very subject of the murder in my book.'

Chapter 2

One week prior…

The Valley Literary Society had been known to be a rowdy bunch, despite the expectation they were learned and artistic.

'Not your best work, Jones, get off,' one harsh critic yelled to the young man on stage reciting a poem from a book he hoped to publish to great acclaim. There were cheers and jeers – some at the critic and some at young Jones, who threw his hands up in the air, ground his cigarette into the floor, and gave up mid-recital.

'What rhymes with sex?' a well-inebriated patron at the table behind author Linton Turner asked as he scribbled notes, writing amidst the writers and poets present.

'Vex,' Linton Turner called over his shoulder in all seriousness and got a round of laughs from the colleagues around his table. He chose his friends carefully – they indulged him, pandered to his ego, and were happy to bask in his success. Nearing his fortieth year, the men in Turner's circle ranged in ages but mostly younger. All were affluent or had patrons that allowed them to live the bohemian lifestyle of an artist. Turner did not need patronage; his books' success made him a self-made man. Although the manner in which he frivolously spent, did give rise to some lean times between publication.

'You can't keep us hanging, Linton, give us the last chapter tonight,' his friend, a fellow writer, said, as he arrived back at the table of six men with a round of drinks and dropped into a chair opposite.

Turner took the offered drink, thanked him, and raised the glass in a toast to success. Arms met in the middle of the table, clinking glasses, before taking the first gulp of the goodly spirit. Turner sat back and ran a hand over his moustache as he thought about the request. The book was complete, what harm would it do to read out the ending, given most of the members would not spend money from their own purse to buy it, and find out for themselves the conclusion?

A woman flitted by and touched his shoulder as she passed him. Turner grabbed her hand and kissed it with affection, before releasing her and earning a look of adoration. He was a renowned ladies' man and heartbreaker, and easily the most successful of the writers amongst the members of the Valley Literary Society. There were many women present this evening, keen to mix with the artistic types and lead their eccentric life, and not all were ladies of the night. Singers, actresses and dancers counted amongst their mix, but rarely a female writer was seen in the club.

'What do you say, darling? Shall I?' Turner asked the young woman seated on his lap with far too much bosom showing and far too much rouge on her face.

'I think you best read it,' she said in a child-like voice, looking up at him with adoration. 'Otherwise, that poor lady in the pyjamas will be a source of worry for us all.'

He laughed and kissed her forehead. 'Well, we don't want you not sleeping at night in *your* pyjamas, my dear.'

'I don't wear anything to bed,' she teased.

'I'm sure you don't,' he said, feeling his body react in a way expected. He cleared his throat. 'Right then, I shall give you the final chapter and the fate of the lady in blue silk pyjamas.' His group cheered. Linton Turner nudged the young woman off his lap and settled her on his friend's lap beside him. She quickly adapted to her new surroundings.

He made his way to the stage with much applause and cheers. Through the hazy, smoky, and dim room, he could see there was a full house tonight and the drinks and entertainment were flowing. They had been a good audience for his writing, and several of his colleagues provided constructive thoughts in the cold light of the next morning when their heads were clearer, and the cloud from last night's adventures had lifted.

Linton Turner took to the stage, seated himself on the chair in the middle of it, and pulled a well-worn pad from his jacket pocket. He flicked to the appropriate page.

'Ladies and gentlemen, I present for your amusement, shock and gratification, the last chapter of my book to be released next week, *The Pyjama Girl Mystery*.'

A hearty round of applause, cheers and boot-stomping preceded and when the room quietened, Linton Turner cleared his throat, sat up taller, and began to read.

Chapter 3

Now…

Detective Thomas Ashdown tried to focus on the scene he was about to encounter – his mentor and partner, Detective Harry Dart had told him that was the best way to avoid trauma in the job. Think about what he might see and prepare for it in his mind before arrival – anticipate and deaden the shock. But his thoughts kept drifting to Matilda. It was two months until they married and then he wouldn't have to see her fleetingly; he would return to her every evening, hold her, have the honour of providing for her, and see her first thing every morning. He would also be vexed, frustrated and worried constantly about her, especially in her role with the *Women's Journal*, but that was a price he was prepared to pay, for now.

Often as he lay in bed at night, he thought of the time he had barged into the Hayward house with Daniel by his side, worried she had been attacked, to find her sitting with the housekeeper Harriet, applying a salve to her bruises.

Matilda's hair was loose, her shirt unbuttoned to the base of her creamy throat. The image had not left his mind. Soon, he would be privy to seeing her like that as often as he desired, and no one else would have the privilege. It had been a long friendship leading to his courting, and worth the wait.

The hansom cab driver stopped as close as he could get to the church, where an audience of onlookers and the press had gathered. Thomas groaned at the spectacle. He jumped down from the cab, paid and thanked the driver, and hustled his way through the crowd. The light was fading now which he hoped might drive some of the on-lookers home. He saw his partner, Harry, talking with one of the junior constables. He knew the day was approaching when he would not find Harry's face amongst the crowd. But Harry assured him that was a couple of years away, despite his wife having other plans and dreams, and hoping Harry would retire sooner. Thomas suspected she would win.

They were well partnered – Harry the experienced older detective and mentor, and Thomas the young gun, who between them had achieved the best success rate for solving crime in the state. He stopped near the constable and turned to the crowd.

'Ladies and gentlemen,' he raised his voice for attention. 'If you were a witness or have something to contribute, please remain and our constables will get to you as soon as possible for a statement. If you are not, please leave now, as we will close this crime scene shortly, and anyone remaining will be here all night.'

Of course that wasn't true, but it worked. He glanced to Harry, who hid his smile and noted the constables looking confused. How one closed a crime scene in a public space was a mystery to them all, short of bringing in ropes and tents. But for now, it was working as people departed, having the luxury of returning to their homes tonight, which the young lady in her pyjamas on the step did not have.

'Nice work,' Harry said.

'It'll be short-lived.' Thomas sighed. 'A fresh round of passing busy-bodies will no doubt replace them shortly.'

Thomas took the half dozen large, wide stairs to the church entrance where, on the top step, the body lay. He stood and observed the area before studying the young lady. He saw Harry step back and direct the constables again to speak with the few remaining people who claimed to know something. Harry was well aware of how Thomas operated. Thomas needed to study the scene and commit it to memory – get the big picture in case it represented something. He had missed a clue at the scene of the crime in his last case, but fortunately, or unfortunately, Matilda had picked it up and advised him the murder scene resembled a painting. She expected to be included in the investigation from then on, which he could not deny was fair enough.

He felt no inspiration from this scene – a young woman dead on the church step, like an orphan or a child abandoned. Her face hidden as her back was visible from the stairs and the street. Thomas moved closer to study her and recoiled. She was but one-and-twenty or younger perhaps, with fair hair, loose around her shoulders like an actress or artist might wear it. He could hear Matilda's aunt, Audrey, calling the victim "a modern miss" with a tinge of disdain.

He moved to a different angle. The facial damage was severe; identifying her would be a challenge and distressing for the family. She lay on her side, her hands joined as if in prayer and placed under her head, her knees and feet together. Her body was completely covered in pale blue silk pyjamas, which were buttoned at her neck, and finished at her wrists and ankles. The scene from behind was not unpleasant, but for the fact she was dead. To see her face was a different story. There were no visible wounds on her body, but Thomas could see the front of the skull had caved in, and given there was no blood on the stairs, it was likely she died elsewhere and was placed here.

'Poor little thing,' Harry said, joining him as they waited for the coroner. He beckoned for Constable Robinson to join them. The young, ambitious man hurried over.

'What do we have, Constable?' Thomas asked.

'Sir, Mrs Goodburn, over there,' he indicated a portly older woman carrying a tired bunch of flowers, 'found the body around 4pm. She does the church flowers, Sir, and was departing with the old bunch, having replaced them.'

Thomas interrupted. 'So, the body wasn't here when she arrived?'

'No, Sir.' He quickly checked his notes. 'She arrived an hour earlier. I guess she couldn't have missed it if she came in the front entrance.'

Thomas nodded and the constable continued.

'From the little she could see of the lady, she didn't

recognise her and is confident she is not a parishioner. Several other witnesses saw the body but thought it was a woman just sleeping.'

'In this heat, on stone steps in the late afternoon?' Thomas asked incredulously.

'There are often homeless people to be found around here, Sir, including women occasionally.'

'Sleeping it off in her pyjamas,' Harry said with a shake of his head.

'Thank you, Constable,' Thomas said, dismissing him to return to assisting the other constable with statements.

They saw the coroner arriving – the neat, dignified, and greying Dr Patrick Nevins, who looked older than his fifty-plus years, partly due to the limp and cane he sported. Thomas was pleased it was Patrick, the best in the business, and not his new gruff offsider. Patrick's limp was more pronounced at the end of the day when his walk was weary. He tapped with his cane across the path to join them, taking the stairs with caution.

'Gentlemen, I was just about to go home, dinner calling, but instead, I get to enjoy your fine company,' he joked.

'Ah, the same here,' Harry told him. 'Who would want to miss out on the adventure?'

'It's a bit different this time,' Thomas said, with a glance at the young lady.

Dr Nevins looked around Thomas. 'Indeed. Are you finished your observation?'

'I am, thank you,' Thomas said, and Harry nodded in agreement.

'Then I shall get to work. The lads will arrive shortly to remove the body.' He moved around them and squatted down beside the woman.

'Why don't you head home, Harry? We can look at this with fresh eyes in the morning. We won't be catching any killers tonight, given it looks like someone dumped rather than murdered the young lady here,' Thomas suggested. 'We have a crime scene to find in the light of day.'

Dr Nevins looked up. 'Thomas is right, this is a very clean death scene, and from the blow to the young lady's head, the death would not have been a clean one. There would have been a good amount of blood spilled. It won't be easy to identify her. The poor lass's face has taken a beating.'

'Dreadful,' Harry sighed. 'Alright, I'll head off then if I can't be of any more use. I'll tell the constables to leave once the body is removed.'

Dr Nevins rose, pushing his steel-rimmed glasses further up his nose, and waved over the two men who had arrived with a stretcher, and horse and cart to remove the body.

'Give me a few hours in the morning to study her,' he told them. 'After 11 o'clock I will have something for you. After midday would be even better.'

'Thanks, Patrick. I'll stay a little longer,' Thomas said, studying the young woman as she was being lifted and removed.

'What are you thinking?' Harry asked.

'That she looks very familiar.'

'Not a young woman you've had relations with?' Dr Nevins asked alarmed and Thomas gave him a wry look.

'No, I tend to remember them,' Thomas said, and Harry chuckled. 'Does she not ring any bells with you, Harry?'

Harry studied her again as she was put onto the stretcher. 'I'm sorry, Thom, but I can't say she does. Perhaps I have seen too many dead.'

'I know how you feel. They are my best company,' Dr Nevins joked.

The three men stood back and watched as the body was removed. Then Thomas brightened. He might get to pay a call on Matilda tonight after all.

Chapter 4

Matilda snapped her book closed, placed it on her dresser, and raced down the stairs for dinner. Harriet had already given her a hurry along, and now she was cutting it fine. It wasn't that her father was a stickler for dinner time, but Mary, the cook, was and she liked her meals to be eaten when ready. Matilda entered the dining room just as Mr Hayward was about to be seated. Daniel had entered seconds before her.

Harriet gave Matilda a wink as she placed bowls of roast vegetables and a gravy jug on the table beside the large cob of bread and serving of butter. 'It must be a riveting book.'

Matilda grinned and slipped into her seat beside her father, and opposite Daniel. 'I shall lend it to you when I am finished, Harriet, but best not to read it at night.'

Mr Hayward thanked Harriet as he selected a slice of bread and looked at his second eldest son, Daniel. 'Well, Matilda and I are most pleased to have your company tonight, Son,' he said with a smile. 'Is it a special occasion or were you just in the neighbourhood? You still live here, do you not?' he teased.

Daniel chuckled. 'On and off, if I may?' he asked in jest. 'But maybe not for long. Now that I have a reliable job illustrating at the court, I need to look to the future.'

Matilda's eyes widened with delight, and Daniel laughed.

'Yes, surprising as it may be, I am planning my future. I am, after all, six and twenty.'

'Good for you, Daniel. If I can be of assistance, just ask,' Mr Hayward said.

'Thank you, Pa. I may need your legal services, or Amos's if you prefer,' he referred to the eldest Hayward brother, a lawyer like his father, who had taken over Mr Hayward's practice.

'You are going to ask for Alice's hand in marriage?' Matilda clapped her hands together in glee.

He nodded. 'Someday soon. But first I need to get a home in order. Not a word,' he warned Matilda.

'Of course not,' she said, looking most indignant. 'But I'm very excited. Who would have thought that meeting my friend from the *Women's Journal* that fateful day at the Freak Show, of all places, would lead to such happiness?' She sighed. 'At last, I shall have a second sister!'

Just as Harriet brought in a large platter of roast turkey to the table, the front door opened and through the doorway, Matilda saw Elijah enter with Thomas by his side.

'Are we too late?' Elijah called out as they removed their coats and hats. 'Will Mary throw us out?'

Matilda stood with delight to welcome them both. Her

brother, now a doctor, rarely made it home for dinner, but Thomas was a surprise. He always had an open invitation to the Hayward household since he was a young lad, but more so now that he was engaged to Matilda.

On hearing her name, Mary stuck her head out of the kitchen. 'It's a good thing I always cook extra,' she said, pretending to be stern. 'Look at you two hungry boys, sit down and eat.'

Thomas gave her a grateful smile and Elijah gave Mary a quick kiss on the cheek, which made the mature Irish cook redden with pleasure, and she disappeared back into the kitchen. She had known the boys since they were lads.

'You made it!' Matilda said after Thomas had greeted her father – the head of the Hayward family – and taken a seat beside her.

'I didn't think I'd get away, but there was little we could do until tomorrow.'

'Perfect timing and we are glad for it,' Mr Hayward said. 'If Gideon was here, we'd have all the household present, Amos and Minnie excepted of course, now they are married.'

Elijah cleared his throat. 'Speaking of Gideon, I am worried about him,' he said of his twin and the youngest Hayward boy. He had the attention of the group now as they passed plates, serving out Cook's excellent fare.

'He seems to be enjoying the gallery work though and has proven himself to be a successful manager,' Daniel said, confused.

Elijah nodded. 'He has achieved a great deal already managing the gallery, but I fear he is a bit lost at the moment.'

'Pray, do tell,' Mr Hayward said, concerned.

Elijah sighed. 'I am worried if he keeps drinking with his current group of acquaintances, he will soon end up in one of Thomas's cells.'

Thomas grimaced. He couldn't show favour to a friend and soon-to-be brother-in-law, but he would be expected to do so. He could sense an uncomfortable scenario emerging.

'Is he still in the company of Miss Chappell?' Mr Hayward asked after Gideon's recent interest – Miss Lily Chappell, who held a flame for Elijah, and when that was unrequited, met his twin Gideon and moved her affection to him.

Matilda lowered her voice. 'They fight quite a bit, don't they?'

'Too much,' Elijah said. 'I think it will soon be over. Gideon has lost interest in going to non-stop social events, dances and theatre and Miss Chappell loves nothing more. For fear of being indelicate, I think she has a new beau and I think Gideon is both insulted and relieved.'

Matilda stiffened. 'Then we must occupy Gideon. I shall think how.'

'You seem to have done well with your matchmaking of late,' Thomas said. 'Elijah and Miss Urry, Daniel and Miss Doran. Work your magic on Gideon.'

Matilda smiled at her beau. 'Thank you, Thomas, how kind.'

He smiled at her excited little face.

'I shall work on it,' she said, tapping her chin in contemplation of whom she knew that was single, attractive and could suit her rather active brother with the short attention span.

'We best work on keeping him out of trouble then,' Daniel said with a glance at Thomas and his brother, Elijah. 'The gallery suits him as every month it is a new event, but clearly, we need to worry about his after-hours life.'

'Where is he tonight?' Mr Hayward asked.

Elijah shook his head. 'I dropped by the gallery and he had left. I came here, hoping to find him.'

There was a silence as everyone worried about the wayward member of the family. Finally, Matilda cleared her throat and said: 'Tell us about the crime, Thomas. Was it a lady in her pyjamas?'

Thomas looked to Mr Hayward for saving. 'Hardly dinner conversation,' he said.

'Indeed,' Mr Hayward agreed. 'But we all know you will have no rest until you do tell, Thom, so proceed if you wish to do so.'

The men around the table chuckled at Matilda's wry look.

Thomas gave a small smile and shook his head. 'There is not much to tell yet, not until I see the coroner in the morning.'

Matilda looked less than satisfied. 'Then I shall tell you about it,' she said.

He raised an eyebrow in her direction. 'Is that so?'

'Yes. You found a woman who has perhaps just come of age, with golden hair, loose and worn out in a modern fashion. She was wearing pale blue silk pyjamas and lying on the second top stair outside the church. Her hands were joined in prayer and placed under her cheek, like a child sleeping, and she lay on her side, her back to the street.

She was brutally murdered with a hit to the face, but there was no evidence at the scene. She will be hard to identify,' Matilda added, her voice saddened.

The room was stilled with just the sound of cutlery in use as they listened to Matilda's recounting.

Thomas looked annoyed. 'Did you go there after all?' He looked at Daniel, who shook his head in surprise and answered before Matilda.

'Neither of us left the premises.'

Matilda agreed. 'I assure you, we did not. But was I right?'

'To the letter. How did you know?' Thomas asked. 'I shall reprimand my officers if you have heard it from anyone on the force.'

Matilda shook her head. 'Do not stress yourself. It is the plot of the book I am reading. A book that has just been published and I have been assigned to review for the *Women's Journal*. That is the very crime that happens in the first few chapters… now it has come to life.'

Thomas looked at her with astonishment.

'If the plot continues to be emulated in real life, then like in the book, I suspect you won't be able to easily find her identity,' Matilda added.

'A sad affair indeed,' Mr Hayward said.

'Who is the author? What is this book? Is it a true story?' Thomas asked.

'No, it is a mystery tale. I shall get it for you. Excuse me, please,' she said rising and the gentlemen around the table rose at the same time. Thomas excused himself and waited for Matilda at the bottom of the stairwell.

Descending, she handed him the book and he read the cover. '*The Pyjama Girl Mystery* by Linton Turner.'

'It is quite explicit,' she said.

'Can I take this?'

Matilda frowned.

'Just for tonight. I'll send a constable out to purchase a copy tomorrow and return this to you.'

'Will you bring it back personally?' she asked, teasing him.

He leaned forward, close enough to place a kiss on her lips but did not; he was in the Hayward household. 'I promise.'

She handed over the book and he reached for her hand, kissed it, and asked her to convey his apologies as he hurriedly departed.

Chapter 5

Thomas headed up the small path to his modest home which was in darkness. Compared to the large estate of the Haywards' household at Highgate Hill, his timber cottage with the neglected yard was cosy at best, but it would be the perfect house for him and Matilda, and a small family if they were blessed with one. It was once his parents' home and big enough for them, Thomas and his older brother, Sewell. Although Sewell was thirteen when Thomas was born, and was gone from the family home before Thomas had reached his tenth year.

Hearing a voice call out his name, Thomas turned to find his nephew, Teddy, arriving behind him from his cooking job at the prison.

'Ah, there's good timing,' Thomas said. 'Just finished?'

'Yes, I prefer the breakfast shift. But it's only another week of late duty.' At eight-and-ten he was a big man, slightly ruddy with his reddish hair, but with a youthful countenance. The job had settled him and staying with his uncle, a detective, had kept him in line. Thomas's brother, Sewell – Teddy's father – had hoped for that. The men were not dissimilar in age, with seven years between them. They entered the house together and removed their hats. Thomas shrugged off his suit jacket, pleased with the cool relief, and placed the book, *The Pyjama Girl Mystery*, on the timber kitchen table.

'I prefer you working the morning shift, too. I like coming home and not having to light the place,' Thomas said, seeking a lamp from the kitchen bench.

'Ah, won't be long until you'll have Mrs Ashdown waiting for you with the lamps lit and dinner ready.'

Thomas laughed. 'I suspect Matilda can't cook; I'll be hiring a cook and housekeeper.'

'Speaking of which, have you eaten?' Teddy asked.

'A half-eaten dinner at the Hayward's but enough. I have some reading to do. You?'

'On the job. But I'll put the kettle on.'

Teddy prepared tea as Thomas entered the dark hallway and lit the house. On his return, he heard Teddy chuckling.

'I wouldn't have thought you'd have time for reading books,' Teddy tapped the cover.

'And you'd be right. Matilda is reviewing this for her *Women's Journal*, it's just been printed. But, I have a murder and she believes there are similarities.'

Teddy's eyes widened with interest. 'The pyjama girl at the church?'

'Word travels fast.'

'I saw a headline in the late evening edition of the paper

on the way home, and one of the prison wardens mentioned it before I left.'

They sat at the table to take their tea.

'How did he know about it?'

'He said he was reading a story about that very subject. Guessing that's it,' Teddy said with a nod to the book on the table.

Thomas sighed. 'Great. My list of suspects is going to be the author, the publisher and everyone who bought the book! Might as well just…' He stopped mid-sentence.

'What?'

'I need to stop the book from being sold until we have more information.'

'It'll be on sale all over the country, won't it?'

Thomas threw up his hands. 'You're right.' 'Let's hope someone confesses then.'

They talked of other matters and then finishing his tea, Thomas rose and grabbed the book. 'To bed to begin.'

*****

Thomas washed and stripped down. It was too hot for a sheet or nightshirt but he kept his clothes nearby should an emergency present itself, and it often did. He set himself up with his lamp and began. After the first dozen chapters, he had to concede, it was well written; Linton Turner could tell a tale. He skipped the romance bits with Turner's detective and his beloved, and then decided he might learn something, so read them as he went along.

The plot was just as Matilda said, to the letter. Why? Did someone have a vendetta against the author, Linton Turner, or was this the actions of his biggest fan? Thomas flipped to the back of the book to see what other stories he had written in case they were to come to life as well. He had half a dozen other mystery murders – *The Missing Corpse, The Bathtub Murder, Death at the Lighthouse, The Man with no Face* and one he could attest to, *Death and the Desperate Detective*.

'Great,' he mumbled.

He stopped to think about the twist in the book. The woman in pyjamas is eventually identified but as two different people and one of them is already dead and buried, so her family now think they may have identified the wrong lady.

'Please God, let the imitation stop with the body and the pyjamas,' he silently prayed, and Thomas was not a praying man.

He read until the early hours of the morning, and then leant over and extinguished his light. Thomas took some time to fall asleep, despite the hour. The woman in pyjamas soon left his thoughts – he was well familiar with crime scenes and select ones haunted him, but not tonight. He replaced the woman in pyjamas with thoughts of Matilda and their pending betrothal. In a matter of months, she would lay in this very bed with him.

If Thomas were honest with himself, he would have to admit he was as nervous as he was excited. What would that first night together be like? He had given his heart to Matilda at an early age. Presented his first flower to her when she was one-and-ten and he was grown-up and three years her senior. He even put up with the teasing from her brother, his best friend, Daniel in the bold display of his feelings which were, to his delight, reciprocated. Thomas gave Matilda the best ring he could buy the year after and promised her his hand in marriage. He smiled at the thought of them as young and innocent, promising each other a future life together.

But regardless, he had not let her win at their games and races. He needed to be a hero for her and to show he could be strong and protect her; she was fast though, for a girl. Now Thomas had presented his hand and a genuine diamond ring that had set him back a considerable sum, and the girl he had always loved had accepted.

How would that translate for them when it came to being husband and wife in the marital bed, he pondered. Would they feel awkward or passionate? He swallowed at the thought. Thomas had no one he could discuss his concerns with or seek counsel. His father who lived some distance away would not entertain such a conversation. There had been little intimacy between father and son growing up. He could not speak to Daniel, his best friend, given Matilda was his sister. Or to any of the Hayward brothers for that matter. Teddy, his nephew, was out of the question, he did not wish to display his concerns to him, and Mr Hayward, despite having five children all now adults, was not appropriate to consult. His only confidant that he could think of, should he wish to discuss his concerns, was his partner, Harry. Maybe, if the time and place were right, he would raise the subject.

He took a deep breath and felt the smallest of cooling breezes through the curtain on his skin. Despite the prospect of seeing Matilda with her hair loose and her layers of clothing removed, her soft skin revealed, and kissable lips open to him, sleep eventually came.

Chapter 6

*T*he *Economic Undertaker* of Tribune Street, South Brisbane, was open for business. Julius Astin arrived at work first; he usually did. Unlike his business partners – his grandfather, sister, Phoebe and brother, Ambrose, he was an early to bed, early to rise person. Years of working around the dead taught him there wasn't a moment to waste, but truth be known, he was always a morning person. Regardless, he did not turn the front door sign to read "open", that was his grandfather's job – the front-man of the business, Randolph Astin. His customers trusted a more mature face when it came to managing grief, and Randolph appreciated being busy.

Julius was proud of his work. Being an undertaker did not appeal to everyone, but he was there for the families of this town when they needed him most, and looking sincere was one of his strengths. Handsome ran in the family; he was tall, dark, and striking – he had been accused of brooding which boded well when dealing with the dead. At eight and twenty, he was older than his years. His parents' death had affected him more than his siblings, being the eldest, and he grew up that day, even though his grandparents stepped in and resumed their care.

Besides, Julius had ambitions and one of them was for the business to be the best undertakers in the city. He tapped into the classes that could not afford the expensive funerals the other businesses coerced with guilt and shame – he had witnessed this firsthand with his grandparents struggling to pay for his parents' funerals and give them a deserving farewell. The Astin family offered a modest but caring funeral and Julius and his siblings led a good life from the profits of the dead, in return giving them a respectful and economic send-off. A win-win for everyone.

Julius licked his finger and flicked to today's date in his grandfather's appointment journal for the business. It was a busy day ahead: two morning collections which he and Ambrose would undertake – one from a private home to the cemetery for burial, and prior to this a body to collect from the hospital, the corpse to be returned to their funeral parlour. This meant his sister, Phoebe, the artist and presenter for the business, would have her work cut out for her trying to make the deceased look warm of feature and natural should any acquaintances come to pay their respects before burial, as no family had claimed them.

There was a job crossed out in his grandfather's handwriting – a family had requested a death portrait but changed their mind. Julius was aware his British counterparts still undertook this practice, but the Brisbane heat was not conducive to post-mortem photography of the corpse – the sooner the dead were buried, the better, and *The Economic Undertaker* strived to do so within a day or two of death.

He continued reading the diary entries for the day. Grandpa had to meet with two bereaved families with recently deceased to book in their funerals, and there was also an afternoon funeral which he, Ambrose, and Grandpa would officiate. All wearing black in the heat. Julius looked at the package chosen by the family – it included the mourning coach with two horses and no plumes – not the cheapest, not the dearest. That would make the family feel better and was part of Julius's pricing plan… everyone liked to think they hadn't settled for the cheapest. Flicking ahead, they had two funerals tomorrow. Last week they buried nine of the town's former residents. He wished more people would die at convenient times, preferably in winter – there's no hurry to reach the other side, surely.

The bell over the door tinkled and he looked up to see his sister, Phoebe, entering.

'Just me, good morning, Julius,' she said, flouncing in, her long blonde hair unconventionally loose around her shoulders and her cobalt blue dress bringing out the blue in her eyes. She was strong but feminine, decisive but demure, a mixture he had not found in the women in his circle who were keen to capture his heart, their mothers more so given he was a man of means and a successful merchant.

'Morning, Phoebe,' he said, 'big day.' He tapped the diary.

'I know, hence my early arrival. The dead beckon,' she joked.

'Well, you look most becoming for your guests,' he complimented his sister on her style and worried, as he often did, for her future. It was a peculiar profession that most likely made her less desirable to the town's courting gentlemen, and she was three and twenty now.

Phoebe laughed. 'I am sure Ma and Pa are rolling in their graves at my dress reform stance and even more so at your acceptance of it.' She ran her hand down her loose dress favoured by the aesthetic movement, with its flowing fabric and uncorseted waistline.

He gave a small shrug. 'You have never been conventional, Phoebe,' he said. 'Who would have you any other way?' He offered a rare smile.

'Thank you, Brother. At least I have a career and financial means, so if I am left on the shelf, so be it. I will not be a burden on the family,' she said, happy with his support. She removed her hat and placed it along with her bag under the counter.

'Never a burden,' he said. 'Although, I confess I was once worried that such modernism was not ideal for business, especially in such a formal environment. But I have found the bereaved to be less interested in our appearance and more interested in ensuring their own mourning clothes are appropriate,' he mused. 'If I were to start another business, I would buy a tailor store and place it next door to provide mourning wear.'

Phoebe cocked her head on the side. 'Why, that is a very good idea, Julius. Perhaps we should pursue that. Speaking of business, where are those lazy partners of ours?' she asked, teasing her other brother and grandfather as the door opened and the two men entered.

'We heard that, and I am wounded to the heart,' her grandfather, Randolph, said with a wink in her direction. He removed his hat and ran his hand through his distinguished grey hair.

'Damned hot already,' Ambrose complained, 'and we've got collections to make out in the heat. Let's get going then,' he said to Julius. Collections being the recently deceased requiring removal from their home to a place of final resting.

'So inconvenient, the dead,' Julius agreed. 'Our first collection is a male from Brisbane Hospital at 9.30am, followed by the funeral of Mrs Raymond, to be collected from her home at Spring Hill at 11.30am… the less salubrious area,' he clarified, seeing his brother's surprised expression that the deceased's family chose *The Economic Undertaker*. 'She is going to Toowong Cemetery,' he continued. 'The next is Mr Tritton to collect at his residence at Logan Road, at 2.00pm for the South Brisbane Cemetery.'

Julius thanked his grandfather for the record of the day's activities and took up his hat again. 'Phoebe, we shall return with the hospital body for you. If you could prepare the corpse for a funeral late afternoon or tomorrow morning and if there is anyone to visit the poor deceased fellow, Grandpa can open our new mourning room.'

'It is gratifying to have the hospital contract,' Randolph said, 'but I can't help but feel sorry for the souls with no one to claim or bury them at the end of their life,' he said and sighed.

'Well the Astin family shall see them off to the next world as if we were their family,' Phoebe said, and planting a kiss on her grandfather's cheek, she swanned off to her room downstairs and at the back of the office which was cooler and suited to her work.

Randolph was happy they could at least do that much. He turned the sign on the door.

'Open for business,' he said, with a smile, and the men dispersed to begin their duties. Later that day the body delivered would bring the detectives to their doorstep.

*****

The office of the *Women's Journal* was abuzz with energy when Matilda entered. She greeted the ladies on hand as she walked through each of the areas – past the artists, the editors, the full-time writers, the typesetters, and female compositors. As always, she glanced to Mrs Dora Lawson's office in awe of the editor, who was in a meeting with her deputy editor, Betty Purcell.

Matilda placed her bag down and sought her closest friends, Georgina and Alice, whom she found in the kitchen making a cup of tea to begin their day. One day, she hoped they would both be her sister-in-law after some fortunate match-making on her behalf.

'Did you hear about the pyjama woman?' Alice said on seeing Matilda. 'Is it true it is similar to the plot of the book you are reviewing?'

'It is the very plot. Quite frightening,' Matilda said. 'So very mysterious.'

'Mrs Lawson will have a word to say about it, I wonder how she'll handle it,' Georgina said.

Matilda glanced out the kitchen door to see the deputy editor stick her head out of Mrs Lawson's office. All the ladies looked up as Betty's voice called staff to the morning meeting. Matilda and her friends hurried back to their desks to get their pads and pencils, before bustling into the editor's office where everyone took their prescribed seats, presenting a happy, industrious bunch of no less than a dozen ladies around the table.

'Well, most peculiar and sad indeed,' Mrs Lawson said drawing the meeting to order. 'I imagine you have all heard of the finding of the lady in her pyjamas on the church step?'

Matilda and the other ladies agreed. Mrs Lawson expected her writers to be informed and no employee of the *Women's Journal* wanted to disappoint their editor.

'Of course it is early days and we don't wish to interfere with the police investigation, but there is a story there already, is there not, Matilda?' Mrs Lawson threw the spotlight on her, and Matilda straightened to attention. Fortunately, she had read most of the book and was not caught unaware.

'Indeed, Mrs Lawson. It is the plot of Linton Turner's latest story, *The Pyjama Girl Mystery*.' There were gasps from the ladies surprised by the course this tale was taking.

Betty, the deputy editor, called for order.

'Then, this is what we shall do ladies,' Mrs Lawson continued. 'We shall write a piece on the increase in violence against women in our fair city. Betty shall assign that story. Include quotes from the police service, family and victims if possible. Also, conclude with some advice on how ladies can take safety precautions.'

Betty nodded and made notes.

Mrs Lawson continued: 'Matilda, aside from that angle, will you write an article highlighting the similarities from the mystery book and the crime as they appear to date?'

'Yes, Mrs Lawson,' Matilda said, keen to do so.

'We will keep that story as up to date as we can before we go to print, so please liaise with Betty if changes or additions come through to ensure its accuracy.'

'I will, Mrs Lawson,' Matilda said.

'Then Betty, will you find a writing partner for Matilda?' She paused and added. 'Perhaps Alice, as you both worked so well together once before on the artist's muse story. What do you think, Betty?'

The two young ladies looked at each other and smiled, happy for the pairing.

'Alice it is,' Betty said. 'I will give you a break from the suffragette stories for a little while,' she said with a wink to Alice. 'I know several of the other ladies are keen to take up the mantle.'

'Excellent,' Mrs Lawson said. 'Matilda and Alice, I would like you to procure an interview with the author, Linton Turner. Try the publishing house and the bookstores as well and include their opinions. Let's see how the death of this poor unfortunate lady is affecting the author and his work, or if there is a theory why the murder reflects the plot of the book.'

Matilda and Alice jotted down notes.

Mrs Lawson turned to the illustrators. 'Ruth, over the coming days, will you and Georgina draw the cover of the book, and do a representation of the death scene on the church steps, as it is written in the newspaper?'

Ruth, who was in charge of the illustrators' department which consisted of herself and Georgina, happily agreed.

Mrs Lawson moved on: 'Now, to other stories, we need an update on the Blue Ribbon meeting…'

Matilda's mind raced ahead with all the possibilities and angles for her story. First, she wanted to see the scene of the crime and could legitimately venture there now without looking like a nosy sightseer. Then, a trip to the police station was in order to retrieve her book; she needed Linton Turner's *The Pyjama Girl Mystery* back from Thomas, today!

Chapter 7

Detective Harry Dart recognised a restless spirit when he saw one; he was once short of temper and time, but boxing had helped expend his energy on a suitable outlet and one that would keep him out of trouble. To this day, he was still a most capable boxer, but not as restless. His calm demeanour was perfect for mentoring a young, Detective Thomas Ashdown. Harry saw in Thomas a look of impatience and frustration, and the day had barely begun.

'It is a little early to call on the coroner for the results, Thom,' Harry said, once they had finished reading through the witnesses' reports compiled by the constables.

'These amount to next to nothing, except for Mrs Phillipa Goodburn who found the body,' Thomas said, and closed the folder with a sigh.

'Nevertheless, I would like to call on Mrs Goodburn this morning, in case she has remembered anything now the shock has worn off,' Harry said. 'I would also like to return to the scene of the crime again.'

'As would I, and since we will be in that area, I need to drop into the *Women's Journal* office if you have no objections? It'll only take a minute,' Thomas said.

'Not a lovers' tiff I hope,' Harry said, rising and preparing to go.

'No, we don't see each other enough to fight,' Thomas said with a look of dismay.

'That will change very soon,' Harry said with a smile that was returned by his protégé. 'So why do you need to drop into the *Women's Journal* office then? Not that I object.'

Thomas retrieved a book from his desk and handed it to Harry. 'It's a new release Matilda is reviewing for her publication and given the topic, Matilda leant me the book last night on the promise I got it back to her as soon as possible.'

Harry took the offered book, his eyes wide with surprise. *The Pyjama Girl Mystery* by Linton Turner. 'What is this then?'

'What indeed,' Thomas said, grabbing his hat and following his partner out of the office and down the hall. 'The author, Mr Turner, has written a murder before it happened and so far, it is to the letter.'

'Goodness me. We'll need to speak with him as soon as we hear what the coroner says.'

'Yes, and Mr Linton has other titles which are equally dramatic. I am hoping now that we don't have a spate of strange literary murders throughout the city,' Thomas said as the two men left the Roma Street Police Headquarters and walked towards the omnibus stop. 'We have enough crime without authors suggesting some new ones to the criminal elements out there.'

Harry chuckled. 'I am surprised it did not keep Miss Hayward up at night or give her nightmares. It obviously kept you up.'

Thomas tried to hide another yawn and nodded. 'I read the entire book, finished in the early hours of the morning. I can't remember the last time I read a book.'

They stood back as the omnibus rattled near and stepped on board after several ladies. Once seated, Harry checked the address. 'Mrs Pip Goodburn is first on our journey, then the *Women's Journal* is on the way to the scene of the crime at the church, and then the time will be right to visit Patrick at the morgue.'

'There's our day well planned,' Thomas agreed and momentarily closed his eyes, letting Harry nudge him awake when they arrived at their first destination.

*****

Mrs Phillipa 'Pip' Goodburn lived with her sister, Constance 'Connie', who was of similar age and appearance. The godly women's small apartment was full of religious images. They were bound to get to Heaven before him, Thomas thought.

'We don't have company very often, do we, Sister?' Pip said to Connie.

'No, we do not, Sister,' Connie agreed, 'but we are grateful for it and for the fine work our police force does.'

'Thank you, Connie, Pip,' Harry said, having been invited to address them as such.

Thomas took a seat, frustrated with the process but knowing it was necessary. He did, however, happily accept the offer of tea and hoped the women baked. He hadn't had breakfast and was fading fast on an empty stomach and lack of sleep. He was rewarded.

'Your timing is fortunate, Detectives. I just baked an apple tea cake, and the good Lord knows we love to share the gift of food,' Pip said.

'Then we are well suited, ladies, as we love to partake,' Harry teased them and nudged Thomas to lift his game.

'Indeed,' he said. 'I did not have time for breakfast so that would be most welcomed.'

Connie stopped. 'Oh, Detective. A man of your stature must eat. Do you not have a wife? I cannot believe it.' She turned to Pip. 'So handsome.'

'Very handsome,' Pip agreed, and Thomas reddened under their observation.

'My young colleague is engaged to be married in two months to a beautiful young lady,' Harry told them, and the ladies looked overjoyed.

'What a blessing,' Connie said and served him a portion of cake that was twice the size of the dainty piece she served herself and Pip. Regardless, he did it justice and ate heartily, seeing their looks of pleasure and shared smiles.

Best to keep them happy, he thought.

'You have a lovely home here,' Harry said, accepting the cup of tea in fine China and requesting a smaller slice of cake as he had breakfasted.

'Thank you, Detective,' Connie said. 'We no longer work but can afford this with our modest means.'

'Oh, you worked?' Thomas asked surprised, and the ladies exchanged looks.

Pip lowered her voice as if the good Lord or Mary the mother of God, who featured large on the sideboard in statue form, might be shocked.

'We have led a colourful life, Detectives, and have worked, loved and lived!' Pip sobered. 'But we do our best to keep the faith. Connie worked as a nurse for many years, and I ran an antique store in Paddington. You might know of it – *The Treasure Chest*?'

'Of course,' Harry said. 'Delightful. You sold it then?'

'Some time back,' Pip said. 'I met a sea captain, the romance of my life; he has since passed.' She sighed and waited a few moments before speaking again in honour of his memory.

'Well, I am sorry to hear that, Pip. Life can be fleeting,' Harry offered.

'So true, Detective, so true,' Pip agreed. 'But Cappy – that was his nickname – wanted to start a business. Thus, I sold the antique store, and Connie was bequeathed some jewellery from one of her patients, so the three of us went into the publican business.'

Thomas's eyes widened in surprise.

'Does that shock you, young man?' Connie said with a smile.

Thomas chuckled. 'My fiancée is a very progressive lady, she works for the *Women's Journal*, so I think she may have found kindred spirits in you two ladies,' he said, and saw Harry's pleased look.

'We subscribe!' Pip said and pointed to their magazine rack in the room's corner.

After some more small talk about their former hotel, and a promise from the ladies to look out for Matilda's stories, Harry got to the business at hand.

'May we speak about the terrible incident the other evening?' Harry asked finishing his second piece of cake, which he had intended to refuse but could not. He proclaimed it to be the best he had ever tasted but requested Thomas did not tell his wife, to the great amusement of Pip and Connie.

'Of course,' Pip said. 'You have duties to attend to. Shall I tell you what I observed?'

'Yes please,' Thomas said, 'and any thoughts you might have had since.'

The ladies looked at each other pleased, and Connie encouraged Pip to be strong and continue.

'The young lady in the pale blue silk pyjamas was not on the church step when I entered the church forty minutes prior to my discovering her. I go the same time, three days a week, so I know the timing of my actions,' she said. 'I was carrying flowers, but I would not have missed her had she been lying there.'

'Very true, Sister,' Connie agreed.

Pip continued: 'The church is sizeable, so I changed the flowers on the alter first, some distance away from the steps, and then I changed the flowers near the church entrance before departing. That is close to the steps and that is when I saw something.'

Harry leaned forward and Thomas straightened with expectation.

'There was a couple that appeared to be a little too intimate in their embrace; they were sitting where the body was later found. I noticed because I thought it to be distasteful, especially on the church steps. What happens behind closed doors is no one's business but out the front of the Lord's house...' Pip said.

'Rightly so, Sister,' Connie agreed. 'Thank goodness for closed doors,' she added and Thomas restrained a laugh. The old girls were a formidable pair; no doubt they had been quite unconventional in their prime.

'A man in a dark grey suit with a hat similar to yours, Detective,' Pip said to Harry with a nod at his hat, 'sat with his arms around a young woman who appeared to be in a dark coat. I noticed because it was very warm and I thought it was odd she needed a coat. But now...'

'You are thinking the man carried her or dragged her there looking like it was a romantic liaison, but then removed the coat and left the deceased woman on the stair?' Harry asked.

'That is precisely what I am thinking, Detective,' Pip said.

'Did you see the back of her head or her hair colour?' Thomas asked.

'Sadly no. She had a hat on along with the coat. But I came out of the church only moments after I saw them... it would have been a matter of minutes and the couple were gone but the woman in the blue pyjamas was lying on the step as if asleep. I can't imagine they left and someone else arrived, laid her to rest and left as well. I'm sure I would have seen that.'

'So it is likely that the woman in the coat was the woman in the pyjamas,' Thomas mused.

'Tell them what you did next,' Connie said, encouraging her sister.

Pip nodded. 'I am not a nurse, like Connie, but I leant down to see if I could assist. It was so peculiar to see her laying there in pyjamas, of all things.'

'Mind you, they sound like very nice pyjamas,' Connie added.

'They were, Sister, pale blue and silk,' Pip agreed.

Thomas was past being frustrated now and quite enjoyed the show. He could read the restrained amused look on his partner's face.

Pip continued. 'I removed my glove and touched her face, and oh dear, it was cool. Most peculiar – a bit like Cappy's skin was in death.'

'Would it be rigour mortis, Sister?' Connie asked.

'I suspect you are right, Sister, but she felt coolish in that terrible heat,' Pip said.

'That is odd, unless she has been kept somewhere cool and only just placed there moments before you found her,' Thomas said. Then realising that may have been too much detail, apologised. 'Forgive me, ladies,' he said, 'that was indiscreet of me.'

'Not at all,' Connie said. 'The sights we saw nursing and, in the hotel, ensured our constitutions are quite formidable.'

Thomas smiled at Connie. 'I can but imagine.'

'What did you do then, Pip,' Harry asked.

'Well, I felt for a pulse as I had seen Connie do before, but there was not one to be found. The young lady would not stir, so I stayed guard and called for a constable.'

'Marvellous work, thank you,' Harry said.

Pip smiled, pleased with herself. 'It was quite an adventure. So do you know who she is, Detective?'

Harry shook his head. 'Sadly, not yet. But we hope someone claims the young lady soon.'

And then the sisters surprised the detectives again.

'I am reading the book, Detectives,' Connie said. 'The very one today's newspaper said the crime was similar to… I picked it up from the downtown bookstore on the day of its release, without knowing what might unfold.'

'Sister loves a good mystery,' Pip said.

'I do,' Connie agreed.

'Do you think the author might enjoy the notoriety attached to his book, Detectives?' Pip asked, but didn't wait for an answer. 'I believe it has sold out of copies, or so Mrs Ratchett told me this morning at the grocer.'

'I suspect you might be right, Pip, and spoken like a true businesswoman,' Harry said. 'The dreadful crime has no doubt increased book sales.'

'We will attempt to speak with the author himself,' Thomas agreed. 'But thank you, now we also have a suspect sighted by you.'

They departed after much thanks and on the way to the *Women's Journal*, Harry chuckled. 'What interesting ladies.'

Thomas grinned. 'Yes, I suspect their penitence now is making up for a life well lived.'

'We should all be so lucky,' Harry agreed.

Chapter 8

Men were rarely seen in the offices of the *Women's Journal* unless delivering mail, boxes of the fortnightly magazine just off the printer, or a bouquet to a lucky lady, so when the two detectives arrived at the reception, all heads turned to view them.

'You have just missed Miss Hayward, Detectives,' the neat, pressed and middle-aged woman at reception advised. 'Allow me a moment and I shall find out where she ventured if you will?'

'I can help,' Miss Georgina Urry said, arriving just in time to overhear the conversation and dropping some mail in the tray on the reception desk. She greeted Thomas whom she had just seen a few days ago at Sunday lunch at the Hayward household. Georgina was a regular guest since courting Matilda's brother, Dr Elijah Hayward.

'Miss Urry! How delightful to see you again,' Harry said, stepping out from behind Thomas.

'And you, Detective Dart. We last saw each other at

the asylum… neither of us needed committing on that occasion,' she joked.

Harry laughed. 'Let's hope that is still the case,' he teased. He greatly admired the large-framed country girl who was never afraid to say what she thought. She was no shrinking violet or a lady prone to swooning, but a handsome woman of sorts and practical of nature.

'Matilda and Alice went to the church where the murder occurred of late,' Georgina informed them. 'They are writing a piece on the book and similarities to the death of the poor lady in her pyjamas. You know the book?'

'Indeed,' Thomas assured her. 'I am here to return Matilda's copy.' He patted his jacket pocket.

'Did you want me to leave it on her desk, Detective?' the receptionist asked.

'Thank you, but I best return it in person, or I shall be in trouble,' Thomas said and Harry chuckled.

'Best you do then,' the receptionist laughed.

'I am heading to the church myself,' Georgina said. 'Mrs Lawson has commissioned me to illustrate the scene and to do my best to include a drawing of the poor lady from what I gleaned in the daily newspaper.'

'Ah, that is where we are heading. Allow us to escort you,' Harry said.

'Thank you, Detective Dart. I would welcome the company,' she said.

'We'll even give you our first-hand perspective of what we saw if you don't mention your source?' Thomas offered.

Georgina gasped. 'Wonderful, thank you. And yes, I shall

take the source of inspiration with me to the grave! Oh, that probably wasn't the right thing to say with a woman dead, was it?'

Harry chuckled. 'You won't shock us, Miss Urry. We've seen aplenty.'

'No doubt. Please one moment, I'll grab my pencil and pad, and we shall be off!'

'No need to rush,' Harry said as he watched Miss Urry rush off. He turned to Thomas, a look of surprise on his countenance. 'That's not like you to offer an insight to a crime scene. Softening, are you?'

Thomas gave a small shrug. 'Miss Urry is a practical woman. She would have recreated the scene from the journalist's reports, so why not give the *Women's Journal* an advantage? Besides, it may help us too.'

'Ah, here she is,' Harry said, and the three departed for the omnibus and to the scene of the crime.

*****

Matilda and Alice studied the very place where the poor lady, believed to be around their age in years, had been found dead yesterday.

'I always expect to feel something,' Matilda said, frowning as she gazed at the stair and then glanced upwards towards Heaven.

'As do I!' Alice took her arm, supportively. 'It feels wrong that a life can be lost on this very spot, and life goes on today as normal.' She gave a small shrug. 'Perhaps it is a good thing too.'

Dressed in their fashionable and practical skirts and jackets, they moved away from the groups already gathered to make some of their own observations.

'In Linton Turner's *The Pyjama Girl Mystery,* the very clever detective made several assumptions,' Matilda said in a low voice.

'Do tell,' Alice encouraged her, closing her parasol as they moved under the shade of several large trees.

'He wrote that the lady left on the steps might have been done so as an offering to God.'

Alice nodded. 'Yes, I can see how she might appear like a sacrificial lamb. So, her killer left her to redeem himself in the eyes of God?'

'Yes, exactly,' Matilda said and opening her bag, reached for her fan, and snapping it open began to fan them both, even though they were standing in the shade offered by the trees and the church steeple. 'I am so glad I am marrying in autumn.'

'As am I,' Alice agreed. 'We will all be more comfortable. Especially the men in their suits.'

'Won't they be handsome?' Matilda said with a smile.

'I cannot wait to see them in their morning suits,' she said, and gave a small squeal of delight. 'Oh, and your dress, Matilda, have you had a final fitting?'

'Next week. It feels so strange – it makes me feel beautiful.' Matilda coloured as she said the words; her life had not been one of frocks and ribbons, especially with no sisters.

'Of course. You will be so beautiful on the day, Matilda,' Alice said, 'and I cannot wait to see Thomas's face when he sees you walking down the aisle towards him. Are you frightened? You know, about what will follow?'

Matilda looked around and lowered her voice. 'I have thought about it a great deal, but I'm rather looking forward to, well, to the intimacy,' she said in a whisper, and then laughed a little.

'As am I, with the right man. Hopefully your brother,' Alice said and smiled, 'but please, do not tell him that! How mortifying.'

'Of course not,' Matilda assured Alice. 'Best they do not know we are speaking about them with a thought to being disrobed and in the bedroom. Goodness.'

They both giggled and let their blushes subside and then Matilda put her chin up and said: 'Sorry, I led us astray. To work then...'

'Indeed. What other theories did the author's detective suggest?'

Matilda nodded. 'Another of the theories was that the woman was a religious person, perhaps Catholic, given in the book someone left her on the stairs of a Catholic church. He surmised that she may have broken her marriage vows or one of the commandments, and thus been killed for it.'

'So much for "*Thou Shalt Not Kill*" then,' Alice said and they shared a small laugh.

They studied the area for a while longer and agreed there was no inspiration to be gained.

Alice asked: 'Shall we venture to the bookstore and speak with the owner?'

'Let us, and hopefully he can connect us with the salesperson, who can connect us with the publisher and author.'

'I imagine the author will get a lot of requests for interviews, I hope we get one,' Alice agreed.

They walked a few paces when Matilda stopped and smiled. 'There's Thomas and Detective Dart, and Georgina arriving! Georgina must have gotten away after all. What a shame she couldn't come with us.'

'I think Ruth thought we might all have too good a time of it,' Alice giggled.

She saw Thomas looking around as if for her, and then they locked eyes and he smiled and looked pleased to see her, which was not often the case at one of his crime scenes. Matilda and Alice made their way over to the three, staying in the cool of the shade as much as possible.

'I was allowed to escape,' Georgina joked, 'and I found two very capable escorts.'

'We did our best,' Detective Harry Dart agreed. The men greeted the ladies and then Detective Dart accompanied Alice and Georgina to the exact position where the lady had been found, so Georgina's drawing would be accurate.

Matilda smiled up at Thomas. 'Do you have any insights for me?' she asked, hopeful.

'Yes,' he said and her eyes lit up with anticipation.

'I love you and cannot wait to marry you.'

Matilda laughed with delight. She did not swoon however, as she had known Thomas since she was a young girl, and swooning was not in her nature.

'Well, that is not quite the insight I was looking for,' she teased him, 'but it is much better than what I expected.'

He took her hand and kissed it, before releasing it again and maintaining the appropriate distance.

'We shall be husband and wife in fifty-six days,' she said. 'Are you nervous?'

'No,' he assured her. 'Happy, excited, hopeful, but not nervous.' He promptly asked: 'Why, are you?'

'No, I have big plans for us,' she said enthusiastically and made him laugh.

'Lord help me.'

'You are in the right spot for that then,' Matilda said with a glance to the church.

Harry, Alice and Georgina re-joined them and they spoke of the crime.

'It must have been a dramatic sight,' Matilda said, looking at the top stair, 'seeing a lady lying so vulnerable and so exposed.' She put her hand to her heart at the thought of it.

'It was a striking scene,' Harry admitted, as he had done previously to Miss Georgina Urry. 'Especially as she looked so peaceful, did she not, Thom?'

Thomas nodded. Matilda watched him with curiosity, knowing he was not one to talk about cases with anyone, let alone ladies.

'Her hands were under her head and she was on her side, looking like a child sleeping peacefully,' he offered.

'And I read in today's newspaper that she was found in pale blue silk pyjamas as if she had come straight from her bed to the church step in the late afternoon,' Alice said.

Georgina frowned. 'I fear my pyjamas are far less glamorous. If you were to find me on a church step in them, you most likely would have thought me a poor, deserted and homeless person.'

Her humour lifted the group and Matilda laughed. Georgina was one of a kind as Matilda's brother, Elijah, discovered to both of their delights. A conservative soul was Elijah and she brightened his world considerably. Fortunately, Georgina did not reveal what she wore to bed but Matilda turned to see Thomas looking at her. He abruptly looked away.

'So, where are you off to now, Detectives?' Matilda fished for a clue.

'We can't tell you, it's official police business,' Thomas said before Harry could respond to her.

'Oh phooey,' Matilda said. 'Then we shan't tell you where we are going either.'

'I shall sit here for an hour, sketching,' Georgina said, telling everyone where she would be in the foreseeable future. 'Hopefully the crowds will ease a little so I can get a clear view of the steps and church.'

'People are peculiar, are they not?' Alice said, studying the onlookers. 'I am sure I would not have come here to look if it were not for work.'

Matilda frowned. 'I am sure I would have.'

All eyes turned to her, and she gave a small shrug.

'It is significant and in today's news, I cannot help myself,' she offered by way of explanation.

'Where are you going next?' Thomas asked Matilda and

then looked to Alice for enlightenment, should his fiancée not answer.

'We will tell if you tell,' Matilda said, placing her hand on Alice's arm to ensure she did not reveal their next move.

Thomas rolled his eyes and Harry laughed.

'We're going to the morgue to speak with the coroner,' Thomas said.

'Ooh, that will be interesting,' Matilda said, wide-eyed.

'And no, you cannot come,' Thomas added.

'I know that,' she said, with a wry look that made Harry laugh. 'We are going to the town's largest bookstore to seek interviews for our story.' She looked at Alice with a sense of self-importance.

'If you get a contact for the author, we may just beg that from you, Miss Hayward,' Harry said, 'save us chasing up the same.'

Matilda turned to Harry. 'Of course, Detective Dart, we are only too happy to assist the good men of our police force.'

Matilda laughed as Thomas rolled his eyes again, took her hand and with a quick kiss that he could not resist, despite the audience, bid her and the ladies' farewell.

Chapter 9

Miss Phoebe Astin stood back, adjusted the curtain in her work room at *The Economic Undertaker* and despite the heat, allowed as much light in as possible for just a moment. She needed to be sure that her efforts, when viewed in the light of the mourning room and church, were acceptable. The cotton wool was gone from the deceased's eyes, and the handkerchief removed from his jaw, no longer necessary as rigour mortis had set in and the mouth was closed forever in a peaceful repose.

'You look very dapper, Mr Kilgour,' she said to the gentleman lying deceased on her table. 'I am sorry we don't have long for the elaborate preparations common in the old country, but your new country's climate does not allow for it.'

Phoebe was content that she had improved Mr Kilgour's colour, ensured his thinning hair was appropriately combed to look more bountiful and arranged his clothing to cover the ligature marks around his neck. She reached for the small paintbrush and a little bottle from her wooden kit, and touched up a mark around his left eye.

'That's better,' she observed, standing back. 'I declare you as good in death as in life, Mr Kilgour. Maybe even better,' she teased. Phoebe often spoke to the dead; she was quite at home in their company.

A tap at the door caught her attention and her grandfather entered. He moved to view the deceased.

'Another excellent job, my dear,' he said.

'Thank you, Grandpa.' She smiled, closing the curtains again to keep the room cool.

'And what did Mr Kilgour have to say for himself?' Randolph asked.

'He was the quiet type,' Phoebe joked, and they shared a smile. 'Why do you think he did it?' she asked in a low voice, not wishing to disturb the dead.

Randolph sighed. 'I believe his son was accidentally killed, and he had lost his wife from illness but a few years prior. It was not a happy life thereafter for Mr Kilgour.'

'He had his share of grief,' Phoebe agreed. 'His neighbours insist it was an accident. We want him buried in consecrated ground.'

'He deserves to lay next to his wife and son,' Randolph agreed. 'A good death is not given to everyone. Let's pray we are more fortunate.'

'I promise you, Grandfather, should you depart this earth before me, I will have you looking as handsome as you do today,' she teased.

'Good Lord, I best depart this world before you, my dear,

that is the natural order. And thank you, I will sleep better at night knowing you will all see me out appropriately,' he said, with a chuckle. 'Although I worry Ambrose might be inclined – since I'm family – to cut corners and wrap me in brown paper and bury me as is,' he joked of his youngest grandson.

'He's not one for ceremony,' Phoebe agreed.

They mused on that for a few moments before Randolph spoke again to his granddaughter: 'Have a little break. The boys have just arrived back with two bodies; a child and an elderly lady await your special touch. Come, I shall put the kettle on before my next family arrive to discuss their preferred burial package.'

She turned to Mr Kilgour and covered him with a sheet. 'Rest now, Mr Kilgour, all is at peace.'

*****

Detective Thomas Ashdown breathed a sigh of relief as he entered the coroner's cool room. He was prepared to put up with the smell that always accosted his particularly sensitive nose, for the relief of being cool.

Dr Patrick Nevins looked up from the body on his table and laughed as he saw their faces. 'Being in the lower basement had its benefits besides keeping the corpses preserved and preserving my complexion from ruddiness,' he said.

Harry chuckled. 'Good morning to you, Patrick. I suspect you are more popular in summer than winter,' he said, enjoying the chill in the room.

'Yes, I can't say that I'm the first choice for a social call, but summer seems to make me more popular to visitors,' Dr Nevins agreed. He saw Thomas's focussed expression and added. 'I have completed my autopsy and am ready to discuss the lady in the silk pyjamas. It's ah, most unusual.' He warned the men as they came closer. 'And it is not a pretty sight, I'm afraid, prepare yourself.'

Thomas and Harry approached closer to the table and saw what they could not see yesterday, when the young woman lay on her side, her hands joined as if in prayer under her head. Lying on her back, as she was now, one side of her face was concave from a heavy blow.

Thomas recoiled slightly and Harry shook his head, saddened.

'I shall call her the Pyjama Girl rather than the unknown deceased,' Dr Nevins began. 'Height approximately five foot four, fair hair that parts in the middle, clean nails, well nourished, and no bones broken elsewhere in the body now or previously. Repeated blows to the skull were the cause of death.'

'A vicious crime indeed,' Harry said, with a shake of his head.

'How long do you think she had been dead before being laid on the church stairs?' Thomas asked.

'Well, that's what is most peculiar. She may have been dead for a long time, hard to say... she's embalmed,' Dr Nevins said.

His comment had the expected reaction – stunned silence.

'What does that mean?' Thomas asked confused. 'The murderer has embalmed her to preserve her but then dumped the body on the church steps. Where has she come from? A grave? A home, a morgue, a hospital?'

'That, sadly, I cannot tell you,' Dr Nevins said. '

'Good grief, Patrick,' Harry said. 'I am amazed that after all these years in the job, I am still shocked by crimes.'

Dr Nevins smiled. 'Perhaps that is a good thing, that you are not cynical and jaded. It surprised me that no one had come forward to say their wife, sister or daughter is missing, but now, I am not so.'

'Because she is embalmed?' Thomas asked.

'Precisely. She may have been missing or died some time ago, she may have even been buried.'

Thomas gave a soft groan. The case was getting more and more difficult.

'Identifying her will be difficult,' Dr Nevins added. 'The wounds to her face are traumatic. If I can make a suggestion?'

'Please,' Harry encouraged him.

'Let's continue to preserve the body, and have a face mask made. Or find a clever artist who is not fearful of such sights and can recreate or draw her face for identification. I am sure the newspapers will run the illustration which will speed up identification.'

Thomas nodded. 'That is a good idea. If no-one comes forward, it might be the best chance for finding her next of kin and likely murderer.'

'I can organise preserving the body,' Dr Nevins said.

'Thank you, Patrick, let's do so,' Harry said. 'And should

no one own to this poor lady in the next day or so, I know just the person to create a death mask or drawing to help us seek her identification.'

'You do?' Thomas asked, pleased.

'Yes, a young lady, with quite a talent for it,' Harry said, and saw Thomas and Dr Nevins surprised expressions. He elaborated. 'Several years ago, before they partnered me with Thom, I had a similar case – a young man unidentifiable after a terrible accident. Miss Phoebe Astin, a talented and composed young lady, assisted.'

'I can't imagine it,' Thomas said, amazed.

'They are very stoic the fairer sex,' Dr Nevins said. 'I recently read a medical journal study that claimed they displayed more patient endurance than we males in matters of pain.'

'Heavens, let's preserve them from that,' Harry said. 'Thank you, Patrick. Thomas, shall we search the missing persons' files first, see if anyone has visited the police station to claim the young lady, and then, tomorrow if needed, pay a visit to *The Economic Undertaker*?'

'Whatever for?' Thomas asked.

'That is where we will find Miss Phoebe Astin, who prepares the bodies for viewing and burial as required and is an embalmer as well. She is also a dab hand at drawing. We can enquire if she can reconstruct the pyjama girl's face and sketch it for us. Let's get this young lady identified and buried by her kin.'

Chapter 10

The bookseller shook his head as if saddened at the thought of a lost sale. He placed his hands in his suit pants, rocked slightly on his heels, his portly frame apparent by the tightness of his waistcoat and sighed.

'We've sold out ladies, I'm sorry, but I can put you on a list and reserve you a copy when the next print run arrives,' he said of Linton Turner's book, *The Pyjama Girl Mystery*.

'We have a copy, thank you,' Matilda said, pulling it from her bag and showing him.

'I don't recall serving you,' he said. 'You bought it elsewhere, perhaps?'

'No, a colleague purchased it here,' Matilda said. 'That's why we are here, hoping you might assist us to get an interview with the author, Mr Linton Turner.'

Before the bookseller could turn them down, Alice explained: 'We work for the *Women's Journal* and we would like to interview you too, please, about the book, your thoughts, its popularity, your impressions.'

'Oh,' he said, standing straighter and looking more important. He ran his hands down his waistcoat. 'Well, of course, I am the biggest bookseller in town. Trevelyan Moore at your service, ladies.' He gave a small bow.

Matilda introduced Alice and herself, and took a lesson from Alice. With four brothers, a father, and no mother alive, and very few females in her household, Matilda had learnt to be direct, but Alice understood the benefit of charming her subject and Matilda took note. She engaged Mr Moore in his opinion before asking more about the author.

'Isn't this book coming to life the most peculiar of situations, Mr Moore? How do you believe it has come about?'

'Indeed, very odd,' he agreed. 'But not so unrealistic if you know the circles that the author, Mr Linton Turner, moves in.'

'Goodness,' Alice said, 'in the company of those capable of murder?'

Mr Moore tapped his nose. 'That's not a statement I would want to make, however, he has eclectic tastes. He enjoys his clubs and bars, drinks with great gusto, and is a gregarious personality. He frequents the Valley Literary Association gatherings in the Quill Club, haunts the place, I believe. There are some very artistic types, both male and female, frequent there if you get my meaning.'

Matilda looked at him a little confused. 'I am not sure we do, Mr Moore. So, you are saying in these circles he might have spoken of the plot before the book was released, and the calibre of patron might be the type to have brought his vision to life?'

He gave a small shrug. 'It must be one theory.'

'It could be someone who loves his work and seeks to pay tribute to the author,' Alice suggested.

'Yes, but the book was only released for one day before the crime took place. Is it not more likely that someone heard or read the work in advance?' Mr Moore mused.

'Yes, indeed,' Matilda said agreeing with him.

They paused their conversation as Mr Moore assisted a young man with a book sale. The purchaser looked to the ladies and gave a small bow, greeting them.

'That is a marvellous volume of poetry,' the bookseller, Mr Moore said, finishing the sale and wrapping the book before handing it to the buyer. They watched the young man depart the store before resuming their conversation. It did not go unnoticed by the ladies how dashing the buyer was, but of course, as both ladies had beaus, neither showed any interest other than to return his greeting with a small curtsy.

And then Matilda practiced being charming and secured the author's address on the promise she would not declare where she got it from, and would not share it with another soul… a promise she might have to break if Thomas asked for it.

*****

Thomas slipped off his jacket and placed it on the back of the chair. In front of him, his partner Harry had placed the recent Missing Persons' volumes on the table for them to peruse.

'I can't do this,' Thomas said, and paced.

'It won't be easy, but we physically know her traits so I suggest we go back about five or ten years,' Harry said.

'No, it's not that,' Thomas said and exhaled.

'What's wrong? You've had no sleep. Go home, grab a few hours and I'll start on the books,' Harry offered.

'What? No, I'm perfectly fine to work,' Thomas said, and saw Harry's confused look. 'I can't just sit down and go through the files. I need to document it.'

Harry understood. 'Of course. Let's do that before we start with the Missing Persons' books.' He knew how his young partner worked and went to the blackboard. 'Are you ready to part with this last case?'

Thomas smiled. 'Yes, consider it done.'

'Then let's begin,' Harry said, wiping the board with a cloth and arming himself with chalk, he wrote along the top – "The Pyjama Girl".

Thomas paced for a few moments before speaking, working out where to start, and then he threw his hands up in the air. 'We have no identification. We have no suspects except a man in a coat.'

'Then that's where we will start,' Harry said, knowing that once a few words were written, ideas would flow. He drew two columns and wrote in one, "Suspects". He coached the younger detective: 'Sometimes the easiest way to start is to get one thought down.'

'Yes, you are right,' Thomas conceded. 'So, a man wearing a coat and hat, with a woman dressed the same,' Thomas started.

Harry scribbled down the notes. 'What do we need to do?' Harry guided Thomas to the side of the board where they would have more to elaborate on. He started listing the people they needed to speak with: 'Author, publisher, bookstore owners, missing person files...' he paused and looked to Thomas.

'Yes, that's better,' Thomas said seeing it laid out on the board. 'Plus add sellers of blue, silk pyjamas, associates of the author, and embalmers.'

'Good,' Harry said, and drew a line under and wrote, 'public assistance with identification if needed.'

'Let's hope we don't have to display the body. The boys down south had to do that a few months ago,' Thomas said.

Harry shook his head. 'It's macabre and draws out the curious; even so, it may be an option if we're desperate.'

'Early days yet.' Thomas felt better for their attempt at documenting the crime.

'Are you okay now?' Harry asked, and Thomas nodded looking a little sheepish. 'We all have our systems, Thom, that's perfectly fine.'

'Thanks, Harry.' He was grateful yet again that he wasn't partnered with an arrogant cop who disregarded his methods.

Thomas sat down at the table in his office and Harry put down the chalk and joined him. Harry slid him a journal and took a large volume to wade through.

'Luckily this handwriting is better than mine and easy to read,' Harry said.

The two men methodically worked their way through

the entries of missing persons as reported by their families. Thomas jotted down a possible match – a young woman who went missing after church one Sunday, last seen near the river. She was in the right age group, but her colouring was darker. Nevertheless, it was worth checking. The rest of his list of the town's missing persons were too young, too old, or had already been found or claimed.

An hour later, Harry closed his volume with a decided thud.

'I have two possibilities,' he said, 'but one of them belongs to Burton and Lou – a missing person case they worked on for a few months. If memory serves me, I think she's been claimed.' They compared notes.

'I've got one lady who is a reasonable match to the pyjama girl's description,' Thomas said. 'Let's go check with Burton and Lou first, and then we've got three families to visit, bringing good or bad news depending on how you look at it.'

Harry rose and collected the volumes to return them to the desk. 'I imagine you always live in hope that your loved one would come home alive.'

'Knowing one way or another must be better than a life of never knowing and being in limbo,' Thomas said, rising and putting on his jacket. 'Never being able to move on would be a terrible state of affairs.'

The men pondered this as they sought out their two counterparts in all the likely places – their offices or the canteen. They found them in Burton's office going over their files.

'Ah, feeling stuck, boys?' Thomas joked seeing their morose looks.

Burton grimaced at the two detectives. 'Never. Just a pause to get our thoughts together. Don't tell me... the department's finest want our help again?'

His partner Lou, grinned and folded his arms in front of him. 'It appears that way. Luckily we're generous souls.'

'That you are,' Harry laughed.

'The pyjama girl?' Burton asked.

Thomas nodded. 'It appears she might be a missing person. No one has claimed her yet or come forward to say she is a relative or a friend is missing.'

'We've got three possible matches,' Harry continued. 'We think it might be two now, if you've claimed one of the young women.' He read out the lady in question.

'Yeah,' Burton owned to her. 'Edith Dobin – a theatre-lover and church goer apparently, poor young thing. Mrs Dobin couldn't identify her daughter because the body had been in the river for days, but in the end, she thought a mark on her daughter's leg and a mark found on the corpse's limb were similar. The husband agreed.'

'They buried her last week,' Lou added.

Harry sighed. 'That's a pity. I wonder if the pyjama girl might be Mrs Dobin's daughter and she identified the wrong girl.'

Lou shrugged. 'Too late now, and she was happy to bury someone.'

They all looked at him and he justified himself. 'Well, you would be.'

'Unless it's the wrong body,' Thomas said. 'Well, thanks lads, we'll check out the other two missing persons we have and try our luck there.'

'And if you don't have any luck and they are not a match, are you going to go stir up our case which we are in the process of closing?' Burton asked, not looking happy.

'No,' Thomas said. 'We'll see if we can get the public to help identify the pyjama girl. We're acquiring the services of an artist to draw the pyjama girl's face since she's been brutally bashed.'

'And if that doesn't work, the pyjama girl becomes another lost soul,' Harry said.

Chapter 11

Sydney Fenton did not love lightly. It was his best and worst trait according to those who knew the melancholy young man, and few knew him well. He woke up late, after 11am, and rose to take his breakfast. He was a kept man. Handsome at twenty and six, adored by his mother, Jane, who never got over the loss of her beloved husband, Sydney's father. Mr Fenton senior was from old money from the mother country and arriving in Australia, invested well, before he upped and died from consumption.

Sydney, unlike his father, had no head for business and even less interest in it. His mother had business advisors who ensured their investments kept them, their property and staff in the life they afforded. Sydney had more important matters at hand – creating his poetry. He moved in artistic circles as a member of the Valley Literary Association who met regularly at their club to share their musings.

The night before had been a night of passion ending with a spark of hope. He thought back on it as he dressed to go downstairs, and the words of his friend and fellow poet, Percy Sutton.

'Come now, Sydney, love and loss, it is what makes us better poets,' Percy had said, pushing a glass of whiskey to him as he returned to their table with their drinks.

Sydney raised the glass, toasted their health and grimaced as he sipped the whiskey.

'But how I loved her, Percy,' he said, and took another sip before professing, 'alas, I was not enough for her.'

'Sara was always a restless soul. You wouldn't have it any other way.'

Sydney grunted.

'It is true and you know it. Not being able to possess her completely made her so much more worth possessing, and you, my dear friend, were the only man she truly loved.'

They drank in silence while both men thought on Sara and watched the milling crowd.

Percy spoke: 'Will you read it tonight? The poem you wrote for her? I would love to hear it and it has been a while since you have presented.'

Sydney nodded. 'Most likely I shall. But only if the quality of the other offerings is fitting company. Last week was drivel.'

'It was immature work at best, although I thought young Hugh showed promise,' Percy agreed. 'Share with me a verse, something poignant to accompany my drink.'

Sydney knew it by heart; for weeks he had worked on the verses, trying to capture his pain and loss with words. He took a deep breath and looking at Percy said:

I do not wish to be warm when you, in your grave, are cold;
But jealous I be of your earthly blanket, and all which it holds.
Rest and wait for me in your grave mound,
Until again in your love, I am bound.

Sydney finished and his voice hitched on the last words. Percy leant over and tapped his shoulder with affection.

'You have done her justice, Sydney. That is fine work.'

Sydney nodded his thanks. Percy continued before Sydney could become too maudlin.

'I saw a young lady today who was a beauty to behold,' Percy said with a grin and finished his drink with a large gulp.

'And did you work your charm on her?' Sydney said with a smile, encouraging his amorous friend.

'No, she was not for me. For you. She was so much like your Sara.'

Sydney sat up a little further in his chair and leaned over to his friend. 'Where did you see this beauty?'

'In a bookstore, while picking up a volume of poetry I ordered. The fairest of hair, the rubiest of lips, eyes that shone with life.' Percy waved his glass for Sydney to get the next round. 'I thought of you immediately.'

'Who was she, this beauty?'

'I cannot be sure. She was enquiring after Turner's new book.'

Sydney groaned. 'Turner again, damn him.'

Percy continued. 'A dark-haired companion also of considerable beauty accompanied her. I believe they said they were both writers.'

'A wordsmith,' Sydney said in a low voice, fascinated. 'And her name?'

'I overheard from some distance when they introduced themselves to the bookseller, so I may not have heard correctly.'

Sydney sighed. 'And thus, I am bound never to see or meet her or even know if the name upon your lips is her name,' he said melodramatically. 'Her name, what did you believe it to be?'

'Matilda.'

Sydney repeated the name softly, as he departed the table to freshen their drinks.

Now, in the cold, hard light of late morning, as he reflected on that conversation, and basking in the success of his poetry reading of which his work was held in high acclaim, he had to confess there was hope in his heart, a quickness in his step and light in his eyes that had not been there for some time. Love was just what he needed to buoy him again, and he intended to pay a visit to the very same bookstore. This Miss Matilda might return or at the very least, he would find out more about her.

*****

The front door of the compact timber cottage opened and a small lady, dressed neatly in a clean, simple grey dress looked stricken to see the two men on the verandah.

'Good morning, Madam, Detectives Ashdown and Dart,' Thomas said introducing them both.

'Have you found her?' Her voice rose in anxiety.

'There's no cause for alarm, Mrs Moorehouse,' Harry assured the woman who he assumed opened the door with trepidation and hope every day since her daughter went missing a year ago.

'We have no news as yet,' Thomas said but before he could elaborate, Mrs Moorehouse interrupted.

'Forgive me,' she said remembering herself, 'please come in.'

'That won't be necessary, but thank you,' Harry said. 'Are you home alone, Mrs Moorehouse?'

'No, my husband is in the garden out the back,' she said, her hand going to her heart again expecting bad news.

'There is a young lady that was found recently—'

'The girl in pyjamas?' Mrs Moorehouse asked. 'I saw the story in the paper and my husband and I went to the morgue straight away.'

'So, you have seen her?' Thomas asked surprised. They had not been informed.

'No, they would not allow it then. But our daughter had a very distinct burn mark from childhood on her back, and the gentleman was good enough to go and look. It was not on the girl in pyjamas,' she exhaled.

'Right then,' Harry said.

'Was that the only lady you were here about today?'

'The only one,' Thomas said. 'We are sorry to have alarmed you.'

Mrs Moorehouse's face dropped with relief. 'No, thank you both, detectives. I am grateful that she continues to be in your thoughts. But I confess I am torn between relief and disappointment that it is not her.'

'Of course, perfectly understandable,' Harry said. 'We are sorry to raise false hope for you, Mrs Moorehouse. We shall bid you good-day.'

She thanked the detectives again and closed the door. Harry turned to Thomas who exhaled.

'Poor woman,' Harry said.

'What agony,' Thomas muttered. 'To the next household then.'

'Let's hope we don't cause the same pain,' Harry said, taking to the footpath and crossing the road to walk on the shady side.

Their next port of call was within walking distance but it would have been more comfortable to take a hansom cab. Finding one proved tricky and they decided to venture on foot. On arriving and knocking on the door of a dishevelled home that appeared to be shared by two families via two separate entrances, they found the reception to be less than welcoming.

'She's run off many a time, so if it is her, she's got what she deserves,' a large man wearing brown trousers, a white singlet and no shoes, told them.

'Caused you a bit of stress has she, Mr Osbourne,' Harry asked, trying to engage the middle-aged man for the purposes of getting the pyjama girl identified and off their books.

'Only from the moment she could walk,' he said. 'I've seen all the stories about the pyjama girl. It's her you think might be Florence, isn't it?'

'We are hoping,' Harry said. 'We'd love someone, a family member, to claim her.'

'I can tell you now, my daughter wouldn't be hanging around a church and I imagine she'd be wearing something more outrageous than pyjamas!' Spit flew from his mouth as he became angrier with the telling.

'By any chance, would you have a portrait or a photograph of Florence as an adult, Mr Osbourne, and then we can eliminate your daughter and find the pyjama girl's rightful next of kin?' Thomas asked, hopeful.

He nodded and strode off, leaving them standing on the doorstep. They heard him speaking to someone, possibly Mrs Osbourne, but he returned on his own moments later with a family portrait photograph.

'The wife had us sit for this on our 25th wedding anniversary. Florence is one and twenty.'

Harry accepted the photograph and both men looked at Florence. She was not the pyjama girl.

'Thank you, Mr Osbourne. It is not your daughter,' Thomas said and Harry returned the photo to the large man.

'Thought as much. Good luck finding that one's folks then.'

They bade him goodbye and stepped away. Harry spotted a hansom and hailed it to their great relief. It was too hot to be walking, especially in their suits.

'So, the only other missing person who comes close to the age and description of the pyjama girl is the one recently claimed and buried – Burton and Lou's case,' Thomas reminded his partner.

'Yes, but let's see if the wider public can identify her before we bring in the wrong parents and dig up the dead.'

Chapter 12

Late afternoon, Matilda and Georgina walked along the path looking for the terrace house of author Linton Turner. A parade of trees along the path provided a cover of shade for the young ladies who felt the heat of the day in their corseted undergarments and fitted skirts and blouses.

'I cannot believe he lives locally,' Matilda said in a low voice. 'I was sure Linton Turner would live in Sydney or Melbourne.'

'We are so lucky,' Georgina agreed. 'I cannot believe the bookstore owner shared Mr Turner's address with you. You charmed it out of him.'

Matilda smiled. 'I learnt from Alice that one must use what one has to get ahead. She is very charming and successful at getting quotes and contacts when needed. I've been understudying her.' Matilda laughed at the thought. 'Having four brothers, I've not been privy to the feminine wiles of women or how to use them. My role model, Aunt Audrey, is terribly practical and my sister-in-law Minnie is quite demure.'

'Minnie is, and very traditional. I truly admire your Aunt Audrey. I've always liked practicality – my mother is much the same,' Georgina said, and gave a small sigh.

'I am sorry, I did not mean to make you homesick.'

'Not at all, silly of me,' the pragmatic Georgina said, brushing away her melancholy. 'My parents are not far away and I will go visit them soon, Elijah will come along as well. They did take a shine to him.'

Matilda smiled with happiness. 'I am so delighted that you and Elijah are together, and Alice and Daniel too. I hope we will be sisters,' she teased and Georgina blushed with pleasure at the thought, even though she was not the blushing type.

'Here it is,' Georgina said, stopping out the front of the townhouses and checking the number. 'It is the one with the black door, number three. A very nice residence.'

'Indeed. Let's just hope Linton Turner is home and he agrees to see us without an appointment,' Matilda said lowering her voice.

'I'll leave the charming to you,' Georgina said and chuckled.

'It is a bit naughty of us but we can always say we came to make an appointment and can come back any time that suits him.'

Matilda knocked on the door and stood back a little. They heard footsteps coming which sounded too light to be that of man, and the door swung open. A young girl wearing an apron, her light brown hair pinned up, and looking hot and flustered stood in the doorway.

'Mr Turner is not receiving,' she said before Matilda opened her mouth. 'I'm the house manager,' she said standing tall with importance.

Matilda nodded. 'Well thank you, Miss?'

'Elsie,' she said, offering only one name.

'Miss Elsie. I am Matilda Hayward and this is Miss Georgina Urry. We work for the *Women's Journal.*'

'My mum says that is bluestocking nonsense and I'd be better off working hard than wasting my time reading it,' Elsie said.

Matilda suppressed an involuntary laugh and she heard Georgina beside her do the same, smothering it with a small cough. It was not the first time they had received that reaction.

Georgina spoke up: 'We were hoping to interview and illustrate Mr Turner for our magazine. Many of our readers are great admirers of his work.'

'Or perhaps make a time with Mr Turner for the interview,' Matilda added.

Elsie shook her head firmly as if it were out of the question. 'Mr Turner said to turn everyone away. Sorry. I've got to go; I have lots to do.'

'Elsie,' a loud male voice boomed behind her and she rolled her eyes and turned to look behind her.

'Yes, Mr Turner.'

'I believe I need a writing break, so I have time for the ladies from the journal. Show them to the drawing-room please.'

Matilda and Georgina smiled with delight as Elsie scowled and moved aside to allow the ladies to enter.

Women's Journal
Tuesday, 12 February 1889
Fortnightly edition Vol.1, No.34.
Price, 3d.

The Pyjama Girl Mystery

An interview with author, Mr Linton Turner, about his latest book coming to life.

Report by Matilda Hayward.
Illustration by Georgina Urry.

--OOO--

Accomplished author, Mr Linton Turner, was surprised and distressed when his intriguing book, The Pyjama Girl Mystery, came to life.

The newly released tale that depicts the murder of a young woman, whose body is left on the steps of a church, came off the page when a young woman was found in her blue silk pyjamas in the same manner as featured in the book.

'They say imitation is the sincerest form of flattery,' Mr Turner said, 'but that is far from the truth in this case, when the death of a young woman is involved.'

The book tells the story of a young independent woman with grand ambitions to succeed in the world of stage theatre. She has dancing and acting skills, and is considered very beautiful.

Mr Turner's character is loved by many, including two men who cannot have her and without wishing to ruin the story for readers yet to acquire their copy, the young lady's future does not bode well.

'The moment I heard of a young lady's body dressed in pyjamas lying on the church step — as my victim is left in The Pyjama Girl Mystery — I was very worried,' Mr Turner said.

'I contemplated, was this someone who is out to harm me or my reputation, or is it a terrible and insensitive prank?' he asked.

Mr Turner refused to believe it could be a gift to the author or flattery.

'It would be a very unhealthy mind that might think I would take any comfort or delight in seeing this scenario play out,' he said.

None of Mr Turner's other books had

experienced a reaction of this nature, and as we are yet to learn more about the young lady left on the church steps, time will tell if her life imitates art, and if she too won the heart of two men and met her death at the hands of one.

The young lady in question is yet to be identified, but the detectives on the case are hopeful that her family will soon claim her. If you have a loved one or a friend missing, please direct your query to Detectives Ashdown or Dart, Roma Street Police Headquarters.

Chapter 13

Aunt Audrey – Mrs Samuel Bloomfield – was a regular attendee at the Hayward household of which her brother, James, was head of the family. She believed it was her Christian duty to offer guidance to her niece and nephews. This intent was often lost on the younger family members namely Daniel, Gideon and Matilda. The visits included birthdays, of which, including her own, there were six occasions, as the twins' Elijah and Gideon shared a birth date. There were the celebrations after mass for the holy days of obligation including Christmas and Easter, and every Sunday after church for lunch, which was a family tradition.

With the death of James's wife at a young age, and her own beloved husband, Samuel, Aunt Audrey was a welcomed maternal presence in a household full of men, except for Matilda. This evening was Amos's birthday, her favourite Hayward nephew. Elijah – for whom she insisted on meeting the costs of putting through medical school – followed a close second.

Satisfied with her grooming, her silver hair affixed firmly atop her head and expensive but tasteful jewellery selected, Aunt Audrey departed her abode. She liked to arrive earlier than the other guests, precisely on the hour at five o'clock, to oversee preparations. Her brother was inclined to let the household staff manage as they pleased; fortunately, as Harriet and Mary had been with the family for decades, this was proving to be satisfactory.

Aunt Audrey's impressive carriage pulled up out the front of the stately home in Highgate Hill, and she alighted with the assistance of her brother, James, who she found in the garden at the time of her arrival. No sooner had she greeted James than Matilda arrived, coming up the path with far too much haste for a young lady.

'Aunt Audrey, Pa,' Matilda said, breathless, giving them both a kiss on the cheek. 'This heat,' she fanned herself.

'Indeed, and at the speed you were walking young lady, no wonder you are hot. Remember young ladies do not run. Although the colour in your face from the exertion is most becoming,' she said, praising her niece.

'And you are out of black, Aunt Audrey! It is so lovely to see you in colours,' Matilda said.

'Indeed, Audrey, most becoming,' James agreed as they walked inside to the cool.

'I have mourned Samuel long enough. I cannot bear one more summer in black, I'm sure he would understand,' she said, with a glance to Heaven and then down at her fawn-coloured dress.

'Two years, not fifteen, is a respected mourning period,'

Mr Hayward teased her. 'You have been respectable above and beyond the call of duty.'

'We have a full house tonight,' Harriet said, greeting Aunt Audrey and Matilda at the door and assisting Aunt Audrey with her hat and gloves.

'I have had to add the extension to the dining table,' Mr Hayward agreed. 'The garden conservatory is coming along nicely and soon we'll have our gatherings out there.'

'What is that book you are reading?' Aunt Audrey asked, seeing a book tucked under Matilda's arm. 'Do not tell me it is to do with that dreadful pyjama murder.'

Matilda hid the book behind her back. 'One and the same, Aunt Audrey, but I was reviewing it for the *Women's Journal* before the murder happened.'

'Lord save us,' Aunt Audrey said, and with a roll of her eyes. Matilda smiled and gave a small shrug before racing upstairs to put the book away with Audrey's voice ringing in her ears: 'You will be a married woman in two months, Matilda, surely your husband will not approve of such a book.'

'Don't be so sure, Audrey,' Mr Hayward said, 'it happens to be his case and where Matilda's concerned, Thomas has a lot to manage.'

'That girl,' she said shaking her head and excusing herself to go inspect Mary's cooking in the kitchen.

*****

Closer to dinner time, Mr Hayward stuck his head in the kitchen to find Mary flushed with the heat but with everything under control.

'You survived inspection?' he asked in a whispered voice and Mary, the Irish cook, laughed.

'I'm still here, don't you be worried about that, Mr Hayward,' she said with a laugh.

'I will ensure you receive a bonus, Mary, for these days when you have to cook tea for such a large, raucous lot. We are taxing you.'

'I won't hear of it, Mr Hayward,' she said, standing tall as if affronted. 'You know I love a large brood and having my cooking appreciated. The other days when it is just yourself or two or three of the family provide plenty of ease for me. Do not be thinking of any such bonus. Besides, the lovely country lass brought a tart with her. She's a thoughtful one that.'

'Georgina is indeed. Let's hope Elijah snaps her up.' He gave Mary a smile and nod, before disappearing and would ensure she received a bonus. Entering the dining room, his heart swelled at the size of his brood around the table; Amos, the birthday boy, 29 today with his lovely wife Minnie, now herself in the family way. Daniel with Alice, Elijah and the 'lovely country lass' Georgina, Matilda and Thomas, and Gideon on his own today and looking a little worse for wear. Elijah was right to be concerned.

Mr Hayward started with a toast. 'To my eldest son, Amos, nine-and-twenty today. I remember the day you were born like it was yesterday. Your mother and I were so thrilled – this fair-headed little lad who changed our lives. The house was peaceful for a while,' he teased.

'Thank goodness I came along next and put an end to that,' Daniel joked.

The family chuckled and Mr Hayward continued. 'You have borne a lot as the eldest, Amos, especially in the dark days with your dear mother's passing and you being of age to have felt it most keenly. And despite your brothers and sister,' Mr Hayward said, lightening the mood, 'you have grown to be a fine young man, found yourself a beautiful wife and will soon have a family of your own. My heartfelt best wishes on your birthday, Son,' he said and raised a glass.

The family joined in.

'You'll want a good influence on that child of yours too,' Gideon said, teasing the conservative Minnie. 'I guess you are looking at me as a godfather?'

Minnie's eyes widened with alarm and Gideon laughed. She smiled at him.

'You are wicked sometimes, Gideon,' she teased him.

Aunt Audrey agreed. 'Amos, praise the Lord, gave us much to be proud of, and Elijah of course, but Daniel, Gideon and Matilda, well you all appear to be settling down a bit at last.' She sighed. 'As for you, James...' she addressed her brother.

'Uh oh,' Mr Hayward said, and earned laughter from around the table.

'I have introduced you to no less than four lovely ladies now, and not one has captured your interest. Mrs Vaughan has similar interests to yours and has been widowed these past five years. I can't imagine why she was not suitable,' Aunt Audrey said.

'My dear Sister, you have done your best and I invite you to hang up your matchmaking mantle. The ladies are all delightful, including Mrs Vaughan. But I could not keep company with a member of the Woman's Christian Temperance Union.'

'Good God no,' Gideon agreed, and took a large sip of his alcoholic beverage.

'I don't believe she strictly abides by it,' Aunt Audrey said.

'Nevertheless, I like my afternoon port and cigar and shan't be abstaining from the evil of alcohol,' he joked.

The conversation broke into small groups during the meal, and Matilda and Alice were most keen to hear news on the pyjama girl case given their vested interest. Georgina and Elijah were having an animated discussion with Gideon and Aunt Audrey which splendidly distracted Aunt Audrey from the inappropriate discussion Matilda launched.

'I have nothing new to tell you,' Thomas said, and tried to focus on the superb roast dinner Mary had produced. His diet had improved since his nephew, Teddy, moved in, but no one cooked like Mary.

'I find that hard to believe, Thomas,' Matilda said. 'We have news for you.'

He looked up interested but expected the conversation would be shut down as soon as Aunt Audrey heard wind of it.

'We went to the main bookshop in town,' Alice said, 'and spoke with the owner.'

Matilda nodded. 'He had some interesting things to say about the character of the author.'

'Is that so?' Thomas asked. 'Perhaps you can tell me later. I'm sure Daniel doesn't care to hear about it,' he said and looked to his closest friend for rescue.

'Quite the contrary, I hope it comes to court and I get appointed the illustrator,' he said. 'I'd love to sit through this mystery.'

Thomas rolled his eyes.

'What?' Daniel asked and then grinned.

'You are no help,' Thomas said.

'No, none at all. Surrender, Thom, you should know better than to go up against Matilda and Alice.'

'I shall trade you,' Matilda said, 'one snippet of information each apiece.'

'I'm sure I can't speak with my mouthful, that would be bad manners,' Thomas said, and shoved a reasonably sized piece of baked potato in his mouth and smirked at her.

Daniel laughed. 'Clever move.' He shrugged when he saw the look his sister gave him.

'We are no longer children, Daniel,' she reminded him sternly. 'Then I shall go first,' she said, placing her hand on Thomas's arm to prevent him from using his fork for another mouthful and making Alice laugh. 'The bookstore owner gave us Mr Turner's address and Georgina and I paid a visit to him this very afternoon.'

Thomas promptly swallowed and shook his head.

'You cannot be serious?' he asked, his jaw locking. 'You and Georgina could have been in great danger. We don't know if he is involved or not.'

'Don't be silly, Thomas. It was broad daylight, his house manager Elsie was there and I didn't go alone, as I said.'

Thomas shook his head again. 'We are going to talk about this. Later.'

'Do you want his address or not?' she said. 'The bookstore owner asked me not to give it to anyone, but if the police insist on me handing it over... and I did promise I'd share with Detective Dart.'

'Yes, please,' Thomas said. 'And you can tell me everything he said later too.' He shook his head again.

'Your turn,' Daniel said, ribbing him.

Thomas frowned at his friend and resigned himself to playing the game. 'This is all between us, not to be reported in the *Women's Journal*, unless you source the information yourself?'

'Agreed,' Matilda said and Alice nodded.

'We have had no success trying to identify the young lady as yet, and there are only two missing women who might resemble her. There was a third, but a family recently claimed and buried her.'

'Oh, that is good for her, unless...' Matilda stopped mid-thought.

'Yes, the identification was not conclusive, so let's hope they did not identify the wrong woman. Your turn.'

Matilda nodded to Alice.

'Mr Moore, the bookseller, said that Linton Turner was gregarious and led quite an active social life at his club,' Alice said. 'Mr Moore says he could have been speaking about the subject of his book for months before it was published.'

'Great,' Thomas muttered and sighed.

Matilda nudged him. 'Your turn.'

'This is all I have, my last piece of information for now.'

'Good, because we are out of news too,' Matilda said, keenly leaning forward. 'Go on then.'

He frowned at her enthusiasm. 'We are considering having a sketch drawn of the young lady for distribution but need to consult with an artist to recreate it.'

'Because her face was damaged? I read that in the paper,' Matilda said, and Thomas nodded.

'Imagine doing that job for a living – painting the faces of the dead for presentation,' Daniel mused. 'He must be a dry fellow this artist.'

'It's a lady actually,' Thomas said and Matilda's eyes widened. 'A young lady, very talented according to Harry. She is also a mortician and embalmer.'

'How wonderful! Have you met her?' Matilda asked enthusiastically.

'Not yet.'

Matilda looked to Alice. 'Mrs Lawson is always looking for women to profile who are in interesting careers. I must meet this mortician and embalmer!'

Thomas was about to protest when the group was distracted by a small ruckus that broke out at the other end of the table. Gideon clearing his throat, rose and excused himself and strode to the front door and opening it with haste, departed. Elijah stood to follow, but Mr Hayward rose and pressed his son back to his seat.

'Let me see to him, Elijah,' he said and followed the way of Gideon.

'What on earth has happened?' Matilda asked the group to her left of the table.

Elijah lowered his voice. 'Gideon has not had a pleasant week. Despite the success he has made of managing the gallery, the owner has decided to sell it or close the business when the lease expires, depending on which comes first.'

'Oh no!' Matilda exclaimed.

'He is so good at managing people and his creative ideas have brought people in; he has put that gallery on the map,' Daniel said with a shake of his head at the pending outcome.

'Gideon has also parted company with Miss Chappell,' Elijah added.

'Then we must occupy Gideon as best we can,' Matilda said.

'Agreed,' Aunt Audrey proclaimed. 'Gideon is a reasonable rider, is he not, Elijah?'

'Yes, Aunt. He is very good in the saddle.'

She nodded. 'I have a new horse that needs to be ridden regularly and to have a firm hand ride him. I shall seek Gideon to assist me. Time in nature is a wonderful remedy for many ailments including distress of the heart.'

'That's excellent, Aunt Audrey,' Elijah said, 'I couldn't agree more.'

'I wonder...' Georgina started.

'Go on,' Elijah encouraged her.

'I was thinking of offering lessons in art to those who might be interested. The idea only came to me because several people have asked would I instruct them.' She looked at the group. 'Daniel, too, is an illustrator. If we were to offer lessons after hours and weekends, occasionally, I wonder if Gideon might find a space and make a business out of it.' She shrugged. 'It is probably a silly idea.'

'It is a marvellous idea,' Aunt Audrey exclaimed. 'I can help as a silent partner with funds and I know many mature ladies who would enjoy art classes.'

'I would be happy to do some teaching,' Daniel agreed.

Matilda saw the look of adoration Alice gave Daniel.

'It would be a great drawcard to take lessons from a court illustrator and a *Women's Journal* illustrator,' Alice agreed looking from Daniel to Georgina and back. 'I am sure Gideon could sell that. Not to mention other classes that Gideon might procure in different forms of art, like pottery, perhaps.'

'Georgina, you must put it to him, it was your idea,' Matilda said, and Elijah agreed, smiling at his clever belle. Matilda continued: 'For my part, I will seek a suitable match for Gideon. Someone unique and creative like him; I shall think on it.' Matilda looked to Aunt Audrey. 'Fear not, Aunt, I also have a lady in mind that I wish to introduce to Pa. I shall put my plans in action.'

Beside her, Thomas smiled. 'Brace yourself, everyone. They are bound to work then.'

She playfully hit his arm but did not stop scheming for the rest of the evening.

Chapter 14

Mr Hayward found his youngest son in the garden, sitting on a bench near the conservatory that was a work in progress. Gideon smoked a cigarette, his legs extended out in front of him, a frustrated look on his countenance. As he walked towards his son, James Hayward marvelled at the wonder of Gideon – he was a striking looking young man, and with an energy for life that added to his allure. Mr Hayward sat beside him.

'You shouldn't have left the party, Pa, I am fine.'

'The party will go on without me. I am worried about my youngest boy.'

Gideon scoffed. 'Three and twenty! Not so young anymore, and out of your hair.'

'When you have sons and daughters of your own, you will know they are never out of your hair, even if your hair is thinning,' he said, and accepted a cigarette from his son.

They sat and smoked in silence for a while.

'I don't know why he would want to sell when we are now

the largest and best-selling gallery in town. All that work,' Gideon shook his head.

'And that is why,' Mr Hayward reminded him. 'You have a gallery at the standard at which he will make a handsome profit. If it was never really his passion and merely a business interest or a passing fancy to dabble in the arts, you have made it profitable for him.'

'I feel like I've wasted the last two years of my life,' Gideon muttered.

'Or your work has been a wonderful achievement which attests to your business acumen for the next project you undertake, or employer you seek. You could start your own business or make him an offer.'

Gideon scoffed again. 'I may be a good manager, Pa, but I am not a good saver. Perhaps if I'd guessed this was coming, I might not have been as reckless with my money. I am no Amos,' he said of his sensible eldest brother.

Mr Hayward studied Gideon. 'You know, Son, even though your mother passed away when you were but seven, you were a source of constant wonder to us; you still are to me.'

Gideon looked at his father. 'Why? Because I am the most reckless, the most unreliable?'

'Sometimes,' Mr Hayward agreed, 'but no. Because we often thought you were the best of both of us.'

Gideon looked away, thinking about his father's words and a little uneasy with the emotion of it.

Mr Hayward continued. 'Your mother was like Matilda and Daniel, quite a free and happy spirit, which you are.

But unlike you, she had no sense for business or interest in it, finding it dreary. But she could write, draw and was very musical. I was all serious when I met her, all about getting ahead and settled, planning and providing for a family as Amos and Elijah are today. I was very good at management, even if I say so myself, and turned many a business around. You have the best elements of both of us. A passion and energy for life like your mother, and even as a child you were strategic in how you went about your activities. Being the youngest son, and with a dash of youth thrown in accounts for the recklessness, but that will pass. You are the best of us both.'

Mr Hayward could tell his son was thinking on his sentiments, his feelings heightened, and now with his father's endorsement, Gideon swallowed his emotion.

'Thank you, Pa,' he said and rising, quickly made his way to the street, leaving the house without looking back.

*****

Thomas was sitting with his nephew, Teddy, enjoying a late-night drink after the Hayward dinner and Teddy's return from the late shift. Fortunately, he had not changed; he heard the gate opening and a person heading up his path.

'This can't be good,' Thomas groaned, expecting to be called back to work.

'I'll get it,' Teddy said.

'No, stay comfortable. It's bound to be for me,' Thomas sighed and rose, heading to the door as the intruder knocked loudly. He opened it to find one of the senior constables from his station on the doorstep. A man in his early thirties, he was a reliable policeman and due for a promotion.

'Begging your pardon for the late intrusion, Detective,' he said.

'Not at all, Constable. Am I needed?'

'Well, that is up to you, Sir. I thought it best to let you know there's a man in our cells asking for you. He's had a bit to imbibe and worse for wear,' the constable said discreetly. 'He can just sleep it off there with the others that we've brought in as well.'

Thomas sighed. 'Would his name be Gideon Hayward by any chance?'

'That would be him, Sir.'

'Thank you, Constable. I appreciate you taking the time to fetch me. I'll go directly there and take him home.'

'Sir,' the Constable said with a tip of his hat and departed the way he came.

Thomas closed the door and met Teddy in the hallway.

'He's had a bad week, needs a bit of sorting out,' Thomas said by way of explanation.

'Happens to us all,' Teddy said. 'I'll come with you and give you a hand.'

'I'll be right. Hopefully, he's not that bad.' Thomas returned his glass to the sink and thought about the situation. 'Perhaps I'd better bring him back here and he can sleep it off on the couch rather than take him home to the Hayward household.'

'Probably best. Let me assist. Come on, the sooner we're

there, the sooner we are home. Just be glad it's not me,' Teddy joked. 'I'm a lot bigger.'

'Yeah, I'd probably leave you there,' Thomas teased his nephew, as they grabbed their hats and coats and went to retrieve Gideon from his night of wild abandonment.

Chapter 15

T he morning was the only time of the day to experience a little coolness, but as the summer departed, that was slowly being extended. Thomas undertook his dressing early and had sent word to Daniel where he might find his brother. Hearing a hansom cab arrive out the front, Thomas met Mr Hayward and Elijah at the door as they alighted and headed up the path. He was a little disappointed, but not surprised, that Matilda had not accompanied them. This was a man's problem and it was best that Gideon's father and his twin took him home.

'Thank you, Thom,' Mr Hayward said, extending his hand. 'I hope Gideon did not place you in a difficult situation with your work.'

'No, it's fine. It's not like he's a regular in the cells,' Thomas said, and his expression conveyed that it best stay that way.

'Renovations are coming along nicely, Thom,' Elijah said, taking in the improvements since his last visit on a Wednesday evening when the boys all met up for dinner, port and cigars. 'Still needs a woman's touch,' he teased.

'I know just the woman,' Thomas said with a grin and led them to the lounge room where they found Gideon sprawled on the couch. He stirred as they entered.

'Uh oh,' he mumbled, and sat up, running a hand through his dark unruly hair. 'First the constabulary, now Pa and my double.' He squinted as Thomas opened the curtains in his living room.

'I shall leave you to it then,' Thomas said.

'No need to leave on our account, Thom,' Mr Hayward said, 'we shan't be long.'

'Don't rush, Mr Hayward, but I'd best get to work. I have much to do today. Teddy is still asleep in the back room – he's on the late shift, so just close the door when you leave,' he said and bade them farewell.

He was happy to depart and let Elijah and his future father-in-law sort out Gideon; he had enough dramas on his plate with a case that was still very much up in the air.

*****

Mr Hayward took a seat nearby and studied his son, as Gideon ran a hand over his unshaven face and winced as he sat back on the couch. Elijah sat at the end of the couch vacated by Gideon.

'What is the time? I have to get to work too,' Gideon asked.

'They'll smell you coming,' Elijah said. 'And you have ample time, it is not yet seven.'

'Why are you both here so early?' he asked, frowning at them.

'Why indeed,' Mr Hayward said. 'Gideon, I want your full attention.'

Gideon sighed and nodded, wincing again straight after. 'I'll do my best.'

'This stops now,' Mr Hayward said. 'Your brother has been worried about you for some time, as have I, and this is the course of action we'll be undertaking—'

'You need not be worried about me,' Gideon cut his father off and looked to his twin. Neither young man said anything but a look of understanding passed between them. Mr Hayward had seen their silent communication many times over the years – nuances, glances, signals.

'We will worry about you,' Mr Hayward said, 'although Elijah has 300 patients at the asylum to worry about as well, but I suspect you are top-of-mind.'

Elijah smiled. 'If I could have you committed, I could keep an eye on you all day.'

'Don't even jest about it, please,' Gideon said, rubbing his temples.

'Son, your attention please,' Mr Hayward said, and Gideon stopped his action and nodded respectfully.

'I have a business arrangement to discuss with you.' Mr Hayward noted the look of interest in Gideon's eyes, the spark of life.

'I'm listening,' Gideon said.

'Your aunt, Audrey, and I have recently been discussing business ventures—'

'You don't have to back me,' he cut his father off again.

'Gideon, listen,' Elijah, the eldest of the twins ordered his brother.

Mr Hayward continued. 'As you know, I have a handful of business ventures that I am involved in as a silent partner or active member. Audrey has her fingers in several pies, mainly community-focused activities. We have been looking at a couple of ventures to invest in together, but your situation creates a perfect opportunity for us. We discussed it after the family dinner last evening.'

He stopped; Gideon did not interrupt, so Mr Hayward continued.

'Audrey and I will provide the capital as silent partners to buy the gallery for you,' Mr Hayward held up his hand as Gideon went to speak. 'We wish to be investors, so we will own a half share each. You will continue to run it as a business, paying off the interest-free loan of my half investment to me. When you have paid it off, which given the gallery's success of late, should be prompt, my half ownership will be transferred to your name. We will structure the payments to ensure that you can maintain the business and current staff level; there is no hurry to pay.'

'There's more, just wait,' Elijah said as Gideon opened his mouth to speak again.

'Are you following so far, Son, given the state we find you in this morning?'

Gideon looked a little contrite given the trouble he was causing.

'I am,' he said, and could not hide a small smile. His eyes gave away his rising level of excitement.

His father continued. 'As Audrey insisted on paying for Amos's law degree and Elijah's medical degree, she insists on her half of the investment being gifted to you after you have paid back the loan to me. So you will then own the gallery outright. All your hard work, all your creative ideas, the freedom to develop it as you wish, will be yours.'

Gideon put his hands to his face, exhaled, and then lowered them.

'You don't have to do this, Pa,' he said once more, his resolve for turning down the gift, lowering.

'We want to do it,' Mr Hayward said with a smile. 'Last night when you and I spoke of your mother, it reminded me of the necessity of having some creative outlets in my own life. I will enjoy seeing the gallery prosper when I know it is your gallery. There is a condition with Audrey though.'

'Alright,' Gideon said warily, 'what is it?'

'You know she holds a lot of community functions amongst the elite set for fundraising. She would like you to consider hosting a selection of them in your gallery – cocktail parties where the town's influential residents gather. It will showcase your gallery to the business leaders of our town.'

'That'd be brilliant,' Gideon said, leaning forward, clasping his hands. 'That's hardly a condition.'

'Georgina and Daniel were also throwing around some good ideas last night that you missed when you left early,' Elijah said. 'My very clever lady, Georgina, suggested you could offer after-hours and weekend art classes on the premises if you had room to do so. She for one, and Daniel, are both illustrators and would happily consider teaching. Charge a small amount, bring people to the gallery, and so on.'

'That's brilliant too,' Gideon said. He sat back and looked to the ceiling with a grin on his face.

'Right, Son, well, I shall leave you to negotiate the price.'

'Do so today if you can, so you do not miss out,' Elijah added.

'Yes,' Mr Hayward agreed, 'and remind him you have made the gallery what it is and that should be factored into his price to you. I am off to see my banker now. Audrey and I will be ready to pay the bill of settlement once agreed upon, and Amos has offered to do the legal contracts, free of course,' Mr Hayward said and rose from his seat.

Gideon stood and embraced his father. Mr Hayward patted him on the back.

'You're welcome, Son.'

Gideon pulled away, smiling. 'I'm going to be a gallery owner and manager.' He sunk back down on the couch again, a wide smile and excited eyes.

'Not if you don't bathe and try to hide the smell of brewery about you. Not to mention making that offer sooner rather than later,' Elijah said.

'Right, you are Brother,' Gideon said, rising and hugging his twin as well, making Elijah laugh with relief at seeing him happy again. Gideon stepped back, swayed and rubbed his head. 'I'm going to be a gallery owner.'

Mr Hayward and Elijah grinned at his enthusiasm. The three men departed to start their business day.

Chapter 16

Matilda was quite determined to get several things done today – her day out of the office, and she was up early with a view to doing so. She also had a fitting for her wedding dress late morning with Aunt Audrey and her sister-in-law Minnie. There wasn't a great deal she saw eye-to-eye on with Minnie, but given Matilda intended to wear a very traditional wedding dress, it was the perfect time to invite Minnie along and spend some time with her. It also pleased her eldest brother, Amos, that Matilda included his wife.

She joined Daniel in the breakfast room before he headed to his morning session illustrating at the courts.

'Where is Pa this morning?' Matilda asked seeing his place at the head of the table empty. 'He is not ill, is he?' she turned to Harriet who entered the dining room with breakfast items.

'Nothing like that, do not alarm yourself,' Harriet said. 'He and Elijah have gone to retrieve Gideon from Thomas's house.'

'Thomas and Teddy collected him from the cells last

night for being drunk and disorderly; he slept the night off on Thomas's couch,' Daniel informed his sister.

'And they have gone to collect him? I would have liked to have gone too,' she said, most put out.

'I suspect they knew that,' Daniel said, 'but calling on Thomas early is not advisable. I've seen him first thing in the morning, save the shock until you are wed,' he joked and Matilda laughed.

'I shall tell him you said that.' She sighed, thinking of Gideon. 'What of Gideon, is he alright?'

'He'll be fine. Pa and Aunt Audrey spent many hours last night talking and are going to offer to buy the gallery for Gideon to pay off and own. Pa will tell him this morning.'

Matilda clapped with delight. 'It is just what he needs, and imagine what he will do with it. I am so relieved.' She smiled and felt lighter knowing Gideon would be happily distracted. Matilda thanked Harriet and reached for some toast and jam. 'I shall call in on him today at the Gallery while I am on my outings and see him. I imagine he is so excited.'

'It will buoy him indeed,' Daniel said pleased. 'Now, we just need to fix his love life.'

'I'm working on it, and Pa's too,' Matilda said.

'Good grief,' Daniel muttered.

Matilda grimaced at her brother. 'You have done very nicely out of my matchmaking Daniel, so don't you dare start.'

'I wouldn't dream of it.' He gave her a wink. 'You have my eternal gratitude.'

'Eternal? How long does that last?' Matilda teased.

*****

John, the crusty, reliable sergeant on the front desk at the Roma Street Police Station shook his head.

'No one has come forward to claim the young lady in pyjamas, detectives. Sorry to be the bearer of bad news.'

'A great shame,' Harry said. 'Thanks, John.'

'Damn,' Thomas muttered.

Harry turned to Thomas. 'Right then, let's get that illustration of the deceased young lady done and get it to the newspapers and onto noticeboards.'

'It's our only course left,' Thomas agreed.

'A trip to *The Economic Undertaker* is in order and we'll see if Miss Phoebe Astin can accompany us to the mortuary to do the illustration, or if she wishes us to bring the pyjama girl's body to her.'

Thomas nodded. 'I also want to visit a mercantile store and ask about those pyjamas. Plus, I have the address for the author, Matilda gave it to me,' he said, patting his jacket pocket as he followed Harry down the hallway.

'At a price?' Harry teased.

'No doubt I'll pay for it somewhere along the long,' Thomas said with a smile. 'We can follow up with the author after the mortician. Let's get this case moving along. I feel like the lady in pyjamas is not the only one slumbering.'

'I feel the same. But I wonder if we should leave the author for a little longer until we have the illustration, and see if they are connected.'

'As you wish,' Thomas said.

The two men exited the police headquarters and hailed a hansom to take them to the business premises of *The Economic Undertaker*.

When seated next to his partner, Harry asked with a smile: 'Is Miss Hayward ahead of us with her investigation?'

'It would not surprise me.' Thomas chuckled, and shared what Matilda had gleaned from the author. When he finished, he looked out at the passing trade and workers but saw little, a frown upon his face.

'Soon you will be able to have her insights every night, and her company of course,' Harry joked. 'It is lovely to come home to your Mrs and the lights burning.'

Thomas returned his smile. 'I am looking forward to it, but it will be strange at first.'

'Are you concerned about how you will manage when you are married; if the pressure might increase on you to share your work with Miss Hayward?'

Thomas gave a small shake of his head. 'We will establish boundaries, eventually. But that is not what I am concerned about,' he said, his voice dropping and the sentence hanging in the air.

Harry waited, not pushing; he was used to Thomas's manner. Eventually, Thomas explained a little more.

'It's because we have known each other since I was seven and Matilda was but four years old. I spent more time at the Hayward household than my own home when growing up.'

Harry nodded his understanding. 'You are worried, because of familiarity, that your duties as a husband might be awkward or—'

'Yes.' Thomas cut him off. 'It's nothing.'

'You cannot speak of this with your best friend, as he is Matilda's brother. Or your father?'

'Never.'

'I see.' They drove in silence for a short while, both thinking their own thoughts.

Harry cleared his throat. 'If I may?'

Thomas gave him a consenting nod and Harry continued, understanding what was required of him. He had been a mentor to Thomas for some years now and regarded him with great affection. Harry lowered his voice, even though it was just the two of them and the driver above was unlikely to hear.

'When I was a young man and quite a successful boxer, I attracted a lot of women. Lovely girls, but not the type I would take home and introduce to my mother.'

Thomas smiled, paying attention.

'When I met Terese, ah, she stole my heart, I was gone for her,' Harry said with a grin.

'At the hospital?' Thomas asked, even though he knew the story but he wanted to hear it again.

'Yes. I was in there after getting roughed up on my police rounds – outnumbered,' he explained and Thomas grinned.

'No doubt. You're still good with your fists, so there must have been a few of them.'

'In my early years I was partnered with a cranky old bugger, and he couldn't fight his way out of a paper bag. I held my own but I couldn't fight for two against five. Anyway, I'm lying there in the ward and next to me is a pleasant fellow, about my dad's age who was in for a small operation. His lovely daughter, Terese, paid a visit, and ended up visiting me as well.'

Thomas laughed, and then Harry got serious.

'Like your Miss Hayward, Terese was a good girl and I was experienced. I've never strayed and never dishonoured her, but if I can offer several pieces of advice?'

'I'd welcome it,' Thomas said.

'In strict confidence? This reflects on my relationship too,' Harry said.

'Of course,' Thomas agreed.

'Lead. I believe a lady – from the timid to the most capable – likes a confident man.'

Thomas nodded his understanding. 'And?' he asked.

'You have nothing but time, Son. Enjoy learning together, and laugh at anything that does not go according to plan. That is most important because it ensures neither party feels embarrassed or frightened to try again.' Harry tapped his nose as if imparting a great secret. 'Call it "practice" and you must do homework to get it right,' Harry chuckled. 'Then there is no end to how many times you can lay together, and try to ensure both of you are happy.'

Thomas smiled. 'Step up, don't take yourself too seriously, and relax.'

'That's it in a nutshell. But that's just the ramblings of an old bugger,' Harry said, with a shrug and a smile.

'No. I appreciate it. Thank you, Harry, thank you,' Thomas said, sincerely.

'My pleasure, Son.'

Chapter 17

Phoebe Astin was not at all what Detective Thomas Ashdown was expecting to find in the dour rooms of *The Economic Undertaker*, despite what Harry had told him of the young lady. At Harry's age, he was inclined to consider a young lady was still in her fourth decade, so Thomas remained dubious of his descriptions. However, this time, he was accurate regarding Miss Phoebe Astin. Young, attractive, of medium height, and somewhat unconventional – her blonde hair was tied back loosely with a ribbon, not held in pins in the traditional fashion, and her dress was free-flowing with no corseting. She entered the reception and smiled with delight at seeing Detective Harry Dart.

'I told you your skills would be called upon again,' Harry said after introducing Thomas to Miss Astin and her grandfather, Randolph Astin, who was similar in age to Harry.

'Oh good, what do you have for me?' she asked, her eyes wide with excitement.

'If we may call upon your services, we have a lady in pyjamas,' Thomas said, declining the offer of a seat as the small group remained standing in the large foyer area of *The Economic Undertaker*, Randolph behind the desk. Thomas did not want to linger; he felt the same every time he visited Dr Nevins in the morgue, despite the pleasure of being cooler.

Phoebe looked to her grandfather and then back to the detectives.

'Oh, I did wonder if she had been claimed and taken to another funeral director; my brothers have gone to the morgue regularly to collect the deceased we are to bury, but she has not visited us.'

'Such a pitiful thing when a person is not claimed,' Randolph said, with a sigh. 'We see it more often than you can imagine.'

'Sad indeed,' Harry agreed. 'But this unclaimed lady is somewhat complex, and we will understand if you do not wish to take it on, Miss Astin. She is not a comfortable sight.'

Phoebe smiled and her grandfather chuckled.

'My granddaughter has a cast-iron stomach,' Randolph said, 'more so than her brothers.'

'It is true,' Phoebe said. 'Besides, I would very much like to help you and the lady. What might I expect?'

'We are hoping you might illustrate her face so we can print copies for the newspaper and noticeboards. However, it may require some creative license,' Thomas said with delicacy.

'She has a facial injury?' Phoebe asked.

'One side of her face has been struck and best you know it now… it is caved in.'

Phoebe's eyes widened and her hand went to her heart. 'The poor lady. If she is not identified by the drawing, will you attempt to present her for a viewing? Do you need me to somehow make her a little more viewable? Perhaps I can hide the injury with a scarf and reveal enough of the side I repair with my kit to make her respectable for identification.'

'Yes please to the illustration and if necessary, presenting her,' Harry said.

'There's another strange thing,' Thomas said, 'she's embalmed.'

Phoebe's mouth dropped open and she looked from Thomas to Harry. 'Embalmed?'

'I gather you do not know who undertook the embalming or you would seek identification there?' Randolph asked.

'Exactly,' Thomas said. 'What do you know of the practice that might help us?'

'Well, there are many of us trained in it, including Phoebe, but it is rarely used here because we bury rather quickly. The heat demands it,' Randolph said. 'Bodies are not on show but rather in the ground within two days. No need to embalm.'

'Hmm, that is interesting,' Harry said, 'and creates more questions than it answers.'

'Such as?' Phoebe asked, curious.

'How long has she been dead? Was she embalmed and on display for some time? Has she come from further afield than our region?' Harry said.

Thomas continued. 'Was she previously buried? Where was she embalmed? Where has she been all this time? Why is she not on our missing files?' he said.

'Goodness, you have your work cut out for you,' Phoebe said. 'If it is possible, I would prefer to work on the pyjama girl here so that I can keep my other appointments and work on her around them. I shall apply whatever makeup I can to make her look like she might in life and then commit her image to paper. It will be quicker that way.'

'Excellent, thank you, Miss Astin. And your fee —' Harry began.

'The Police Force has an account with us, Detective, we can use that if you have permission to do so,' Randolph said.

Harry nodded and thanked him.

'I won't do any more than necessary at this stage,' Phoebe assured them, 'and we can look at the presentation aspect later, should she remain unidentified.'

Randolph looked at the diary. 'Shall I send Julius and Ambrose just after midday to collect her from the morgue?'

'Perfect, thank you both,' Harry said. 'I shall advise the morgue to expect them for the pyjama girl's collection.'

Thomas was only too pleased to get out of the funeral directors' offices. Death had a smell that he could never get out of his nostrils, whether it came from a crime scene or the funeral cortege, he could always smell it.

*****

Gideon laughed as Matilda released him from her embrace. She removed her hat and gloves and greeted his assistant, Miss Warren, who briefly appeared to say hello and disappeared just as quickly.

'How exciting!' Matilda exclaimed.

'I know,' Gideon said his smile wide, his eyes alive with excitement. 'I have a meeting with the owner this very afternoon.'

'Does he know what the meeting is about?' she lowered her voice in case Gideon had not mentioned it to Miss Warren. 'That you are going to offer to buy the gallery?'

'I told him I have a proposition and he was most interested,' Gideon said. 'I have told Miss Warren too and assured her of her job security, but she is sworn to secrecy.'

'Wonderful. I can't imagine why he would not accept the offer. Who better to sell it too and he has not had to advertise or pay an agent the commission for his sale.'

'Let's hope he sees it that way,' Gideon agreed. 'Pa visited the bank this morning and he and Aunt Audrey have given me a limit to spend to, but I intend to get much lower than that.'

Matilda looked around the gallery. 'To think this might soon be yours, and look at all the artists you represent.' She turned her attention back to Gideon and sniffed slightly. 'You do smell like you had an excessive night though, Gids.' She baulked slightly at the strong scent of alcohol wafting from him.

He groaned. 'I have changed and tried to freshen up, but I drank a skinful last night.' He rubbed his forehead. 'I also have a throbbing headache.'

'I suggest you have a strong coffee and I shall go to the chemist for some Rowlands' Kukonia powder.'

'Make-up? I don't look that bad, do I?' he asked alarmed.

'Not make-up, just a dusting of powder which might absorb some of the alcohol smell coming off your skin.'

'Oh, well nothing to lose, thank you, Tillie, that would be great.'

She smiled with pleasure. 'I'll be calling back the favour.' She saw his smile fade to a look of suspicion.

'Okay, but I don't want to come to the theatre with you, I've had a lifetime of that,' he said, still upset by the recent end of his cordial relationship with Miss Lily Chappell, which remained close to the surface of his conscience.

'Good grief, no. Besides, I have lots of people I can drag to the theatre before you, should I wish to go,' she assured him. 'But I may need to pay a visit to a funeral home and once I get my research completed, I was hoping you could escort me.'

'Well, that's different. Anyone dead that I know?'

Matilda smiled. 'No, it's for a story, if Mrs Lawson agrees.'

'Consider it a deal. Now... the powder if you please?'

'Back soon.' Matilda exited and hurried off to purchase it. She was keen to suggest the story to Mrs Lawson for a profile piece on an interesting woman with an equally interesting career. And, if Thomas advises that the mortician is an attractive young lady and single, then she will insist Gideon accompany her for the interview. The lady mortician would not be a conventional choice of lady to romance, but Gideon was not a conventional man either. Their artistic outlooks may just match and Matilda would get a great story out of it too! It really was a lovely day.

Chapter 18

Having attempted to make Gideon somewhat more respectable, Matilda entered the dressmaking salon for her private appointment with Parisian modiste, Nicolette Emmanuel. Nicolette was the only dressmaker to make the wedding dress, according to Aunt Audrey who waited with Minnie for Matilda's arrival. Aunt Audrey had insisted on paying for Matilda's dress and that of her bridesmaids. Generously and somewhat emotionally for Aunt Audrey, she pointed out it would be the only niece's wedding she would have the opportunity to enjoy, given she only had one niece. Aunt Audrey spared no expense.

'The Honiton lace is perfect,' Aunt Audrey said, putting her spectacles on to look more closely at it and admiring the patterns of butterflies and lilies. 'Well done indeed, Mrs Emmanual.'

'Nicolette, please,' she reminded the ladies with her melodic French accent, 'and thank you. It is a beautiful lace and I think it will make this dress unique.'

Nicolette directed Matilda behind the curtain to change as the ladies continued their banter. After some prodding and poking, Matilda emerged and the two ladies gasped.

'Oh Mrs Emmanuel, you have outdone yourself,' Aunt Audrey said, disregarding the request for first-name basis informality.

Matilda stood before them in the fitted and elegant wedding dress. A high neck bodice covered in delicate lace flowed to long sleeves and into a full silk skirt and train. The trim around the sleeves and skirt was a Liberty silk satin trim, and on her small feet, Matilda wore satin shoes.

'It is truly breathtaking,' Minnie agreed and sighed. 'It's so lovely being a bride.'

Matilda smiled with delight, as she looked at her reflection and turned to admire the dress.

'You have taken the tomboy out of me,' she said with a laugh that Nicolette reciprocated.

'That was not hard, Matilda. You have a very feminine figure and face,' Nicolette said, moving to pin an area that she felt needed attention. 'You are correct, Mrs Bloomfield,' she addressed Aunt Audrey. 'The lace is the perfect touch.'

'Aunt Audrey, I cannot thank you enough,' Matilda said. 'It will make me feel so special on the day.'

Aunt Audrey smiled. 'Perhaps it will start a new tradition. Your daughter might wear it and her daughter after her.'

Matilda smiled. 'Wouldn't that be wonderful?' Her smile dimmed a little.

'What is it?' Minnie asked. 'I should not ask, but do you not want children?'

'Oh, indeed I do, we both do,' she said assuredly. 'There is only one thing that makes me a little sad about my wedding.'

'Your father,' Aunt Audrey said, and Matilda nodded.

'I hate to think of him alone in the house or at meals. I fear he will be lonely.'

Aunt Audrey sighed. 'I understand and I have done my best to introduce him to suitable women who could enrich his life, but he is most stubborn and particular.'

'I am not sure Pa is lonely though,' Minnie added, addressing her father-in-law as a new daughter-in-law would. 'Amos has needed help and offered work to Pa, but he was not keen to accept. He said the work no longer held interest for him and he was content filling his days.'

'Minnie is right,' Aunt Audrey said. 'James still has three sons who live at home and come and go, Harriet is always there, along with that cook of yours that I've been trying to poach for years.'

'Yes, I am being sentimental,' Matilda said, turning as directed by Nicolette who was working on the skirt length. 'Besides,' she said, and narrowed her eyes mischievously, 'I have a lady I believe might be a delightful partner for Pa. I will tell you about it over our lunch, but I intend to put my plan into action over the next few days.'

Minnie clapped with delight. 'Would that you succeed!'

'I also have a lady in mind for Gideon, but I have not as yet finished my research on her.'

'Well young lady,' Aunt Audrey said, as Nicolette declared today's session finished, 'let's hope all the family members have a guest on their arm for your wedding.'

'Including you, Aunt Audrey?' Matilda asked wide-eyed with surprise, knowing Aunt Audrey had no interest in remarrying.

'Not in the manner in which you are scheming, Matilda, but a companion perhaps.'

Matilda and Minnie exchanged looks.

'Not another word about it,' Aunt Audrey warned them. 'Now hurry and change and we can discuss this woman for your father over lunch.'

Matilda had one more long look at herself so she could remember the moment and went to change. Everything was going to plan, she mused, which meant it probably wouldn't!

*****

Blue silk pyjamas by the box load. Thomas sighed as the vendor indicated the current stock on hand.

'I sell about a dozen pairs a week, sometimes more on the weekend,' the middle-aged salesman said stroking his moustache as he thought. 'Sid, down the street at the markets, stocks them as well and sells just as many.'

'So, you wouldn't remember the ladies who buy them, or have a record of them then?' Harry asked anticipating the answer.

'Lord no. No idea. We have them in pink too if you'd like a pair for your missus,' he said with a look at Harry then Thomas.

'No, thanks,' Thomas said. The last thing he wanted was Matilda wearing pyjamas he saw a dead girl in.

The men thanked the vendor and returned to the Roma Street Police Station to find Julius Astin looming large at the reception desk. The eldest of the brothers from *The Economic Undertaker*, his height and bearing gave him a formidable stance and many heads turned as they passed him in the hallway.

The Desk Sergeant, John, looked up at hearing Harry's voice talking with Thomas.

'Ah, detectives, a gentleman to see you,' John said and waved a hand at Julius.

'Mr Astin,' Harry said surprised. The men shook hands and Julius followed Harry and Thomas down the hallway to Harry's office, avoiding the board in Thomas's office where they were collating their investigation. 'What brings you here? Is everything alright?'

'Yes, I believe so, thank you, Detective Dart.'

'Did the morgue not release the pyjama girl to you?' Thomas asked

'No, we have her. It's just that Phoebe thought something might be of interest to you,' Julius said.

'Anything, we'd be grateful for all insights,' Harry assured him. 'Will you take a seat?'

'Ah no, but thank you. My brother waits outside with our carriage. Phoebe wanted me to tell you the embalming was not done by a professional.'

Harry and Thomas were stunned for a moment.

Julius offered a small shrug as if he had wasted their time. 'She said it might not be important.'

'No, it's very important,' Thomas assured him.

'Very,' Harry agreed. 'You just caught us by surprise. So, it may have been done in the home of the killer, by anyone, by a citizen.'

'According to my sister, yes.'

'That is extremely helpful, Mr Astin, we're grateful you came by,' Thomas said.

'Please tell Miss Astin so, and give her our thanks,' Harry said. 'Does she have any other insights?'

Julius smiled. 'Plenty, I suspect she talks with the dead,' he said in jest. 'But she assumed most of her observations would have been passed on by the coroner.'

'Our coroner tends to deal in the physical not necessarily the nuances a lady might pick up,' Harry said. 'Could you advise Miss Astin that we will call on her tomorrow should she find time to give us an audience?'

'I am sure it will be fine, come at your convenience,' he said, and taking his leave, Julius Astin departed.

Thomas turned to Harry. 'How hard is it to embalm someone if you are untrained?'

'I have no idea but Miss Astin and the coroner can no doubt tell us,' Harry said. 'We don't have much to go on, but every bit helps.'

'We have next to nothing,' Thomas agreed and they returned to his office to study the board. 'A woman is found in pyjamas that half of the women of our town own. A man with a coat and hat dumped her on the church steps, his face not visible, but witnessed by a church helper. We have a mystery tale that tells of her murder before it happened and an author who when asked in an interview denies all knowledge. Add to that an embalmed body that does not give us a date or time of death, and was embalmed by an amateur.' Thomas sighed.

'Yep, we're lost,' Harry agreed.

'Not for long,' Thomas fired up. 'With the illustration soon at hand, I feel we will have success identifying our victim.' With that, Thomas called it a day. 'Are you coming around for a drink or staying for tea?' The Wednesday night gents' club, as Daniel had named it, was starting as soon as each man arrived at Thomas's place of abode.

Harry consulted his timepiece. 'One drink won't hurt or get me into too much trouble. The mother-in-law is coming to dinner.'

'That's one experience I'll never have,' Thomas said, given Matilda's mother passed away when he was seven, and that was the year he befriended Daniel. He did not remember her presence in the Hayward household.

The men caught the omnibus and walked the remaining distance to Thomas's house, keen to remove their suit jackets and enjoy a cool ale. Teddy would have the drinks on ice given he was on the morning shift this week.

On arriving, they found the gents' club in full swing with Daniel, the twins – Elijah and Gideon – already present, along with Teddy and his prison chef colleague, Joseph Fieldhouse, who was always welcome for the quality of cigars he brought. Despite the heat, Teddy had cooked up several large shepherd's pies for later. It was an open invitation on a Wednesday evening with one condition – you had to be male.

'I hear congratulations are in order,' Thomas said, extending his hand to Gideon.

'Signed and sealed today,' he said shaking Thomas's hand, the delight on his face evident. Gideon proceeded to tell the rest of the guests why.

'You are looking at the new owner of the *Gallery of Fine Arts*, and a man with a huge loan,' he said, and welcomed the laughs and congratulations from the group.

'I'm thrilled for you, Gids,' his twin, Elijah, said.

'We're a diverse bunch,' Teddy said topping up drinks. 'Detectives, chefs, doctor, illustrator, and a gallery owner.'

'If Mr Hayward or Amos were here, we'd have the law covered as well,' Thomas agreed.

'As scintillating as Pa and Amos might be, they don't bring good cigars like Joseph,' Daniel said satisfied.

Joseph chuckled and Elijah jumped up and reached for his medical bag – he had come straight from work at the asylum, but was rarely without it in case of an emergency.

'That reminds me. A patient passed away last week and her family gifted me a bottle of port,' he said pulling it out of his medical bag.

'Is it safe to drink do you think?' Gideon teased his twin.

Elijah laughed. 'The seal is unbroken, I've checked,' he joked. 'She was a lovely lady and very wealthy. Her family were pleased for her care and for her demise, I suspect.'

He showed the bottle to Harry who had taught himself a thing or two about wines and ports and had a keen interest in them.

'It's an 1879 Seppelt Para Liqueur Port, Harry, what say you?' Elijah asked.

'That's a very good drop, Elijah and ten years old is just right for a port,' Harry said.

'You sure you want to waste it on this lot?' Daniel joked.

'Either that or I'll polish it off myself,' Elijah said.

'Best we help then,' Gideon added, 'I'm always thinking of you, Brother.'

'So, do we only have a few more of these gatherings to go then?' Joseph Fieldhouse asked. 'I hear you are to be wed very soon, Thom.'

'That is the truth, but I assure you, our Wednesday gents' club will continue here indefinitely,' Thomas said. 'Besides, Matilda intends to do her own Wednesday ladies' club. I'm not sure if she's warned her father yet that they will be moving in on Wednesdays or if she intends to have it elsewhere.'

'I'd love to be a fly on the wall at those sessions,' Daniel said. 'I wonder if they'll talk about us.'

'They're ladies, of course they will,' Teddy said, 'just like we're talking about them now!' The gents laughed.

The conversation moved around to Thomas and Harry's latest case – the pyjama girl.

'I can't believe no one has stepped forward to claim her,' Teddy said.

'Once we've got the illustration of her face, hopefully, she'll look familiar to someone,' Harry said. 'It is being drawn for us now.'

'Let's hope,' Thomas agreed. 'She has a distinct style and haircut. Her blonde hair is cut blunt to her shoulders and she has blue eyes and is about Matilda's height.'

'I saw a girl like that not long ago,' Gideon said.

Thomas and Harry turned to him, eager for any insights.

'Lily made me go to some boring arty club so she could hear a poet reading. Some man she loved who was a bit of a fop. A woman just like that was there, flitting around.'

'What was the name of the club?' Thomas asked.

'The Quill Club.'

Thomas looked at Harry. 'The very same club that the author of *The Pyjama Girl Mystery*, Linton Turner, frequents.'

'You might have just made yourself useful, Gids,' Elijah said, watching the detectives as they considered what was said.

'First time for everything,' Gideon retorted. 'We could go there tonight if you like?'

'No,' Thomas and Harry said in unison.

'I need to be a little more prepared before then,' Thomas said. 'But thanks, Gids.' With that Thomas tuned out as his mind spun with possibilities. He needed to go to that club but he had no intention of taking a large group with him. A subtle study of the club surroundings and patrons was in order, and he would do it himself sooner rather than later.

Chapter 19

It was most improper and Matilda knew she should not do it – risk being found visiting, unaccompanied and unwed, at a single man's abode. But regardless she rushed to Thomas and held him, her arms finding the strength of his body inside his jacket, feeling his back defined through his shirt.

Thomas hesitated for a moment – more surprised than bowing to propriety – and then returned her embrace with passion, holding her tightly to him. She was waiting for him on his front veranda, and he pried himself away long enough to lead her inside, pleased to be alone and out of the watchful eyes of the neighbours. She still wore her hat and gloves, and looked most becoming in a pale blue dress with cream lace. Before he had even closed the door, Matilda reached for him and held him again.

'What is it? What has happened?' he asked, hurriedly, concerned and fearing bad news.

'Oh, Thomas, it is the worst of news.'

'Tell me,' he said, trying to move her slightly so he could

see her face and hear her words better. He caught but a glimpse of her face and saw her eyes were slightly swollen from crying.

'Matilda, what has happened?' he demanded firmly but kindly as he searched for his handkerchief from his pocket to offer it to her.

'Thomas, someone has killed me,' she said and tilted her head to look up at him. Her head was caved in on the side and her eyes glazed as if dead.

Thomas yelled out in terror, thrashing in the sheets, caught in the horror of seeing his beloved battered. His bedroom door burst open and his nephew, Teddy, rushed into the room.

'Uncle!' He moved to the bed and shook Thomas, who awoke gasping and looked around in terror. His bedding and bedclothes were askew, his eyes wide, and breathing ragged.

'Whatever it was, it is not true, a dream,' Teddy assured him.

Thomas issued a string of profanities. He swung himself out of bed to a sitting position and wiped his face with his bed shirt before throwing it off.

'I am sorry that I woke you, Teddy,' he panted, a little embarrassed by his calling out.

'You didn't. I was reading in the lounge room, contemplating going to bed.'

'What time is it?' Thomas asked perplexed.

'Just on midnight. You have only been asleep about an hour.'

Thomas rose. 'I'll never sleep again tonight. I am going out.'

'Out? Now? Where?'

'The Quill Club,' he said, and gathered his clothes and started to dress in his suit.

'The club that Gideon mentioned? That's not your scene from what I've heard of that club. Lots of stage actors, writers and artistic types.'

'Exactly, and somewhere that our victim might have frequented,' Thomas said, continuing to dress at a speed that showed he was keen to leave his bedroom and outrun his nightmare.

'I'll come with you,' Teddy said.

'You need not, I'll be fine, I am only observing.'

'I want to; I am on the afternoon shift tomorrow and need not rise early. I'll change.'

Thomas nodded. 'I'd be pleased for the company.'

As Teddy departed, Thomas continued to dress, the terror of seeing Matilda so lifelike and so dead horrifying him. He wanted to go straight around to the Hayward household, rouse her and look upon her face, but he knew he couldn't. He tried to think of ways he could justify it, but it was after midnight, and he did not want to incur the wrath of his soon-to-be father-in-law despite how much he needed to see her to settle himself. He knew he was being irrational but Thomas considered trying to awaken Matilda at her window, however her bedroom on the second level would not be easy to reach, and he could not afford to have his career set back should someone report him for loitering.

The explanation would be most embarrassing. He wasn't a praying man, but he hoped to God that she was safe and peacefully sleeping in between the sheets of her bed, her face whole and pretty on the pillow.

*****

Thomas had calmed a little by the time the two men entered the club. He wished he had an illustration to show to patrons who might be willing to help him, but he also saw the benefit of lying low for the first visit and getting the feel of the place. Thomas and Teddy found the club full of patrons despite the hour being nearly one o'clock. Grabbing a drink from the bar, Thomas directed them to a small table in the far corner where he could observe the goings-on. He had briefed Teddy on the way about the author, Linton Turner, frequenting this club. Matilda had tipped him off, courtesy of the bookstore owner. He was also pleased Harry suggested waiting to talk with the author; much better to view Linton Turner and his habits beforehand.

'They most likely create a verse in the afternoon, come here at night and sleep all morning,' Teddy said, studying the crowd and leaning in to talk with his uncle. 'What a life.'

'A different world from ours,' Thomas said, not averse to the smoky haze, relaxed atmosphere and the opportunity to put Matilda out of his mind for a moment.

A small jazz quartet placed in the corner near the bar, finished a number, enjoyed a rowdy round of applause and declared they were taking a break. Straight away, a young man took to the stage and called for the next recital. There were several interested parties, but the man who took to the stage was given the most encouragement. He pulled up a stool, introduced his work and began a recital of his verses.

'Lord save us,' Thomas muttered. He was not one for poetic verse, least of all bad poetic verse.

Teddy chuckled beside him. 'Have you spotted the author yet?'

Thomas shook his head. He had only the photographic portrait he had seen in a newspaper clipping to go by and Georgina's illustration in the *Women's Journal*.

'Can't see him, but it's not the easiest place to spot someone.'

A glass was broken, a cry went up, and the poet held up his hands in frustration and then continued with his verse.

Thomas said so only Teddy could hear: 'So, the author might have taken to that very stage and read his story about the murder of a girl in pyjamas out to this crowd,' he mused. 'Then one of them has gone away to enact it.'

'True, unless the author brought his book to life. But who is the poor girl that was chosen to be the subject of the re-enactment and why her?' Teddy asked.

'Why indeed?'

The crowd applauded as the poet left the stage.

'I could do better than that after a few rums,' Thomas said, making his nephew laugh.

'I'd pay to see that,' Teddy teased him and Thomas chuckled.

And then the young master of ceremonies returned and

introduced "Everyone's favourite author", asking 'What have you for us tonight, Linton?'

The author that Thomas recognised took to the stage with much stomping and cheering.

'That's *The Pyjama Girl Mystery* author,' Thomas said, leaning forward with interest and studying Linton Turner. 'The bookshop owner told Matilda that Turner haunts this place, he was right.' The author was confident, well imbibed and had an air of arrogance.

'I'll tell you what I don't have for you... is another one of my murder plots,' the author said in jest and smiled. 'While I appreciate the publicity gents, bringing the crime to life is a bit extreme.'

There was much laughing, clapping and jeering. Thomas wanted to jump up and remind them all that a young woman was dead. Instead, he took a large gulp of his drink.

'Tonight, I present for your listening pleasure – hopefully – a page or two from my very first book published fifteen years ago to the day. An anniversary indulgence if you will,' Linton Turner said.

He began to read and Thomas tuned out, studying the crowd. They all looked like they couldn't commit a crime of such a heinous nature for fear of soiling their suits or cravats. He finished his drink, grabbed Teddy's glass and headed to the bar for a refill.

Chapter 20

Harry entered Thomas's office and departed just as quickly, making his way down to his own office. It was rare that he beat his partner in, except on days when his wife, Mrs Terese Dart, had her early morning church gatherings and he went without company and breakfast. Glancing into his own office, he found it empty as well, so returned to John at the front desk.

'I can't find him, John, perhaps he has gone to the dining room,' Harry said. 'I'll head out and call back for him.'

John looked confused. 'He has not come by this way again, Detective, and he was definitely in his office last time I passed.'

'Hmm, I shall check once more,' Harry said and returned down the hallway. He entered Thomas's office completely this time, and making his way to Thomas's desk to see if there was anything that might indicate where his partner had gone, Harry saw Thomas's legs sticking out from behind his desk.

'Good God,' he said racing around, to find Thomas asleep on the floor and startling him awake. 'I thought you were dead.'

Thomas leaned up on his elbows. 'I do feel a little like that, but not today.'

'What's going on? Did Teddy kick you out of your own home?' Harry asked confused.

Thomas chuckled, rose and dusted off. A glance at the looking glass told him he looked like he had spent the night on the street.

'I was up late doing research so I saw no point in returning home given I only finished around four this morning. I thought I would come in here, rest a little and start again when you arrived.'

'Why didn't you come and get me?' Harry asked, remembering the last time Thomas went off on his own to question the doctors at the asylum and it did not end well.

'I hadn't planned on going but couldn't sleep. It was just to the club that the author is said to frequent. Rest assured, I didn't do any interviews, just observed, and Teddy came too,' he said. 'It gave me a chance to view Linton Turner with his guard down.'

'Excellent. Let's have breakfast then and you can tell me your findings. Terese has her church meeting this morning so left before me and I dare not enter the kitchen,' he said with a smile.

Thomas straightened his necktie and ran a brush through his hair. 'Presentable enough?'

'No, but no worse than some of the others,' Harry joked and the men made their way to the police dining room.

Soon after, laden with a hearty fried breakfast and a morning cup of tea, Harry said, 'So did you fit in? I hear that club is a bit highfalutin?'

Thomas grinned and said in his best street accent: 'Are you sayin' I couldn't pass for someone with a bit of culture?'

'Heaven help us,' Harry chuckled. 'So, what did you see, hear or discover?'

'My first thoughts were that most of that lot are too soft to commit a murder of such violence.'

'Ah, but passion has brought out the worst in many a man,' Harry reminded him. 'All through history the worst battles have been fought for love or God.'

Thomas shook his head. 'What hope is there?'

'That's where the ladies come in... they remind us of what is worth protecting in the world,' Harry said, 'and I firmly believe that. So, what else did you observe?'

'Linton Turner was there and admitted as much that he had read extracts of that book, *The Pyjama Girl Mystery*, out on stage and inflicted some of his earlier work out loud on the crowd.'

Harry looked amused. Both men conversed and dined in comfort with no regard for table manners in the male-dominated dining room.

'What's he like?' Harry asked.

'Full of his own importance and surrounded by friends who reinforce his status,' Thomas said.

'Hmm, not surprising. Did you speak with him at all?'

'No.'

'Good. Best we approach him in the light of day, with clear heads,' Harry said relieved.

'I felt the same, but Teddy spoke with him. He was at the bar when Turner also sidled up for a drink. Teddy has the knack of being able to talk with anyone.'

'He does that,' Harry agreed, finishing a piece of toast. 'What did he glean?'

'It was most interesting and I'm keen to see if his story will change when we speak with him. Teddy sympathised with Turner and asked if he had modelled his victim on anyone he knew.'

'Good lad,' Harry said, keen to hear Turner's response.

'Turner said many of his characters from his latest books are based on a beautiful woman he knew, but one in particular that he had feelings for, did not return his attentions. He then joked; he was sure she was still alive and recognised herself captured forever on his pages.'

'Interesting,' Harry said. 'So, is the outcome – that being her brutal death – what he wanted for her since she did not return his affection?'

'And did he inflict it on her, or was it merely a coincidence?' Thomas said. 'You don't suppose… it's a strange thought, but if she has been his inspiration for the last few books, could she have been embalmed and with him all that time?'

'Perhaps discarded when he had finished his work and his need for her,' Harry mused, thinking out loud. 'Let's see what he has to say about that theory. You did well.'

'Thanks,' Thomas said and suppressed a yawn.

'Why couldn't you sleep?'

'I had a shocking dream,' Thomas said with a slight shrug as if it were ridiculous.

'There would not be one soul in this building that didn't have nightmares from the job now and then, from the constables to the hierarchy.'

Thomas sat back with his cup of tea and exhaled. 'It was so real, I had to get up and banish it from my mind.'

'An accident or murder scene we have visited?' Harry enquired. 'I've seen those many a time in my sleep.'

'No,' Thomas said, and frowned thinking upon the dream. 'I saw the pyjama girl, but it was Matilda.'

'Ah, dreadful. I am sorry, Thom,' Harry said, grimacing. 'I understand why you needed to rise and convince yourself it was not true.'

Thomas leaned forward. 'Have you ever not wakened? That would be hell.'

'If that happens, Son, then it is not a dream.'

*****

Sydney Fenton glanced up and winced at how bright the morning was, despite the fact it was nearing noon. He confirmed from the sign above the door he had the correct bookstore. He entered and found no less than half a dozen ladies and two gentlemen scattered between the shelves perusing books.

It did not take long before he heard the whispers; he always attracted them. The Fenton's of the top of the peak in Spring Hill were wealthy beyond imagination and both unmarried. His widowed mother had no intention of marrying again, and Sydney hoped to, but his beloved was gone – her death inspiring voluminous lines of verse. Many a mother had pushed their daughter towards him, which is why he avoided poetry launches and book signings. He was also respected and held in some renown for his volumes of poetry that were critically praised by the literary reviewers. Add to this, his face was handsome beyond compare – a heady mixture, if his melancholy and indulged nature could be overlooked.

The bookstore owner's eyes widened on seeing him enter.

'Mr Fenton, what a pleasure to have you in my store. Trevelyan Moore, owner and manager, at your service. Can I be of assistance?' He asked with a small bow, and a glance around to see who else was paying attention.

'Good morning, Mr Moore, what a fine bookstore you have.'

'Thank you, Mr Fenton. We pride ourselves on being the biggest in the town with a wide representation for all literary tastes.'

'That does not surprise me,' Sydney said, as the skill to charm people and write verse were good companions and came naturally. 'If I may have a moment of your time, I was hoping you could help me find an old friend for my mother.'

'Of course, if I can, I would be happy to assist,' Trevelyan Moore said, standing taller with importance now that his assistance was being sought.

'A colleague of mine was here just recently purchasing a book of poetry from your fine collection and he mentioned meeting two ladies that were discussing books with you.' Sydney held up his hand and looked around with an engaging smile. 'Obviously, you have many lady customers.'

'I do, but perhaps a little more detail and I'll recall,' Mr Moore said, keen to be of service to the esteemed Sydney Fenton.

'He believed one of the young ladies looked familiar and was the daughter of an acquaintance of my mother,' he created a sympathetic story to glean what he wanted to know. 'My mother would love to rekindle the acquaintance, having been in mourning so long.'

'Of course, deeply respectful of Mrs Fenton,' Mr Moore said.

Sydney had very little to go on but prolonged the investigation as best he could to ensure Mr Moore would not be flippant with his recollection.

'The lady was of fair hair, in the company of a dark-haired lady, and they were both writers.'

'Ah yes,' Mr Moore said, and Sydney's heart stopped as he waited with anticipation.

'I cannot recall their names, even though they did interview me,' he said, again ensuring all in the store could hear him. 'But I recall they worked for the women's newspaper... let me see, what is that called?'

An older lady stepped forward, several books in her hand. 'The *Women's Journal* I believe is its name,' she said.

'That is it, thank you, Madam,' Mr Moore said.

'The *Women's Journal*. I shall seek her there,' Sydney said and thanked both parties. He offered a small piece of information provided by his colleague. 'If I have the correct person, her name – the lady who was in your store – was Matilda.'

'Yes, that rings a bell,' Mr Moore proclaimed. 'Yes indeed, I believe you are correct.'

Done! Sydney thought with satisfaction. Now to buy a copy of the *Women's Journal* and find out the lady's surname. He thanked them again for their time and kind assistance and lingered long enough to sign several copies of his books on the shelf, and three more copies for ladies who approached him while in-store before departing.

Chapter 21

Miss Phoebe Astin, armed with her pencil and pad, moved a small chair closer to the body of the pyjama girl and seated herself. Since the body of the young lady had arrived yesterday afternoon, Phoebe had worked on her between clients, touching her up to look more presentable. This morning, she had a block of free time and intended to get the illustration finished and into the hands of the detectives, the younger of whom was particularly handsome but a little gruff. He reminded her of her eldest brother, Julius, who often bore a serious countenance and carried the weight of the world on his shoulders. She preferred a lighter-hearted man, especially given her daily work was so very serious.

'Hello again,' she said to the pyjama girl, studying her momentarily before applying pencil to paper.

'What was your life like prior, my friend?' she asked softly, drawing the lady's delicate eyebrow and estimating where it should be on the other side of her face given it was not visible, covered discreetly by a scarf. 'Were you a sister, a wife, a lover, a friend?'

She drew on, her pencil flowing over the paper, recreating and imagining the full face of the damaged young woman.

'You are quite a beauty,' Phoebe said. 'Did you like to read or dance? I pray your last moments were quick and you were not aware of the injury inflicted upon you.'

She drew the lady's symmetrical nose, and the small, dainty chin. The hair that remained, Phoebe drew loose and straight, ending bluntly and fashionably hanging below the lady's shoulder on her visible side. Phoebe turned, hearing someone enter her room and smiled at her eldest brother, Julius.

'I am checking this has not upset you?' he asked.

'Thank you, Julius,' she said. 'It is sad but no more so than many young people we have seen to their grave.'

Julius studied her drawing and the woman lying in front of him.

'You have captured her beautifully; I am sure she would be grateful.' He frowned and asked of the corpse, 'Who are you, pyjama girl?'

'We will find who you are, my friend,' Phoebe said. 'But for now, rest assured you are in good hands and safe here. Julius is a wonderful protector.'

Her brother laughed, which he rarely did. Not one used to accepting flattery, Julius hastened to the door, to leave her to her work, before remembering the message he had to deliver.

'Oh, the detectives very much appreciated your embalming insight,' Julius said and passed on their thanks. 'Detective Dart hoped they might call on you today to discuss any other observations you might have.'

Phoebe turned to him. 'That is kind. Do tell Grandpa to show them in when they arrive.'

Julius nodded and departed. Phoebe returned her attention to the pyjama girl.

'My brother would be a very good catch if you were here in body, not just spirit,' she told her. 'I live in the hope Julius will meet someone soon. Yes, I am open to love too,' she said as if answering a question from the lady herself. But anyone nearby would have only seen Phoebe working alone.

*****

Thomas did not intentionally mean to slow down as they approached *The Economic Undertaker* but his body physically reacted.

'You surprise me, Thom,' Harry said, with a glance at his partner.

'How so?'

'With all the sights we see – many so challenging – and you never as much as flinch, but you show an aversion to a funeral home.'

'I suppose it is odd,' Thomas agreed as they arrived at the entrance.

'Is there a reason that you care to share?' Harry asked, pausing before entering. But before Thomas could answer, the door swung open and the brothers, Julius and Ambrose Astin, hurried out.

'Detectives!' Julius exclaimed. 'Forgive us, we are late for an appointment, but Grandpa and Phoebe are inside.'

'Thank you, Mr Astin, we won't delay you,' Harry said, and they entered to find Randolph Astin behind the desk and greeted him.

'Detectives,' he responded, 'Good day to you. Phoebe instructed I was to send you to her on arrival.' Randolph glanced at Thomas. 'I gather you are not very comfortable in these surroundings, Detective Ashdown, and Phoebe needs a break. Why don't I show you to our drawing-room to meet?'

Thomas stood straighter and took in a deep breath. 'Thank you, that is most kind, Mr Astin, but we may need to see the body as we talk with Miss Astin. I assure you; I will be fine.'

With a nod, Randolph led the men to Phoebe's room and announced them on arrival. Yet again, Thomas was taken by her different and unconventional appearance. He wondered if Matilda would soon loosen her hair and robes – he wasn't averse to the idea except for his fear it might attract more men to her for the wrong reasons. He couldn't wait to see her long hair down and around her when they shared a bed.

'Thomas?' Harry said.

'I beg your pardon,' he answered, realising he had missed the conversation.

'That is quite alright, Detective Ashdown,' Phoebe said with a smile. 'I am often in my head going through many things and able to ignore my brothers capably.'

Thomas offered her a smile of thanks for her empathy.

'Will you both come into the next room?' Phoebe continued. 'I have laid out the pyjama girl and shall point out my small observations.' As they followed her into a smaller, cool room, one flight down the stairs, she added: 'I hope I have not wasted your time.'

'I assure you, that will not be the case,' Harry said. 'We have so little to go on that everything is significant.'

'The embalming information was most interesting,' Thomas agreed as Phoebe pulled back the sheet to reveal the pyjama girl's face. 'How difficult is it to embalm if you have not been trained?'

Phoebe considered the question. 'There are several good books written on the subject, so the process is not difficult, but getting the materials and solutions, can be troublesome,' she said.

Studying the young woman before her, Phoebe addressed the detectives: 'I shall just say what I have observed, and if you find any of it useful, then I'll be pleased to be of service.'

'Thank you,' Harry said, inviting her to start.

'The manner in which she wore her hair says to me says that the pyjama girl is a confident young lady,' Phoebe said as she walked behind the body on the table, and touched the pyjama girl's blonde hair, bluntly cut and loose in such a modern style. 'I can say in all honesty from adopting a more informal type of dress myself, that it is not always easy to strike out and be different. I am often criticised quite openly and rudely. So, I imagine the pyjama girl either did not care for people's opinions or she wanted to stand out.'

Thomas nodded. 'As a performer might,' he suggested.

'Yes, exactly,' Phoebe agreed. 'There have been a few performers that have rested on my table when they have succumbed to their malady. But it appears an illness is not what ended the lady's life.'

Harry confirmed: 'You are correct, the blow to her head

was the cause of death. The coroner found her free of illness,' he said with a look to Thomas who agreed.

Phoebe moved to the pyjama girl's left hand and removed it from beneath the covering. 'There is a faded mark here on her ring finger, which might suggest she was once married or engaged.'

'We did not see that,' Harry said, moving forward to study the hand. 'Indeed, it is so.'

Phoebe continued, lifting the cover a little from the corpse on her table to reveal from the knees downward.

'The pyjama girl's calves are not well developed. If she was a dancer, they would be more so, I imagine. Your coroner could offer more insight than I on that. But, if she was a performer, perhaps she was an actress on the stage, not a dancer.'

'An excellent observation,' Thomas said, impressed.

'I hope that has assisted you,' Phoebe said.

'It certainly does, thank you, Miss Astin,' Harry said. He smiled at her. 'Did the young lady whisper anything to you?'

Phoebe grinned. 'Yes, but nothing I can repeat.'

Harry chuckled and wished her a good day.

'I shall have the drawing completed in a few hours. I can get one of my brothers to drop it at the station to save you coming back,' she suggested.

'Please do not go to that trouble,' Harry said. 'We are out and about today, so shall swing by again later.'

Thomas joined Harry in thanking Miss Astin. Outside, Harry suggested they visit the author. 'I had hoped to have the illustration to show him, but let us not waste the morning.'

Thomas needed no encouragement to depart the premises and surrounds as soon as he could.

Chapter 22

Mrs Lawson worked her way around the table of writers in her office as the weekly meeting for the *Women's Journal* part-time and junior staff was now in session. She invited each lady around the table, in turn, to provide an update on their progress, and be issued a story or suggest a story if passion dictated.

'Alice, shall we start with you today?' Mrs Lawson said, calling on Matilda's dear friend and writing partner.

'Of course, Mrs Lawson,' Alice said in her crisp British accent. 'I correspond regularly with my sisters in England and a cousin in America, and they know of my work. They share some interesting news stories and angles which we could research and present locally.'

'Most interesting. What did you have in mind?' Mrs Lawson asked.

'Well, the *Chicago Tribune* newspaper ran a story about what happens to women who are divorced.'

There were murmurs around the table and Mrs Lawson

allowed the discussion to develop for a little while to study her writers and their opinions. Matilda did not speak as she had not given the subject a great deal of thought.

'I do not know any lady who is divorced,' she shared with Alice.

'Nor I,' Alice agreed. Several of the ladies thought the act of divorce was scandalous, especially when married in a church in the eyes of God; others were more open-minded. Mrs Lawson soon called for attention adding: 'There are circumstances where it is probably better and safer for a woman to leave her husband. We don't know unless we walk in their shoes. Continue Alice, what did the newspaper article say?'

Alice resumed: 'It was most interesting. They undertook a survey and found 75 per cent of divorced women remarried within a year, 10 per cent were anticipating an offer; 10 per cent had fallen into evil ways as they called it...'

'Goodness,' Mrs Lawson said, 'one dares imagine.'

'And five per cent were celibate and intended to stay so.'

'Most interesting,' Mrs Lawson said again. 'What were you thinking then, Alice, for a story?'

Alice sat straighter in her chair and presented her story idea. 'I thought we might quote these figures but take a broader angle, such as "Life after marriage" and include widows and divorcees. If possible, interview both groups and ask them about their station in life, if they feel stigmatised, lonely, or free. How they manage, and how they view marriage.'

Mrs Lawson smiled. 'Excellent. I like that very much, well done Alice.'

Alice gave a small smile and Matilda subtly squeezed her friend's hand, delighted for her.

'That piece will take some time and research, so perhaps allow yourself several weeks and report back on progress next week.'

'Thank you, Mrs Lawson, I will,' Alice said, excited to get started.

Mrs Lawson glanced around and chose her deputy editor, Betty. 'Is there a story you would like to assign, Betty?'

'Yes, an interesting one. Ladies in Victoria are signing a petition for the commutation of the death sentence passed upon Louisa Collins.'

'Ah, yes,' Mrs Lawson said. 'She was sentenced for killing her two husbands with rat poison.'

'That is her,' Betty said. 'Two years ago, as you remember, Mrs Ellen Thomson was hanged in Queensland and they have hanged no lady before or after. In light of the petition for Louisa Collins, I was wondering should we test the mood of the women of our town about hanging women, given the few years passed may have given us cooler heads? There were many letters written to try to stop Mrs Thomson's hanging and much support from the gentlemen who did not want to see – as one of them said – the fairer sex hanged.'

Mrs Lawson looked around for comment and Georgina spoke up. 'Not that I am a writer, but as a reader, I would think the severity of the crime would need to be discussed and factored in.'

'Excellent point, Georgina, I agree,' Mrs Lawson said. 'There was always some doubt about Mrs Thomson's guilt, whereas if there is no doubt, do we feel the punishment fits the crime? An interesting and topical piece, Betty. Is there a writer present who would like to take that story and develop it? Indicate by raising your hand for Betty if you would like to do so.'

Several hands shot up and Betty assigned it, pleased with the interest.

'Matilda, what have you?' Mrs Lawson asked.

Matilda's heart rate hastened and she quietly cleared her throat to propose a story or a series of stories to Mrs Lawson.

'I have not approached the lady in question yet, as I wanted to see if you thought a series of articles on different ladies' professions might interest our readers,' Matilda said and held her breath.

'Indeed. Who is the first lady you have in mind?' Mrs Lawson asked.

'I recently learnt there is a lady about my age who is working at a funeral parlour as a mortician and embalmer. Her primary role is to prepare the deceased to make them presentable for family viewing if the family does not wish to do so in their own homes, and to do the same for those people who die in the hospital and are unclaimed but need to be washed and laid out for burial.'

Several of the ladies gasped and laughed.

'Imagine that!' Ursula, the typesetter proclaimed, which was the reaction Matilda sought.

'That sounds most fascinating,' Mrs Lawson agreed. 'How we mourn and the funeral process is changing, that is for sure. Once we run one profile, we are bound to have people nominate other ladies. We want to be sure we represent the out of the ordinary though. Good work, Matilda. See if the young lady will agree to an interview and Georgina, could you illustrate the female mortician at work, should she permit you to do so?'

'I would love to, Mrs Lawson,' Georgina said, pleased for the quirky assignment, which was much more interesting than the illustration she just completed of a cake of soap for an advertiser.

'Well done,' Mrs Lawson said and moved to the next writer.

Matilda smiled and nodded her thanks. A glance at Georgina confirmed she was equally pleased. Now Matilda hoped that the female mortician and embalmer would agree to an interview, and be a single lady and just right for Gideon. Aunt Audrey's reaction would be priceless; Matilda amused herself with the thought.

*****

Harry hid a smile as Thomas dozed off beside him on the omnibus on the way to the author, Linton Turner's terrace house. Harry marvelled how anyone could fall asleep on the bumpy ride with the surrounding noise, but apparently, after sitting and leaning his head against the frame next to him, Thomas had succeeded in doing so. It was almost a shame to wake him, but nevertheless, Harry did when they reached their stop.

'Why couldn't he live further away?' Thomas mumbled grumpily.

'Go home and get some sleep, I'll cover for you, especially as you were doing night research,' Harry offered.

'Thanks, but no. I'm not much good at sleeping during the day.'

Harry raised an eyebrow in his direction.

'Usually,' Thomas added.

The terrace house was one of four small sandstone terrace homes adjoining each other in an attractive building, and featuring large iron fencing and railings in black. Each had a different coloured door and Harry, on checking the address Matilda has supplied, rapped on number three, the black door belonging to Mr Linton Turner. It was close to midday and hopefully the man was up and faring better than Harry's partner, Thomas.

It took several knocks before the door swung open and a bleary-eyed man wrapped in a nightgown opened.

'Is it that time already?' he asked.

'What time is that, Mr Turner?' Harry asked and showed his identification.

'Sorry, mistook you for the publisher's henchman, also known as an assistant,' he mumbled. 'I should be up writing so every day at around this time, the publisher sends one of the staff around to harass me to make sure I am dutifully producing words. Come in,' he said and headed down the hallway leaving the two men to follow.

'I could make some tea or coffee,' he said looking around as if he wasn't sure where the kitchen was. 'The girl comes after one o'clock to clean and cook for tea.'

'If you're making one for yourself, then we'll happily partake,' Harry spoke on behalf of himself and Thomas.

'I am. I need one. Come this way,' he said, and ventured into another room and then through to the kitchen. 'Take a seat,' he indicated the kitchen table and busied himself filling a kettle.

'I imagine you've been expecting us, given the parallels to your book and the recent discovery of the deceased body on the church step,' Thomas said.

'I have. It's been great for sales,' he chuckled.

'Not so good for the young lady in question,' Thomas said.

'Who is she?' Turner asked, gazing their way before returning his attention to tea making.

'I know you haven't seen her, nor do we have an image to show you yet, but we were hoping you might tell us that,' Harry said. 'Are you missing anyone in your acquaintance circle?'

'Often,' Turner said, and put three cups and a sugar bowl on the table and filled the teapot. Taking a sniff of the small milk jug and deeming the contents suitable, he furnished the men with what they needed and dropped into a seat beside Harry. 'People come and go in my world all the time. Fame is a fickle thing and artists, and women for that matter, all have their moment in the sun.'

'I see,' Thomas said. 'From your time at the club or spent amongst your colleagues, has anyone bragged of emulating your book or suggested who might have done the crime?'

'Not a soul, although it's not something you're going

to take credit for,' Turner said and ran a hand through his hair which had not seen a brush since he rose from bed to answer the door. 'But no boasting or sinister murmurs, since that's what you're getting at, sorry.'

'Do you have any fellow writers who would consider going to the extreme of imitating your book hoping to besmirch your reputation by incriminating you?' Harry asked.

'Absolutely,' Turner said, 'we are all miserable, competitive, jealous artists. But considering it and doing it are two different things, and I cannot think of any in my circle who would soil their hands on such a crime.' He chuckled. 'If they did, it has backfired on them since my book has received an increased profile as a result of the crime.'

'Might they have paid someone to do it for them?' Thomas suggested, finishing his tea and accepting the offer to help himself to another.

'They'd really have to hate me to do that, and be prepared to forgo their hard-earned pounds. I can't see them going to that extreme.' He looked around. 'I can't even offer you a biscuit, sorry. I'm starving.'

Harry nodded. 'We won't keep you much longer. Did you have anyone in mind when you wrote your character?'

'No, it is purely from my imagination,' Turner said.

'But yet last night you said that your leading lady from several of your books was based on a beautiful woman you knew who did not return your affection.'

'Ah,' Turner said and studied Thomas. 'Did I tell you that?'

'No. You told a friend of mine.'

Turner studied him. 'A friend of yours, hey? Well, when I have a character in mind, it is easier to model them on someone I know. It lets me flesh them out. So, if I know an attractive woman who could be my character, I write with them in my mind. Am I a suspect?'

'Everyone is,' Harry said.

Turner straightened in his chair. 'Well, in that case, I suggest you come back with your illustration of the lady in question and I'll see if I can identify her. After that, best you speak to me via a legal representative then. I have my career to consider.'

'Fair enough, Mr Turner,' Harry said and the two men rose. 'But if you get wind of anyone who is missing, or hear of anyone confessing to foul play...'

'You'll be the first I contact,' he said.

The men bid him farewell and on reaching the street, Thomas said: 'That went as expected.'

They departed Linton Turner's abode and arrived not long after at *The Economic Undertaker* to pick up the illustration Miss Phoebe Astin prepared for them.

'I thought he might have been a little more forthcoming, but he's somewhat defensive,' Harry said.

Thomas swung open the door and entered after Harry to find a young couple wearing black sitting in the waiting area. Thomas and Harry removed their hats.

'Forgive the intrusion,' Harry said, and Randolph gave them a nod and a smile, hurriedly sweeping them off to Phoebe's room, away from the couple who were in attendance to organise the burial of their child.

Thomas felt his necktie tightening, and the hallway to the back room getting smaller and darker, feeling very much like a coffin or tomb. He stopped midway and gulped air.

Randolph turned around. 'Are you okay, Detective?' he asked the younger man.

'I'm sorry, Mr Astin, Harry,' he said addressing them both, his breathing hastening. 'I'll wait outside,' he told Harry and lingered only long enough to get Harry's agreement before turning and hurrying back out again, past the mourning young couple, and into the fresh air and heat of the day. He drew a deep breath and felt better for it.

His partner was not too long in appearing and carried a rolled-up drawing in his hand.

'Sorry,' Thomas began but Harry waved him off.

'It is of no importance. I am not capable around heights, so we will balance each other out.' He waved the rolled-up drawing. 'Miss Astin has done an exceptional job. She had several but I've selected the one I think is the most lifelike.'

'Let's get it to the printing office and get copies distributed. If we can find out who this woman is, we will have something to work on at last,' Thomas said.

'Thank goodness no more characters from his book have shown up, or ladies in pyjamas for that matter,' Harry said.

'Someone knows something, though. And once she is identified, we can shake the tree and see what falls out,' Thomas said with renewed energy in his step.

Chapter 23

Matilda promised Georgina she would do her best to convince the lady artist and embalmer from *The Economic Undertaker* to allow herself to be interviewed and illustrated for the *Women's Journal* and would report back hopefully with good news. She checked with the deputy editor, Betty, and with her permission left the office on her assignment. Matilda decided not to take Gideon just yet, best she determined if the woman would appeal to Gideon – the brother closest in age to her, and the most carefree. While Thomas had responded to her questions and said the lady was handsome, Matilda wanted to see for herself. The mortician needed to be pretty like his recent interest, Lily, but confident and not interested in being seen in the right places. Matilda was sure Gideon would prefer to be seen in the wrong places. She sighed at the thought; he was a little hard to match given his energetic nature – no ordinary girl was going to keep his attention.

Matilda walked to the corner of the street and waited with

several other people until the omnibus arrived. Normally she might have walked into town given the *Women's Journal* was just on the outskirts, but the heat in the day did not encourage it. As she arrived in the street where *The Economic Undertaker* was located, she saw Thomas and Detective Dart passing in another omnibus. Thomas had his eyes closed as if sleeping. He looked particularly handsome and even though she waved at Detective Dart who had his eyes open, he did not see her. Another very handsome man her own age alighted behind her at the same spot as Matilda and gave her a smile.

'Lost friends?' he asked.

Matilda laughed. 'Hopefully not forever,' she replied watching them fade from sight.

'Good day to you, madam,' Sydney Fenton tipped his hat.

'Good day,' Matilda said, returning his charming smile.

She made her way to the front door of *The Economic Undertaker*, and taking a deep breath moved to open the door but instead, it opened gently from the inside.

'Madam.' A handsome, mature man dressed in a dark suit greeted her with a small bow. 'Were you looking for our services,' he asked, with a glance at the blue colour of her dress.

'Yes, in a manner of speaking,' she said. 'And you are correct, I am not in mourning.'

'Please come in. Randolph Astin at your service,' he stood back and Matilda entered. The room was cool which was welcomed but she could not help but think it was tomb-like. The surroundings were modest in keeping with the economic theme of the business. Dark curtains, as expected for mourning, were held back with burgundy rope tiebacks, soft lamps and several large bouquets of fresh flowers – a regular expense but necessary Matilda imagined – completed the picture. Four large tastefully printed chairs were placed against the wall but were empty of occupants. In a side room, Matilda could see a display of coffins from a very plain timber box to a more ornate design but nothing too elaborate.

'How may we be of service?' he asked.

'Mr Astin, my name is Matilda Hayward, and this is a business call, but I am not in mourning or dying for that matter,' she said and made Randolph smile.

'Well, that is a relief.' He looked to his right, where a back door was visible and had opened. Two young men entered, the tallest wiping his brow. Both stopped on seeing a customer in reception.

'My grandsons, Miss Hayward,' he said, assuming as she only wore an engagement ring that she was still a miss. 'May I present Julius and Ambrose Astin?'

The two men acknowledged her with a bow and excused themselves, disappearing into another area out of sight. But there was still no sign of the elusive lady mortician, and Matilda hoped she was in attendance.

Matilda began again. 'I write for a publication called the *Women's Journal*.'

'Ah, I know of it indeed,' Randolph said. 'My granddaughter, Phoebe, subscribes.'

'Oh, good!' Matilda brightened. 'My editor, Mrs Lawson,

has commissioned me to write a series on ladies of our town who have intriguing and different careers.'

Randolph laughed. 'Yes, well that is Phoebe.'

'Do you think she will allow me to interview her, and be illustrated? It will be good for business too, I imagine,' Matilda added, hoping Mr Astin would be an ally for her cause.

'That it would. My granddaughter is a liberal young lady with her own mind, so I cannot speak for her. But I hope she will. Would you like to wait here and I shall ask her to come to the reception?'

'Should I make an appointment?' Matilda asked, not wanting to get off on the wrong foot.

'No, not at all, that won't be necessary. Phoebe will no doubt welcome a small break and her clients are not going anywhere,' he said with a smile and Matilda couldn't help but laugh.

'That is true. Shall I come with you, if that is more convenient?'

'Her work is not for everyone,' he said, cautiously.

'Do not fear, Mr Astin. I am engaged to a detective and quite at home with the unfamiliar. Also, with my work, I have seen several dead people and was not overly alarmed.'

Randolph studied the young woman.

'Goodness, the young ladies today. You are all so talented and brave. My wife prefers to know nothing of our business and worries Phoebe will never attract a gentleman caller given her line of work.'

'Surely there must be many who admire her being so clever and independent,' Matilda said, surprised.

'Of course, but that works to her detriment as well, as you can imagine.'

Matilda conceded with a nod. She thought of Thomas who allowed her to be who she was without criticism, although he was well used to her after the years they spent growing up together. He had, however, made it clear he did not like her meddling in dangerous police business.

Randolph added: 'Phoebe will not give up her work should she marry. Will you be doing so when you marry your detective?'

'Definitely not,' Matilda said.

'Good for you, young lady,' Randolph said impressed. 'Come then, let me introduce you to Phoebe.'

With great hope for a story and a match for Gideon, Matilda followed Mr Astin to the cooler basement room where Phoebe plied her trade.

*****

'Well, she looks familiar, detectives. Very familiar,' the author, Linton Turner said glancing at the illustration that Thomas and Harry presented to him. 'Come in. I am having a cup of tea, join me.'

The men exchanged a glance as they followed a more obliging Linton Turner down the hallway into his living room. The later hour of their visit this time, found Mr Turner dressed and presentable. A housekeeper appeared from the kitchen and bustled off to retrieve two sets of tea cups for the detectives.

Thomas and Harry took the offered seat in the drawing-room and waited patiently as the author studied the illustration.

'I believe I have seen this young lady before, it's the distinct manner in which she dresses and wears her hair, like an actress.'

'Have you met her at your club or is she a fan perhaps?' Thomas asked, keen to move him along, but Linton Turner liked to hold court and enjoyed being the centre of attention.

'Maybe both and I could be wrong but I believe she is a dancer.' He looked up at them as if he had solved their problem.

'A dancer, as in a professional dancer for entertainment productions?' Harry fished with politeness.

'Not quite, although I'm sure she could have got work in that area. She's a dancer at a men's club if I am not wrong. I am sure she has performed a few times at my club,' he said, with a frown and studied the illustration again.

'Do you know her name?' Thomas asked, accepting the filled teacup from the housekeeper with thanks.

'I can't say I do. But certain types at the club always avail themselves of the company of the ladies of the night, if you know what I mean,' Turner said, with a glance at the housekeeper who hurriedly left the room after performing her tea duty.

'So, you are saying she is a prostitute?' Harry confirmed.

'In all fairness to the young lady, I can't say that. But if memory serves me, she did enjoy working the room.'

'When was the last time you recall seeing her alive at your club?' Thomas asked.

'Ooh, now you are challenging me, Detective,' Turner said and sat back in his chair. He crossed one leg over the other and sipped his tea. 'A month at the most I would say. I can't be sure, as I'm there quite often and faces come and go.'

'I see,' Harry said. 'Well thank you, at least we have a starting point.'

The two detectives rose, Thomas finishing his tea in two gulps.

'Don't get up,' Harry beckoned for Mr Turner to stay seated, 'we shall see ourselves out and thank you for your time.'

'I hope I have been of some assistance,' he said with a smug smile.

It wasn't until the men had hailed a hansom and were en route to the station to see if any other citizens had stepped forward to identify the young lady from the posters already distributed, that Harry asked: 'What did you think of all that?'

'I don't like him and don't trust him,' Thomas said, speaking bluntly. 'What did you think?'

Harry hid a smile. Thomas was always straightforward in his assessment of people and even more so when he was tired and grumpy.

'I think he knew more than he was saying and if I had a constable to spare, I'd have him watching the house to see what happens next,' Harry said. 'I wouldn't be surprised if he rushed to his club or to talk with someone about our pyjama girl.'

Thomas gave an unceremonious sniff. 'He was quick to cast aspersions on her character.'

'Let's swing by the coroner's office,' Harry said.

'Why?'

'I don't know if Patrick could tell because she was embalmed, but he didn't mention if she was... intact,' Harry said lowering his voice.

'Good point. To Patrick then.'

Chapter 24

Randolph Astin gently rapped on the door of Phoebe's rooms.

'I have a guest here to see you, my dear, if now is convenient?' he asked.

Phoebe looked up with surprise.

'Of course, Grandpa.' She rose and Randolph stood aside as Matilda entered the room.

Randolph did the introductions. 'Miss Matilda Hayward, may I present my granddaughter, Miss Phoebe Astin.'

'Miss Astin,' Matilda said with a small bow and Phoebe returned the same. Matilda's expression revealed her surprise. Phoebe was about her age, two and twenty, and was beautiful. She wore her hair loose, tied only by a ribbon and no pins, and her dress flowed freely, not restrained like Matilda's fitted and corseted top and skirt. Matilda glanced at the corpse on the table behind Phoebe.

'I'm sorry, does this startle you?' Phoebe asked concerned, and she moved to cover the body with a shroud.

'No, not at all, please don't go to any trouble on my account,' Matilda assured her. 'I told your grandfather, Mr Astin, I have seen several bodies now while working as a reporter for the *Women's Journal*, and also while unofficially accompanying my fiancé who is a detective.'

'Ah, I'm sure you have,' Phoebe said with a smile, looking equally intrigued by Matilda as Matilda was of her.

'I am sorry to have come unannounced.'

'No, not at all. I am always happy to converse with the living,' Phoebe said, and they both grinned.

'You must forgive our occasional humour, Miss Hayward,' Randolph said. 'In the sober world in which we live and work, it reminds us that life goes on and there is much to enjoy about it.'

'Of course, necessary I imagine,' Matilda agreed. 'And I'm sure there are quite a few good situations that would lend themselves to a little humour.'

'Too true. Shall I leave you to discuss business?' Randolph asked his granddaughter who agreed and thanked him.

'I shall see Miss Hayward out,' she assured him.

'Please call me Matilda.'

Phoebe insisted on the same informality. 'So, Matilda, what can I help you with today?'

'I hope to persuade you to allow me to interview you for a feature we are doing.' Matilda told of the pending series and the illustration request, and then she held her breath while Phoebe thought for a moment.

'I would be honoured.'

'Really! That's wonderful, thank you,' Matilda said, making Phoebe laugh.

'Did you anticipate I would say no?'

'I could not tell. You may have been painfully shy or private, or not wished to draw attention to your occupation. However, I think it is marvellous and you have a unique skill.'

'Thank you,' Phoebe said. 'I've never feared the dead and I take satisfaction in knowing I am helping ease the pain just a little of those who are saying farewell to their recently departed.'

'Of course, it would be a great comfort to see them looking peaceful and as family remembered them,' Matilda mused. 'Now, I imagine your day is quite irregular so if I may return with our illustrator, Miss Georgina Urry, we could work around you if we may make a time?'

'I can always continue to work while we talk, should I get busy. If that doesn't cause you distress?' Phoebe asked, with a glance to the middle-aged woman waiting on the table for her now.

'If your clients do not mind and you don't, I am very comfortable with that, as I am sure Georgina will be as well. She is very practical,' Matilda said.

The ladies made a time, and Matilda departed, her spirits raised. Now she just needed to get Gideon to visit with her, somehow. It required a reasonable excuse to warrant his attendance as she didn't need an escort. She hurried back to the office for the remaining few hours of the afternoon to tell her deputy editor, Betty, and Georgina the good news.

*****

Thomas had to see Matilda despite the fact he was dead on his feet. He rarely slept well, but two hours snatched on the floor of his office after the club research with Teddy had left him tired and ill-humoured – more so than usual. Thomas knew he wouldn't sleep tonight until he could hold her, see that she was safe and replace the nightmare image of her mutilated body in his mind. He wanted to steal a kiss too. Once before he had managed to do so in a hansom cab; this evening, that was his mission.

'Last stop for the day,' Harry said, reading his grumpy partner's mind. 'We've got a bit done today and let's hope by tomorrow, someone has come forward to give the pyjama girl a name and claim her.'

They entered the building of the coroner and before entering Patrick's room, paused to look through the glass of the door. Burton and Lou were in there.

Thomas groaned. Dr Nevins beckoned them in.

'I've never been so popular,' he joked, 'sadly I know deep down inside you are here about my clients, not me.' He sighed and got the expected laugh from those that were alive in his room.

'Patrick's busy with important business,' Burton ribbed Thomas and Harry. 'What do you two want?'

'To solve our case again,' Thomas joked. 'How's that coming along for you?'

Burton dramatically placed his hand on his chest. 'Stab to the heart, golden boy,' he said and Thomas shook his head, grinning and ignoring him.

'So, are you finished or what?' Thomas asked. 'We're very busy.'

'We're done. Thanks, Patrick,' Lou said, and with a grin and a nod to the boys, nudged his partner and the men departed.

'The pyjama girl?' Dr Nevins asked.

'Just a clarification if we may?' Thomas asked.

'Of course. Allow me to get the file.'

They waited while Dr Nevins covered the body on his slab, washed his hands and found the file on his desk.

'What can I help you with gentlemen?' he said returning to the table where the two men waited.

'We are hoping, despite the pyjama girl being embalmed, that you were still able to do an autopsy of sorts?' Harry asked.

'Yes and no. Bear in mind, I'm not a toxicology expert. If you have a query related to blood, then you are sadly out of luck – analysis of blood is no longer possible because the embalming fluid has replaced it, but other lesions, injuries and so forth have not materially changed to a great extent.'

Thomas cleared his throat. 'The author of *The Pyjama Girl Mystery* recognised the young lady from our illustration but could not identify her. He thought she might be a dancer and had been with gentlemen at his club.'

'A dancer or a lady of the night or both?' Dr Nevins said and looked at the file.

The men waited. Thomas hoped she wasn't a prostitute, not that he had an issue with the ladies or the service they plied, but he knew she would receive a more sympathetic audience if she was a good girl.

'This young lady is not intact,' Dr Nevins announced from his report, and both men nodded their acceptance.

'So, the author has given us a breadcrumb trail,' Thomas said, 'if he can be trusted.'

'Do you think he is holding something back from us?' Harry asked. He was more inclined to give the author the benefit of the doubt.

Thomas made a harrumph sound. 'I don't trust him.'

'I know,' Harry said. 'Thank you, Patrick. Nothing else that you have thought since the last meeting that might help with identifying her?'

'Sorry gentlemen,' Dr Nevins said. 'I have suggested the shape of the instrument used to inflict the wound to the side of her head. Her general health appeared to be good with no signs of illness or disease. She was fairly nourished, with no deformities or sores. All her organs were present. There is nothing more untoward, but don't hesitate to ask if you require something specific.'

The men thanked him and departed.

'We need to circulate her picture around that club where Linton Turner thinks the pyjama girl was a regular visitor,' Harry said.

'Except I wouldn't be surprised now if everyone clams up,' Thomas said. 'Watching Linton Turner in action in the early hours of the morning, he had his followers. He'll prime them for sure.'

'You are probably right. Let's see what happens overnight… if anyone comes forward to identify her. If not, we'll make our plan in the morning and in the afternoon, visit the management and staff of the club. Go home and stay home,' Harry said, with good-humoured bossiness. 'That's an order.'

'Can I go via the Hayward household first, Sir?' Thomas asked with a smile.

'I give you leave to do so, but you need to be in bed before midnight.'

'Yes, Sir,' Thomas snapped and sharing a smile, the men departed for the evening, Thomas in a hurry to get to see Matilda all in one piece and pretty.

Chapter 25

The deputy editor of the *Women's Journal*, Elizabeth Purcell, or Betty as everyone called her, looked up just in time from her reading to catch Matilda preparing to leave for the day. She contemplated doing the same. Only a handful of ladies were left in the office, and often Betty remained just that bit longer should anyone need assistance and to ensure when she arrived home to her small abode, she had filled in the dusk, was tired and ready for tea. It helped to make the night shorter when she was alone. Betty consulted a looking glass, tidied her blonde hair with the grey strands peeking through, and packed her desk to depart.

The in-between times was when she felt the loneliness – first thing in the morning after waking and just before work; and the dusk at evening after work before preparing tea for one and listening to the radio. She would walk home for exercise and see the couples taking their evening strolls, which she used to do with Mr Purcell before illness took him coming up to three years now. It felt like yesterday.

Twenty-two years of marriage gone in the blink of an eye and now at two-and-forty, she felt adrift sometimes. Her work was her saviour.

Matilda approached and asked: 'Are you leaving, Betty? If we travel in the same direction, we could take the omnibus together? I am heading to Highgate Hill.'

'And I am the stop after. That would be lovely, thank you, Matilda.' Betty smiled and rose, unaware that Matilda was plotting a way to invite Betty in to meet her father. She continued: 'I usually like to walk, but in this heat, I might postpone my walk.'

They bid farewell to the ladies still present and on departing, Betty said: 'I hoped that when you finished Linton Turner's book, *The Pyjama Girl Mystery*, I might borrow it to read. I'm sure a lot of ladies have requested it, but it will help me cross-check facts for our story. Plus...' she admitted with a smile, 'I'm keen to read it.'

Matilda laughed. 'It is a good read. I have finished it and Thomas has a copy if I need to cross-check. It is at home, on the way. Drop-in and I shall give it to you now.'

'Oh, that would be good. I'd love to start it this evening; there is nothing more exciting than beginning a new book. As long as this is no imposition?' she added. 'I don't wish to impose on your family so near tea-time.'

'Not at all, we are very informal. Besides, I never know if my brothers will be there, so it is often just Pa and me,' Matilda said, as they waited for the coming omnibus.

'Oh, your mother is away or has passed?' Betty asked.

'Passed away, many years now. I was but four. Pa has never remarried, but now that I will be leaving home soon, I hope he might focus on the task. He is only in his fiftieth year and has much of life ahead to enjoy.'

Betty smiled. 'It may motivate him to action,' she agreed.

They stepped onto the omnibus, thanking several gentlemen who offered assistance and took a seat.

'I understand your father's reluctance,' she said. 'When my husband, Edward, passed away three years now, I was lost. Finding work has given me a sense of purpose, but he was my great love, we were married twenty-two years. It is very hard to imagine someone else in your life.'

Matilda's heart swelled thinking of her own Thomas. 'I am sorry, Betty, I can't image the grief of losing a husband after so many years together. The thought terrifies me.'

'Then do not dwell on it. It may never happen,' Betty said, brightening. 'Besides, I have my friends, my work, the cricket – and I do love it,' she laughed.

'As does Pa,' Matilda said. 'And you are so terribly good at your job.'

'Thank you, dear. Before I started with Mrs Lawson, I worked as a secretary for the editor at the *Brisbane Courier*. I was always finding errors in the copy he received, so he put me to work reading the copy. But I like the deputy editor role at the *Women's Journal*. Reading copy all day is quite wearing, but now I source stories, manage the team, and still read the copy as well.'

'Would you leave it for love or reduce your hours and days?' Matilda asked, determining just how ambitious Mrs Elizabeth Purcell really was.

'You know, Matilda, if the affection and love was as powerful as my love of Edward, I believe I would.'

Which was exactly what Matilda wanted to hear.

*****

Mr Hayward was pleased with the progress of work on his conservatory. He did not use the large, cool venue often enough and the gardener used very little of it for growing plants, given the garden was well established. Now with his grown adult brood all marrying, and his first grandchild on the way, it would make the ideal venue for future Sunday lunches.

'The glazing repair was easier than we expected, Mr Hayward,' Evan Caird, the conservatory specialist said, standing back and looking at the work done thus far.

'It's looking terrific, Mr Caird. It makes the conservatory look cleaner already.'

'Aye, it does that,' he said with a thick Scottish accent. 'This is a beautiful space, you'll get a lot of use out of it when we've finished, I've no doubt.'

'What are your thoughts on the frame?' Mr Hayward asked.

'It has worn very well. The dry climate is good for that, but the heat is not so. Still, only a few areas that need replacing,' Mr Caird said, running a hand over his chin as he studied the conservatory. 'I've given the floor some thought and I'm still of the belief a slate floor will be best. It will be hearty. I'll get you a price.'

'That sounds like a good plan. Well, I imagine you'll be finishing for the day now. I shall see you in the morning,' Mr Hayward said, and the men shook hands.

He was pleased with the outcome and could comfortably afford the work. It would also be a grand place to sit and read in the winter months with the sunlight streaming in through the glass. As he was about to re-enter the house, he saw Matilda arriving at the gate and waited for her. Mr Hayward then noticed an attractive, fair-haired lady with his daughter, coming his way. As she got closer, he realised she was a mature woman and not a young friend of Matilda's. He hoped he was presentable after a walk around the garden amongst the dust and dirt of the conservatory renovations. He removed his handkerchief and wiped his hands and brow.

'Pa! Perfect timing,' Matilda called on seeing him, and he raised a hand in a wave. The lady next to her smiled a most pleasing smile. Her colouring was not dissimilar to Matilda's; they could have been mother and daughter, or aunt and niece.

'Hello my dear, and good day to you, Madam,' he said.

'Betty, may I introduce my father, Mr James Hayward. Pa, may I present Mrs Elizabeth Purcell, the *Women's Journal* deputy editor.'

'Betty, please,' she said.

'A pleasure,' Mr Hayward said.

'Please forgive me for intruding on your family time,' Betty said, 'I am just here to collect a book from Matilda.'

'You are not intruding at all. My apologies for not

receiving you more appropriately,' Mr Hayward said, noting Matilda smiling happily beside Betty. 'I have been surveying some renovations on the property and look a little dusty and worse for wear.

'As Betty hopefully is not in a rush to get home, perhaps a cup of tea?' Matilda suggested, her implication being there was no one for Betty to hasten home to see.

Mr Hayward realised Betty, too, might be widowed. He added: 'Excellent idea. Will you take tea or a cooling drink? This heat is most wearing.'

Matilda did not wait for Betty's response but led her forward as Mr Hayward escorted them up the front stairs of the veranda and opened the door. Harriet appeared at the entrance.

'Hello Matilda,' Harriet greeted her, reaching for the young lady's hat.

'Harriet, hello. Allow me to do the introductions. Mrs Betty Purcell, deputy editor at the *Women's Journal*, this is our house manager, Mrs Harriet Jarvis.'

'How do you do, Mrs Jarvis,' Betty asked with a warm smile.

'Most well, thank you, Mrs Purcell, and please do come in. I shall organise some cooling drinks. Allow me to take your hat and gloves.'

Mr Hayward led Betty to the room with the most enchanting view of the garden, not seeing the look of promise exchanged between his daughter and housekeeper.

Chapter 26

Thomas arrived at the Hayward household and spotted from afar Mr Hayward showing a mature lady around the grounds. Mr Hayward raised his hand in a wave which Thomas reciprocated and went to the main house.

'Thomas! Matilda will be pleased to see you,' Harriet said opening the door.

He greeted her and took off his hat, hanging it on the nearby stand as they spoke. He had known Harriet since he was a boy and felt awkward allowing her to do duties for him as an adult.

'Is that the lady from the *Women's Journal* I see in the garden with Mr Hayward?' he asked. 'She looks familiar.'

'Yes indeed, Mrs Purcell,' Harriet said, most excited. 'She visited with Matilda to collect *The Pyjama Girl Mystery* book and stayed for refreshments, and a tour of the conservatory renovations.'

'Does she have a husband to go home to?' he asked in a low voice.

'No, Matilda tells me she is widowed.' She raised her eyebrows and Thomas laughed.

'Well done, Matilda,' he said.

'And here she is!' Harriet exclaimed looking to the stairwell behind Thomas.

Thomas turned and raised his eyes to the staircase where Matilda alighted on hearing his arrival. She wore a red dress that looked striking and his sense of relief on seeing her was palpable.

'I shall leave you young people to it,' Harriet said, with a smile as Matilda bounded down the stairs as she did in her younger years when she was keen to head out with her brothers and Thomas.

'You are here!' she exclaimed as if he were an apparition.

'I am. I had to see you. Can we go somewhere private for a change?' he asked, hopeful, and reaching for her hand which she placed in his.

'Is everything okay?' she asked as he raised her hand to his lips and kissed it.

'Perfectly fine.' He studied Matilda's face and touched her hair.

'Have I something in my hair?' Matilda hurriedly patted it.

'No, nothing, it is fine.'

'Is it coming loose?' she said and fussed. 'I should do what Miss Astin does and wear it down from now on.' Her eyes widened with excitement. 'I have to tell you all about my meeting with Miss Astin.' She touched her hair again on the side of her head where Thomas was looking – the side that was caved in, in his nightmare.

'No. It's lovely, I was just admiring you,' he said as she stood on the step above where he stood, and they were eye to eye, her lips in easy reach.

'Do you remember when Gideon put that grasshopper in my hair and I could not find it?' She shuddered. 'They are my least favourite insect.'

Thomas chuckled at the memory. 'You stole his cricket ball in retaliation if I remember. A worthy punishment.'

She smiled. 'I did, but I relented and gave it back. At least he didn't put any more bugs in my hair after that.'

Thomas leaned forward to kiss her and Matilda cleared her throat and leaned back. They were in a very public spot.

'Are you sure you are alright, Thomas?' she said, studying him.

'I'm just tired and would love a moment with you, just us two.'

'Then we shall slip into the library. Pa is showing Mrs Purcell his conservatory renovations and will no doubt return to the drawing-room.'

'I have heard of your noble efforts at matchmaking from Harriet,' he said as Matilda led him to the library and over to the large, comfortable Chesterfield couch to sit.

'It was a genuine visit. Betty needed the book, I said I could reference your copy if I needed to. Can I?'

'Apparently so,' he said, teasing her, and she laughed.

'They have a lot in common,' Matilda said her face alive with excitement.

'How long have you been planning this?' He moved closer to her on the couch.

'Not long. I became more earnest knowing our wedding day was coming. I'm working on Gideon's romantic affairs too.'

'You do have the book to give Mrs Purcell then?' he asked, worried he would have to go fetch his copy.

'Of course I do. I had the book in my handbag the whole time, but I didn't want to reveal that naturally. Wouldn't it be exciting if they formed an intimacy?' she asked and sighed at the thought.

Thomas laughed at her ingenuity as they sat. 'It would be a wonderful thing for your father,' he agreed, 'and would give you great relief after we are married.'

'That is very true,' she added.

He leaned into her. 'Lord, I am tired. I need to be recharged with something… someone beautiful, reminding me of what is good in the world, as Harry always says. Kiss me, Tillie.'

'Here? Now?' she asked, wide-eyed with surprise and glancing around.

'No one is around and we will be married soon,' he said not taking his eyes off her.

He leaned closed and she did not move away. Thomas's lips touched hers, and with all his being, he drank her in, enjoying her touch and the relief of seeing her whole, beautiful and his. Thomas didn't care at that moment if the whole Hayward household walked in including Harriet and Cook. She returned his kiss, their lips discovering each other and then on hearing Mary the Cook talking with Harriet in the hallway, Matilda hurriedly pulled apart.

They looked at each other, their breathing increased.

'Oh my,' Matilda said and Thomas smiled. He sank further down on the couch, reclining in the corner, and closed his eyes, relieved.

'You are exhausted. What has happened today?'

'Just work. But I had a late-night call-out doing research at the club that Linton Turner frequents. I have had a couple of hours sleep, and I was worried about you.'

'Did you discover anything?' she asked, keen to know about the case. 'Why were you worried about me?'

Thomas opened his eyes and grimaced. 'Because you somehow always seem to be involved in my cases and because a young woman has been murdered.'

'I am perfectly fine and very happy; you need not worry. But tell me what happened last night?'

'It was a spur-of-the-moment thing. I couldn't sleep so I took Teddy with me. But I came here not to think about work. How was your day?'

'Oh yes, Miss Phoebe Astin. I met with her, the amazing mortician and artist from *The Economic Undertaker*… which will just make you think about work,' she said with a small shrug.

'True, but continue.'

'She is quite beautiful; do you not think?'

'As mentioned, I thought her handsome, but I have given no more thought to it.'

Matilda gave him a coy look and he laughed.

'Well done, Thomas,' she teased, poking his ribs, and he

grabbed her hands and kissed them. 'I am hoping she might be a match for Gideon.'

'That could work,' he agreed.

As he sat back again, rested and listened to her voice, Matilda ran her fingers gently over his forehead, removing the hair that fell in his eyes. He closed his eyes and enjoyed the comfort of her touch. He had never experienced the true tenderness and affections of a woman as a mother or belle before Matilda. He didn't remember falling to sleep, but apparently, he did.

Chapter 27

Betty happily accepted the book, *The Pyjama Girl Mystery*, from Matilda and placed it in her own handbag.

'Thank you. How exciting, I do love starting a new book,' she said.

'As do I,' Matilda agreed, 'but it is not for the fainthearted. Some of it is quite brutal.'

Betty lowered her voice and pulled Matilda aside in the drawing-room for a moment while Mr Hayward busied himself with the refreshments.

'Would you be uncomfortable if I accepted your father's invitation and stayed for tea, Matilda?' she asked in a quiet voice.

'Absolutely not,' Matilda said, 'I would be delighted, Betty.'

Betty smiled. 'Well, that's settled then.'

'I must warn you though if several of my brothers arrive, we are a rowdy bunch, but it could just be the four of us of course. My fiancée is here at the moment, resting in the library.'

'I think I would enjoy some rowdiness,' she said with a smile.

The door swung open and Daniel barged in.

'Speaking of which,' Matilda said with a smile at her brother.

'Tillie, Pa,' he called, removing his hat and placing it on the stand. He barged into the room and stopped short. 'Oh, I beg your pardon, I didn't realise we had guests.'

'My brother, Daniel,' Matilda said, and to Daniel, 'allow me to introduce Mrs Betty Purcell, the deputy editor of the *Women's Journal*.'

'Mrs Purcell,' he said, politely and they exchanged greetings as Mr Hayward re-joined them, drinks in hand for the ladies.

Daniel joked: 'Have you come to give us a report on Matilda, Mrs Purcell? We know she's a handful and you have our sympathy in advance.'

Matilda gave him a wry look and Betty laughed.

'On the contrary. I can happily and honestly report she is one of our brightest stars,' Betty said.

Matilda nudged her brother. 'So there.'

Mr Hayward shook his head and smiled. 'They never really grow up, Betty, but I live in hope.'

Matilda laughed and keen to push Betty's attributes said: 'Betty is mad for the cricket, Pa, you will have someone who shares your interest at the dining table tonight.'

'I'm afraid I am,' she added, 'and I am most unrestrained in my enthusiasm which is hardly ladylike.'

Mr Hayward chuckled as Daniel groaned and said: 'You

cannot be any worse than Pa. We call him the coach – he freely shares his opinion on what is going right and wrong in the match, even when not called for.'

Mr Hayward laughed again. 'It is true, but only in the spirit of the game.'

'Naturally,' Betty agreed smiling with enthusiasm. 'The only thing I find disappointing is that there is not more of it and the season seems so short. I very much enjoyed the Australian Eleven's victory against the combined team, since it did not include a Queensland team. Otherwise, my loyalties would have shifted.'

'I agree wholeheartedly!' Mr Hayward said, delighted with the conversation. 'The bowlers lifted their game to save the day.'

The conversation continued in good humour and as Harriet entered to advise tea was ready to be served, the door opened again and Elijah entered just in time for dinner and was introduced.

'I thought you were on the night shift,' Daniel said.

'That was last week, keep up,' he ribbed his brother. 'I have the great fortune of dating Miss Georgina Urry,' he said to Betty on discovering she worked at the *Women's Journal*.

'What a marvellous young lady she is,' Betty agreed, thinking of the kind and friendly illustrator, 'and so very talented. She is very taken with her beau, I am led to believe,' Betty shared making Elijah redden with the praise. Matilda saved him from responding, drawing attention to Daniel.

'Like Georgina, Daniel is an artist too, professionally,' Matilda said.

'Court illustrator,' Daniel added. 'My closest friend, soon-to-be future brother-in-law got me the position.'

'Should I wake him for tea, do you think, Pa?' Matilda asked.

'He's here?' Daniel looked around as if expecting him to appear and was awarded laughs from the group.

'Asleep in the library.'

'You've bored him to sleep?'

Matilda gave Daniel another wry look. 'He had a late night on assignment at the club which the author, Linton Turner, frequents.' She gave Betty a look implying she would fill her in later.

'Did he now! He said he was not ready to go there yet. And he went without me,' Daniel said, disappointed.

'I believe it was a spur-of-the-moment thing after midnight. He took Teddy.'

'I'm inclined to let him sleep,' Mr Hayward said.

'I'll go check on him,' Daniel said. 'If he is asleep, I'll remove his boots and make him comfortable. If he wakes, I'll bring him to tea.' He excused himself and headed to the library as the guests made their way to the dining room.

Matilda suggested Betty sit in Gideon's seat, right next to her father and she sat opposite to ensure the conversation flowed comfortably. Daniel and Thomas entered moments later; Thomas patted down his hair as he entered.

'Forgive me,' he said, embarrassed.

'Not at all, Thom,' Mr Hayward said, 'you are exhausted. Come and eat. You are welcome to stay the night here.'

'Thank you, Mr Hayward,' he said, and took his usual seat

next to Matilda. 'But I will head home, Teddy will worry what has become of me if I don't make an appearance at some time during the evening.'

Thomas greeted Betty, remarking on seeing her on several occasions whilst dropping into the *Women's Journal* office with Harry. The dinner was a convivial evening and the start of something magical for Mr Hayward and Mrs Betty Purcell. In the years to come, they would enjoy re-telling the story of how their fates entwined when all the time Matilda had the book in her handbag.

Outside Sydney Fenton's carriage passed by, carrying the artist as he returned to his own home. Now he knew where the young beauty lived.

Chapter 28

The next morning the two detectives were hopeful of a break through as the illustration of the pyjama girl had been widely distributed and printed in the daily newspaper. They sat opposite in Harry's office wading through the statements already taken by the constables from members of the public claiming to know their victim.

'This pile is for people who have seen her but don't know anything else about the pyjama girl. This pile is those who have sighted her but can't remember where so we don't even have a location trail,' Thomas said with frustration. He placed his hand on another pile of papers. 'This lot are idiots,' he said, making Harry laugh, and then placing his hand on the desk where nothing existed but timber, he added, 'and this pile is genuine possibilities.' He pulled another statement towards him for reading as Harry chuckled. They worked silently for another thirty minutes before Harry waved a piece of paper at Thomas and grinned.

'Something useful, at last,' he announced.

Thomas looked up with a look of hope on his face.

'A witness who believes the pyjama girl was an usherette at the Gaiety Theatre in Adelaide Street,' Harry said.

'That's better than anything I've got,' Thomas said and added with a glance at the other piles: 'I guess they are doing their civic duty.'

'Right then. Let's go to the theatre, show them the illustration and see if we can find someone who can positively identify the pyjama girl. Then we'll go to Linton Turner's club later today and talk to management. They should be awake and preparing for this evening's clientele by then.'

'If no luck there, we can return to this lot,' Thomas said, pushing aside the paperwork and rising.

They headed out, Harry advising John on the desk where they were going. Thomas summoned a hansom cab – there were plenty around the town heart and fringes.

'Seen anything at the Gaiety Theatre lately?' Thomas asked Harry as they made their way to Adelaide Street. They could have walked but the heat did not entice them to seek the exercise.

Harry thought for a moment. 'I don't think I've seen anything at the Gaiety ever. We're not theatre folk. Terese likes musicals, but has this thing about being trapped in her seat if she doesn't like the production.'

'You can't just leave?'

'Not until the intermission and Terese is worried someone will see us departing and we'd be considered ill-manner,' Harry said with a sigh as if he could not care a fig what anyone thought. 'I told her we could call it a police emergency.'

'Absolutely. That excuse has saved me from many boring events,' he said, and they exchanged a smile.

The hansom pulled up at the Gaiety Theatre in Adelaide Street and Harry paid the driver. The billboard boasted the latest showing: "*Whittington and his Cat*".

'What do you think that's about?' Thomas joked.

'A man and his cat,' Harry suggested as they entered the theatre, noting the sign out the front listed the venue was under the management of Mr W. Watkins. 'You know the story, don't you?'

'No,' Thomas said. 'Do you?'

'Yeah, it's a popular pantomime, been around since I was a kid.' He looked at Thomas, challenging him to say something.

'Wouldn't dare,' Thomas said, reading his look and Harry chuckled.

'The folklore goes that Whittington was a very successful and wealthy man but when he was young, he was poverty-stricken. So, he sold his cat to a rat-infested country and made a fortune.'

'Sounds stupid,' Thomas said, and Harry chuckled expecting nothing less from Thomas's review.

The first person they encountered in the quiet and musty smelling theatre was a cleaner. She stopped and looked at them with a startled expression.

'The theatre's closed,' she said unceremoniously.

'Yes, thank you, madam,' Thomas said. 'Detective Ashdown and Detective Dart looking for Mr Watkins or whoever might be in charge please?'

'Nobody's here right now except me and the costume lady. She's downstairs getting organised for tonight's performance.'

'What time might you be expecting management?' Harry asked.

'About a few hours before showtime. I'd be saying around four o'clock,' she said. 'Is Mr Watkins in some kind of trouble?'

'No, nothing like that I assure you,' Harry said.

'Perhaps you can help,' Thomas said, rifling in his suit jacket for the folded illustration of the pyjama girl.

'I've not seen anything or heard anything that I can imagine the police would take an interest in.' She shook her head with great conviction and stood taller as if challenging them.

Thomas persisted. 'We are trying to identify a young lady who has had some misfortune, in order to find her family. It was suggested that she works here or once did. Would you recognise her?' He held the illustration up inviting the cleaning lady to observe it.

Her eyes grew wider and she smiled. 'Of course, that's our lovely Sara. She works here as an usherette, but mind you, I haven't seen her for a few weeks. She's away maybe. She could be an actor on stage herself, quite a beauty and her face lights up a room.'

'Do you have a last name for Sara by any chance?' Harry asked, hiding the desperation in his voice.

'Ooh, I don't know, let me think.' She leaned on her mop and looked at the theatre ceiling. 'No, I'm not sure I ever knew it. But there's a list of all the staff that work here in the ticket booth drawer,' she said with a nod to the very same booth. 'In case one of us is away, we can call on someone else. She should be on it.'

Thomas and Harry brightened and followed her to the booth, as the cleaning lady put down her mop and fussed through the drawer.

'Here it is then. Let's see.'

They waited again as she withdrew her spectacles from an apron pocket and placed them on.

'Here she be. Sara-Anne Wilford.'

Thomas repeated the name and felt the relief rushing through him. At last, they were getting somewhere. They had their pyjama girl.

'She's alright, isn't she?' the cleaner asked.

'No madam, sadly she is not,' Harry said. 'Are there any contact details for Sara-Anne written on that piece of paper?'

'Yes, an address. Do you want it?'

It took all of Thomas's restraint not to grab the list from her. He waited patiently as Harry jotted it down. Thanking her and assuring the cleaning lady she had been a great help, the men departed.

The pyjama girl was Sara-Anne Wilford, and now they could release her name and hopefully encourage more public assistance. But just who was Sara-Anne Wilford that she deserved to be embalmed and left in her pyjamas on the church steps?

Chapter 29

'I won't go into great detail, as it is not a topic for the fainthearted,' Phoebe said, 'and it is best to remember our loved ones at peace. But there is much to do after a death and many families, especially those who are new to the country, don't have the support or skills to do that preparation, especially in our climate.'

'So true,' Georgina said. 'I live on a farm, and my mother has made it perfectly clear she wants to be wrapped in a sheet on the day she dies and buried under a tree at the back of our property.'

'Sounds rather lovely,' Phoebe agreed.

'I can't say I have ever thought about my final resting place,' Matilda mused. 'It would be nice to be with all your family though.'

'A big plot is quite common,' Phoebe agreed.

'Can you tell us a little about what you do, Phoebe and how the body changes after death, just for our curious readers?' Matilda asked, keen to know herself.

'Of course,' Phoebe said, and glanced at the lady lying in front of her. 'The body discolours within two hours, that is why coolness or embalming helps for preservation. Then it becomes very stiff, so *The Economic Undertaker* or the family must lie out the body in the pose that we wish their departed one to rest in, then wash and dress the body.'

Phoebe stopped, waiting for Matilda to make her notes and catch up. She continued: 'It is natural for body fluids to seep out – we don't need our body to hydrate us anymore,' she said delicately, 'so we prevent that by padding the body in the appropriate areas.'

'I see. Does your family make the coffins?' Matilda asked.

'No, we have a talented cousin who does that, and they are very affordable.' Phoebe told of what drove her brother, Julius, to seek a cheaper option for families, consenting to Matilda using the story in her article.

'How admirable,' Matilda said. 'But your work is in the preparation stage?'

'Oh yes. I have always enjoyed drawing and I took a particular interest in faces. When my family decided to open this business, my skills were a good fit. I am also qualified in embalming.'

'I can't imagine there are many women qualified as embalmers,' Georgina said.

'No indeed. My grandfather had to convince the course instructor to allow me to do it. They don't like women learning the trade.'

Matilda sighed. 'We encounter that quite a bit though, don't we?'

The three ladies exchanged smiles.

'It will change, I am sure of it,' Phoebe said. 'I also get great satisfaction from assisting the police sometimes with illustrations of the deceased.'

'You have helped them recently, I believe,' Matilda said, pleased to have a chance to raise the subject. 'You have met my fiancé, Thomas and his partner, Detective Harry Dart?'

'I have indeed,' Phoebe smiled. 'Detective Dart and I have worked together several times now. Your fiancé is very serious but has a kind and handsome face.'

'That is him indeed,' Matilda said with a laugh. 'I believe the detectives requested that you illustrate the lady they are calling the pyjama girl?'

'I cannot say without their permission, as much as I would like to – it is a private matter. But should they permit me to tell you what victims I have assisted with, I will happily let you know.'

'That would be most interesting, thank you,' Matilda said and moved along. 'What is the strangest request you have ever had, may I ask?'

Phoebe laughed quietly. 'There have been a few. I had a clairvoyant client once who requested we remove her husband from her house head first instead of feet first through the doorway.'

Both ladies looked at her with blank expressions.

Phoebe explained. 'It is an old custom and superstition, but many families want their dead carried out of the house feet first. It stops their spirit from wanting to return or looking back and taking another member of the family with them to the other side. But of course, the clairvoyant wanted her husband's spirit to return to the house.'

Matilda and Georgina laughed with fascination.

'She was hoping he would return and be with her?' Matilda asked.

'More than that. She hoped he would help with her readings by talking with other deceased parties up above,' Phoebe said, pointing to the sky.

'Good grief,' Georgina laughed. 'We all have quirks in our professions I imagine.'

'Indeed,' Phoebe agreed with good humour.

'Did you ever feel like a spirit was with you, or see any of your customers in their afterlife form?' Matilda asked.

Phoebe hesitated and gave a small smile. 'In my years of working with the deceased, I have never had anything strange happen in my place of work. But I do always feel their spirit.'

'I'm not sure I understand,' Matilda said.

'Because I am recreating them as if in life, preparing them for their final earthly appearance or helping the police to reconnect them with their families, I feel a bond with them. I hope I have served them well. When Julius and Ambrose take them to their family for burials, I farewell them and feel a sense of loss.'

'You have a good heart,' Georgina said, finishing her illustration.

'One might say I know an awful lot of people,' Phoebe said and laughed. 'But most of them are dead.'

'We are kindred spirits,' Georgina joked. 'Most of my closest friends are cattle on the farm.' The ladies laughed.

'Well now there are three of us, all very much alive and friends,' Matilda said, and earned their affectionate smiles.

Phoebe returned to an earlier subject. 'I confess, I have read *The Pyjama Girl Mystery* and found it most intriguing.'

'As did I!' Matilda said.

'I am yet to get a copy,' Georgina said. 'I am not one for mystery books.'

'It is quite confronting,' Matilda said.

'He is a brilliant author; do you not think?' Phoebe asked and continued without waiting for an answer. 'I heard he reads extracts from his work at the Quill Club. Ambrose and I have been there a couple of times – that is, my brother and I. We are going there this very evening. Would you both care to join us?' she asked shyly.

'I would love to,' Matilda said, seeing an opportunity.

'I cannot,' Georgina said, 'but thank you. Elijah is not on night duty, so we have made plans.'

'Another time then,' she said to Georgina, before turning to Matilda. 'Will you bring your fiancé?' Phoebe asked.

'No, Thomas is likely to be working until late. We see each other at odd times. But if you have no objections, I shall bring one of my brothers, Gideon perhaps.'

'Goodness, how many are there?' Phoebe asked.

'Four, and all older.'

Matilda saw Georgina's look – she knew exactly what Matilda was up to.

'Wonderful,' Phoebe said. 'I'm sure our brothers will find something in common, and you and I can enjoy the readings of Linton Turner, should he choose to read.'

Matilda had fully intended to see Miss Phoebe Astin again, and now her plans would fall into place, as the unsuspecting Gideon would soon find out.

Chapter 30

Harry straightened as he stood next to Thomas, ready to deliver a death call to the family of Miss Sara-Anne Wilford before the press caught wind of the discovery of the pyjama girl's identity and released her name.

'Thank goodness we did not have to put the young lady's body on show for identification,' Harry said. 'Too gruesome and the last time we did similar, almost a decade ago now if my memory serves me, it attracted more busybodies than viewers who might have been able to make an identification.'

'I wonder where they think she is or has been, given not one of them has come forward to report Miss Wilford missing?' Thomas said, shuffling in his jacket in the afternoon heat.

'Peculiar indeed,' Harry agreed. 'Unless the family is estranged.' He took a deep breath and knocked on the door. They saw a curtain move slightly and then a woman around the same age as the pyjama girl, answered. On seeing the two men in suits, she looked fearful.

'May I help you?' She looked up at them, her petite and thin frame making her appear more childlike than her years. The men removed their hats.

'Good afternoon, Madam, Detectives Harry Dart and Thomas Ashdown. We are desiring an audience with the family of Sara-Anne Wilford please?' Harry said.

'Sara-Anne? She left here months ago, and she has no family.'

Thomas visibly deflated. Waiting to deliver bad news was a stressful business.

'I am sorry, I have forgotten my manners. Would you like to come in?' she asked.

'Just briefly to get out of the heat, thank you,' Thomas said, and they followed her inside the small stone home which was considerably cooler than outside.

'Can I offer you tea?'

'We would welcome a glass of water, thank you,' Harry said, and Thomas nodded his appreciation.

The men took the offered seats in the small drawing-room and waited for her return. The house was tastefully but modestly decorated. On returning with the two glasses of water she sat opposite the detectives and explained: 'I am a lady's companion and helper. Mrs Moffitt is at her church group today, but will be back by tea time.'

'So, Sara-Anne has no family here on the premises or here in our city?' Harry asked for clarification.

'Both. She came over from England with her parents when she was a child and they both perished on the journey. She was raised at St Vincent's Orphanage by the Sisters of Mercy. We both were,' she added.

'I'm sorry to hear that Miss...' Thomas fished for her name.

'Chivers, Kate Chivers,' she said with a small nod of her head. 'Can I ask why you need to find her family?'

'I am afraid it is not good news,' Harry said preparing her.

Kate gulped in a short sharp breath of air, her hand going to her heart. 'It is her, isn't it? The pyjama girl?'

Harry nodded. 'Did you suspect as much?'

'I saw the illustration and thought it looked very much like her. I would have come forward eventually if no one else had.'

'There is no next of kin then?' Thomas asked. 'Are you the person closest to her?'

'Yes, I think I can claim that honour,' Miss Chivers said.

'Do you know where she has been living since you last saw her or with whom?' Harry asked.

Miss Chivers looked reluctant to speak ill of the dead. 'She was living here for a while. She paid Mrs Moffitt board from her work as an usherette, and stayed in the third bedroom. But Sara-Anne was always in love and always looking for love. Sadly, she could not trust anyone.'

'I imagine with what you have both been through, it is hard to feel stable with people,' Thomas said. He read widely on human nature in the limited spare time he possessed.

'Yes, I believe that is the truth,' Miss Chivers said. 'Sara-Anne was so beautiful. She wanted to be an actor, a dancer, a singer; I think she just wanted to be someone and to have enough financial independence not to need anyone.'

'Did she have a beau? Was she staying with him perhaps?' Thomas asked again in a different way.

'She was in love with a writer for a brief while and may have stayed with him.'

Thomas and Harry exchanged a glance.

'Then there was the poet that she loved madly but Sara-Anne was scared he would leave her. They were always fighting; it was very passionate. What shall become of her body? I could ask Mrs Moffitt to advance me my wages for a small funeral.'

'Do not concern yourself with that just yet,' Harry said. 'We will need to keep her body for a little while in the police morgue, and then we will see what help we can get to save her from a pauper's burial.'

Miss Chivers' bottom lip quivered; she had been particularly brave up until now.

'Thank you, Detective,' she said to Harry.

'We'll be in touch,' he said, 'but should you need us, drop into Roma Street Station and ask for Detectives Dart or Ashdown.'

'Thank you both,' she said, rising to see them out.

'Miss Wilford did not mention the name of either of these men that held her affection?' Thomas asked as they reached the front door.

'Yes, and I only wish I had been more attentive,' she said, scolding herself. 'I think the poet's name was Sydney, but the writer, I could not tell you. I believe he was considerably older. I might know his name if I heard it.'

'Linton Turner?' Harry asked.

'Why yes! That is the name, I am fairly confident,' Miss Chivers said surprised. 'Sara-Anne met them both at a club where the creative people often meet.'

'You have been most helpful, Miss Chivers, thank you for your time,' Harry said, and the men departed with the author, Linton Turner in their sights and a mission to find a poet.

'So, Linton Turner knew who the pyjama girl was all along,' Thomas shook his head, his lips thinned in anger.

'He looked at that illustration, said she looked familiar and as good as called her a prostitute,' Harry added his disgust.

'Most likely because she shunned his advances for this poet, whoever he may be. And why hasn't the poet come forward given her photo has been out there now for a reasonable time?'

'Let's swing by the station and let the inspector know he can release Miss Wilford's name now since there is no next of kin to speak of,' Harry said.

'Then brace yourself for the press are bound to be upon us,' Thomas said with a sigh, 'including the ladies from the *Women's Journal*.' The thought brightened him somewhat.

Chapter 31

T hat evening, Gideon adjusted his necktie, stood back and looked at his reflection, satisfied with his appearance. He wasn't putting much stock in Matilda's matchmaking attempt, but that didn't mean he didn't want to appear at his best to meet Miss Phoebe Astin.

'Passable,' he said but in truth, he was confident he had something to offer. The ladies liked him and with his new business interest, he was becoming a man of means. However, after the experience with Miss Lily Chappell, he intended to be a little more discerning in his choice of partner. Gideon did not want to provide the expectation of a betrothal when it was clear compatibility was not there. He made his way down the stairs where Matilda and Harriet waited for him.

'I was about to leave for the evening, but could not resist seeing you both looking resplendent and heading out,' Harriet said. 'It does my heart good.'

'It must, to see us all grown up and finally out of your hair,' Gideon teased her.

'There is that,' she agreed, giving him a wink.

'Let me look at you,' Matilda said to Gideon, herself looking lovely in a black and gold evening dress.

'I am quite capable of dressing myself,' he said with a roll of his eyes and a quick straighten of his waistcoat. Nevertheless, he ventured forward for Matilda's scrutiny.

She fussed with his cravat and collar and pronounced: 'Most handsome.'

'I am, aren't I? Am I your best-looking brother?' he teased and gave her a wink.

'Since you are the only one here at the moment, I'll agree you are that,' she said with affection and Harriet laughed at their antics.

'I won't tell the others, I promise,' Harriet joked.

'The only one that comes close is Elijah and only because we're identical,' Gideon said.

Mr Hayward entered the room also dressed in evening attire for a planned night out.

'Well don't we all look splendid,' he joked. 'Particularly you, my dear,' he said to Matilda.

'Thank you, Pa. I hope you and Betty enjoy the theatre.'

'It's been a long time since I've been inside a theatre and seen a play on stage, so it will be lovely to return.'

'And in the company of such a beautiful and intelligent lady,' Harriet said.

'Especially that,' Mr Hayward said, delighting Matilda with his newfound happiness. 'Now Gideon, mind your sister this evening.'

'I'll try, Pa, but she'll most likely be minding me,' he retorted and received a grimace from Matilda.

'Where is Thomas by the way?' Gideon asked. 'Is he meeting us there?'

'He hopes to. He sent word that he has a small break on his case,' Matilda said. 'So, we may see him at the Quill Club if his breakthrough has anything to do with the author, Linton Turner.' She turned to Harriet and her father, and added for their benefit: 'Mr Turner frequents there regularly.'

'I'm surprised Thomas would let you go to that club full of lecherous artistic types,' Gideon said.

'I do not need Thomas's approval to do anything, Gids,' she said haughtily. 'Besides, I am devoted to him and he trusts me.'

Mr Hayward gave Gideon a look that said he had been told and Gideon chuckled.

'He is the jealous type though,' Gideon continued to tease his sister.

'Oh phooey, he is not,' Matilda scolded him, allowing Harriet to fuss with the hairpins needing attention at her nape.

Gideon looked to Harriet. 'Do you remember when Elijah had a school friend home for the summer holidays?'

'I do, a lovely young boy,' Harriet said. 'He was a boarder and couldn't get home because of the floods near Maryborough if memory serves.'

'That's correct,' Mr Hayward joined in, recalling the event. 'He spent two weeks with us until the waters cleared. Henry, wasn't it?'

Gideon clicked his fingers. 'Henry it was. He was 15 and you were 13, Matilda, and he thought the sun shone out of you which neither Elijah nor I could understand why.'

Mr Hayward and Harriet laughed at Gideon, and at Matilda's expression.

'He gave you a flower he had picked and Thom was so cranky because you thanked him and gave him a kiss on the cheek.'

'I don't recall that,' Matilda said. 'I do remember Henry though. I wonder what became of him.'

Harriet smiled. 'Thomas was very upset. If I recall, he stayed away for an entire week and refused to come to the house. Daniel had to go to Thomas's house. Unheard of for Thomas.'

'He challenged Henry to a dual,' Gideon laughed.

'No!' Matilda exclaimed.

'True story,' Gideon said. 'But Amos overheard and did his responsible big brother thing and told Thomas that Henry was our guest and there would be no duelling.'

'How very boring,' Matilda said and sighed.

'I suspect Thom was relieved,' Gideon said. 'Henry was bigger, but Thom had Daniel on his side. Speaking of which, where is Daniel?'

'Daniel and Alice are meeting us there,' Matilda said, 'but Elijah and Georgina are previously engaged.'

'Sounds like a splendid night for you, young folk,' Mr Hayward said, 'and Matilda, don't you make that young man of yours jealous,' her father teased.

'I won't Pa,' Matilda assured him and kissed him and Harriet on the cheek

'Right then, let's go,' Gideon said. 'Have a good night, Pa.'

'And you too, my two youngest,' he said with heartfelt affection, as Matilda and Gideon departed, leaving him to take the carriage to fetch Betty.

The siblings walked down the long path to the street, and Gideon handed Matilda up into the hansom cab.

'Look at you all ladylike,' he joked.

'I know, what is becoming of me?' Matilda said and laughed. They settled in for the ride across town.

'What are they like, the couple we are meeting with?' he asked.

'Phoebe is like me, the youngest, but with only two older brothers, and Ambrose is her middle brother. I have only met him fleetingly. He and the eldest brother entered through a back door when I was in the front of *The Economic Undertaker* office, gave me a quick greeting and disappeared through another door.'

'And Phoebe?'

Matilda smiled. 'She's rather amazing. Attractive, interesting, and different.'

'I feel like I'm being romantically managed,' he said, looking less than happy.

Matilda shrugged. 'Phoebe said she was bringing her brother, I said I would bring one of mine. I didn't give any further details about you, your state of being single or a good catch,' she teased. 'Besides, we had a deal... you said you would accompany me in return for buying you the powder. At least I'm not taking you to the morgue.'

'True. I can get a drink at the club.'

'Anyway, Phoebe is bound to attract a lot of suitors. She may not even notice you,' Matilda said casually, and Gideon made a humph sound of disbelief.

'But if you did find each other compatible, we might get discount funeral benefits,' Matilda said, brightening and making him laugh.

Chapter 32

Sydney Fenton's fellow poet and closest friend, Percy Sutton, had already secured them a table when Sydney arrived at the Quill Club that evening. Sydney waved on seeing him, indicated he would get them a round of drinks, and made his way to the bar. He ordered for the two and watched as Percy chatted to some young man while flirting with the young man's attractive companion. Sydney sighed and looked away. And then he saw her; his heart momentarily stopped and he had to look twice – Miss Matilda Hayward was here, at his club. It was definitely her, looking exquisite.

Sydney watched as she smiled and gave her hand to a man who kissed it. Miss Hayward was much more attractive when she smiled, her petite face came alive, and her eyes sparkled. She was introducing a good-looking man beside her to another handsome couple. Was this her fiancé? Sydney turned to accept the drinks and requested for them to be put on his tab. As he walked towards Percy's table, he studied the man beside Matilda. He had seen him before somewhere, but couldn't place where that had been. He'd ask Percy, he would know if this man was someone in their circle. Percy never forgot a face or name; Sydney tried to forget them regularly.

As he waded through the club patrons towards Percy and their table, he caught Percy's eye and saw Percy hurriedly bid farewell to the couple he was speaking with. They left, looking a little disappointed in their 'dismissal' and not getting a chance to meet the poet, Sydney Fenton.

'I thought you would never get here, I've had to talk with half a dozen boring people,' Percy said, slapping Sydney on the back once he put the drinks down. Sydney could turn on the charm if required, but he liked Percy's company because they understood each other. Percy was the life of the party who enjoyed his higher profile as Sydney's closest friend, which allowed Sydney to fade into the background, observe and not make the small talk required as a social nicety, which he abhorred. His accepted quiet persona also gave Sydney the opportunity to observe people – a necessity for his craft.

'So old fellow, what can you tell me?' Percy said on accepting the drink and turning his attention to Sydney.

'Subtly look behind me and tell me who you see,' Sydney said.

'Right then.' Percy played casual, taking a sip of his drink and glancing around the room, including the group behind Sydney in his sweep. 'She's here, that girl from the bookstore!'

Sydney smiled. 'I know, I found out who she is – Miss Matilda Hayward, she writes for the *Women's Journal*.' Sydney had a glance at them and turned back around. 'Who is the man with her? Her fiancé maybe? I know his face.'

'That's not her fiancé. That's Gideon Hayward, he manages the Gallery of Fine Arts. We saw the Marlon Dominey exhibition there, remember?'

'Of course, how could I forget. You fell in love with Marlon's muse,' Sydney said with a roll of his eyes recalling the theatrics at the time.

'It was only lust,' Percy assured him. 'Gideon must be her brother. So, is that other man her fiancé?'

Sydney shook his head. 'I don't think so. I watched her introduce her brother to him. But she's still got the ring on her finger, there's a fiancé somewhere.'

'Let's go say hello,' Percy said, and Sydney looked alarmed. 'Why not?'

'Maybe, let me work up to it.'

Percy chuckled. 'Good idea. We'll have a few more drinks and then you can meet her in the flesh.'

*****

Matilda keenly watched for the reaction between Gideon and Phoebe as she introduced them. She didn't expect to see sparks fly, but she wasn't disappointed. They looked at each other with fascination, and then as the small party sat, Matilda saw them exchanging curious looks. Phoebe looked stunning with her hair restrained loosely by a gold ribbon and a long, flowing dress of red and gold with soft pleats and a small train. Her dress sleeves were long, but gathered all the way along, to create a puffed and feminine effect. Gideon was being particularly charming which satisfied Matilda he liked Phoebe with more than a casual interest, and then she saw Daniel and Alice and waved them over.

After introductions, the men stood around the table talking, while Alice, Matilda and Phoebe sat with their drinks, intermittently listening to the poet on stage and exchanging small talk. When the poet had been applauded and exited the stage, Alice leaned forward to the ladies and gushed: 'Sydney Fenton is here!'

'I know, so exciting,' Phoebe said, glancing in the same direction that Alice was looking.

Matilda looked over. 'He's the poet, isn't he?'

'He's more than that,' Phoebe said, 'He is the official poet in residence for the arts centre for the past three years and the highest-selling poet in Australia.' She smiled and gave a small shrug. 'I am quite an admirer and have all his works.'

'I confess I don't know his work, but I know his family name holds a lot of weight. His mother is a widow, I believe,' Matilda said, 'and they own that enormous mansion on the rise in Spring Hill.'

'Talented and good looking,' Alice sighed, 'just like us,' she added, and they all giggled as they stole looks at him.

'I have seen him several times,' Matilda said, frowning in his direction. 'He was on the same omnibus as I was just last week and greeted me, and I'm sure I saw him near our offices one day.'

'How peculiar,' Phoebe said. Her eyes widened, and her breath hitched. 'He's coming over with his friend, they are coming this way.'

'But why, do any of our party know them?' Matilda asked.

'My brother and I don't,' Phoebe said.

'Nor I, but I can't speak for my brothers,' Matilda said.

'I don't know anyone,' Alice said with a small laugh. She had only arrived from the mother country nine months earlier.

The ladies observed as the men did indeed stop at their table and Sydney Fenton's friend said: 'Mr Hayward, I believe we met fleetingly at your gallery exhibition last month. Percy Sutton and my friend, Sydney Fenton.'

'Mr Sutton, of course, I knew your face but could not place it. Good evening, Mr Fenton,' Gideon said and introduced Daniel and Ambrose and then the ladies. When he introduced Matilda, Sydney's eyes locked on her and did not move to greet the other ladies.

A loud noise and the breaking of a drinking glass startled them all and they snapped around to look towards the bar from where the noise emanated.

'Goodness!' Matilda said, recognising a very inebriated Mr Linton Turner, the author, struggling with another man in some sort of fisticuffs.

There were many calls to settle down and sit down, and eventually, the two men did just that and another drink was placed in front of the author and the man he was fighting.

'Give us a poem, Fenton,' someone yelled out from across the room and Matilda saw Sydney flinch with displeasure.

In moments the audience was calling for him to take the stage and Percy slapped him on the back. 'Your audience awaits you, best not disappoint them.'

Sydney gave a small smile and nod, and handing Percy his drink, headed to the stage looking quite reluctant.

'Does he not like to recite?' Matilda asked his friend, Percy.

'Don't be concerned,' Percy told her and the ladies. 'He likes to recite; he just needs some encouragement.'

'He is certainly getting that,' Alice said, as the roar of the surrounding patrons was most enthusiastic, including the clapping from the ladies present. Soon the room stilled as Sydney took the offered chair and removing a folded note from his pocket introduced his poem.

'This is an unfinished work I have been penning having been inspired by a beauty I encountered of recent,' he said, and there were sighs from the women and cheers from the literary men in his company. Matilda noticed Percy's chest puffed as if he was proud of his friend and responsible for him. When she turned back, she saw Sydney Fenton glance at her as he finished his explanation.

The room was silenced and at the same time, she felt a hand on her shoulder and looked up to see Thomas had arrived behind her. She beamed at him and squeezed his hand. There were so many things she wanted to ask him about the case and his breakthrough but they had to be silent while Sydney Fenton performed on the stage. Thomas leant over, placing a kiss on her hand, before straightening and the pair returned their attention to the poet.

Sydney Fenton began: 'My verse is titled *Second chance*.'
He cleared his throat, reading some lines, knowing the
other lines by heart.

> *'Surely there can be but one true love for me,*
> *'A second true love will never be*
> *'But to imagine no more joy, my heart decries,*
> *'If forever, love should die.'*

Matilda glanced around. The room was so silent you
could hear a pin drop, and given Sydney Fenton was not
only extremely handsome but somewhat melancholy of
nature, his words felt pained, as if talking of an open wound.
She noted he glanced her way again, and she felt Thomas
stiffen behind her, his grasp on her hand a little tighter, his
body moving a little closer. Was that why he was watching
Sydney Fenton so intently, she wondered. He thought his
intentions dishonourable or is there more at stake?

A thought struck Matilda. Could Sydney Fenton be
writing of her, as his second chance at love? No, she almost
laughed at the idea and her vanity. It was but a coincidence
seeing him those few times and didn't all poets write of love?

He continued:

> *'Once loved, could I hope to love anew?*
> *'When the pain is as dear to me, as you.*
> *'When all appears in the world to be lost*
> *'The price more to pay than the cost.*

'Teach me to trust and trust again,
'Though hopes prove false and hearts deceive,
'And whether the world brings loss or brings gain,
'To ever love and still believe.'

He waited for a beat and then the room erupted in wild clapping and cheering. Sydney gave a small smile and nod of thanks and rose, vacating the seat for the next artist. It was then that the mood of the room changed. Linton Turner rose to his feet and yelled out: 'Murderer!' and Matilda knew straight away who Thomas was observing for his case, and it had less to do with jealousy and more to do with murder.

Chapter 33

Detective Thomas Ashdown knew his night was going to end differently than he planned the moment Linton Turner bellowed with outrage: 'You killed her, you killed my Sara!' But at least now, he was fairly confident he had found the poet that loved Miss Sara-Anne Wilford and that Linton Turner had loved her too. Despite Turner's denial, Thomas was sure Miss Wilford was the author's pyjama girl victim.

He sighed. His night with Matilda had come to an abrupt end. He watched her, the look of disbelief on her face as the scene played out. Thomas flinched as a chair was thrown across the room passing near him; women screamed and pandemonium broke out.

'Ladies, under the table,' Thomas hastily ordered, and with Daniel, Gideon and Ambrose, pulled the chairs out and assisted the ladies to hide. Patrons ran towards the door but Turner's supporters were blocking it as Sydney Fenton's allies moved towards them. Other ladies ran for the bathroom to hide. Men ducked below the bar.

Matilda rose slightly to speak with Thomas, and he pushed her down, kneeling to listen. 'Your breakthrough, is it anything to do with Linton Turner's book and now this accusation? Is Sara the girl in the pyjamas?' she asked.

'Yes, we have identified the pyjama lady and her name is Sara-Anne Wilford,' he said, glancing across the room, preparing to intervene. 'Confidentially…' he warned, pulling away from her ear long enough to get her agreement, 'she was said to have been loved by a writer and a poet.'

'I think you have found them,' she said, looking up at him with wide eyes, and if bedlam was not breaking out around them, the desperate need to touch and kiss her would have distracted him. Another table was overturned.

'Please stay here with the ladies until this settles,' he said and rose. He would have to intervene, even though he was hoping it might all be over shortly.

'She loved me and you possessed her and killed her,' Turner yelled, spitting as he spoke and breaking free of the friends restraining him. He rushed towards Sydney Fenton as the poet stepped down from the stage, giving him a good shove. Sydney tumbled backward, his hands grasping for something to break his fall, but he fell hard, from the edge of the stage to the floor.

'Murderer!' Turner said, stumbling to the ground, his hands finding Sydney's throat.

'Get off him.' Percy shoved Turner, helping patrons pull them apart. 'Get the hell off him!'

Percy grabbed Sydney up from the floor. Percy was not the fighting type but he was a big man, and bigger than his closest friend, Sydney.

'For the love of God,' Thomas said, knowing he would have to step in. 'Excuse me,' he muttered grimly to Matilda, 'duty beckons.'

'Of course, but you need help,' she said, looking around and cowering with the noise and fighting. 'Don't go in alone, Thomas, you'll be hurt.'

'I'll get Turner out of here and find an officer on patrol to take him to the watchhouse until he sobers up,' Thomas said.

'I'll help, let's go, Thom,' Daniel stepped up next to his best friend.

Thomas nodded his thanks. Linton Turner and Sydney Fenton had been separated and were being moved well away from each other, Sydney rubbing his throat with discomfort as Percy brushed him down from his fall. Thomas cuffed Linton Turner around the neck to move him outside.

'Police, stand back,' Daniel called, which surprisingly they all did fairly quickly.

'You've had enough Mr Turner,' Thomas said to him, guiding him to the exit.

'You again,' Turner slurred.

'Unfortunately, yes. Let's get you out of here and when you sober up, you can tell me what you mean by accusing Mr Fenton of murdering Miss Wilford.' Thomas led him down the stairs, Daniel at his back.

'I loved her,' he started to wail. 'She should have been mine.'

Thomas looked to Daniel and rolled his eyes. So much for a night out with his girl.

*****

The group fussed over Sydney Fenton on his return, giving him the attention which he enjoyed as most people of importance and profile did.

'Thank you for your concern, I assure you, I am fine,' he said, straightening his necktie. 'Thank you, Percy, for coming to the rescue, again.'

Percy grinned. 'I don't mind a bit of action,' he said with a laugh.

It was then, when seated opposite Miss Phoebe Astin to recover himself fully, that Sydney Fenton's eyes were opened. He had to look twice – how had he not noticed this beauty when introduced. He was standing behind her then, that is why, and focussing solely on Miss Matilda Hayward.

She was Sara-Anne, just like her. Nonconforming, beautiful, confident, and with no ring on her finger. Who was she? What was her name again? From that moment onwards, Miss Matilda Hayward disappeared from his thoughts and his attention was purely focused on Miss Phoebe Astin. He had to know more about this intriguing woman, in her loose flowing gown with her hair restrained only by a small ribbon. What he would give to have that ribbon.

He looked up as Daniel re-entered and joined the group.

'Where is Thomas?' Matilda asked.

'He found a constable on the street and they have taken Turner to the lock-up for the night. He wants to question him while he's in a talkative mood, in case he clams up tomorrow,' Daniel said.

Sydney shook his head. 'He's dangerous and irresponsible.'

'He's jealous, that's what he is,' Percy said. 'He can't stand to think you are a better selling artist, better looking and the girls he likes would pick you for their first choice.'

Sydney appreciated his friend's loyalty but gave a small shake of his head as if indicating the conversation was not suitable for this time or place and his modesty would not entertain it.

'Shall we depart?' Ambrose asked of his sister, Phoebe, and looked wider to the group he came with. 'Go somewhere else perhaps?'

'Fine idea,' Gideon said.

Sydney could see Miss Hayward's brother, the gallery owner, casting glances at Miss Phoebe Astin too. Were they both going to compete for her affections? In which case he hoped Percy was right, and like every other woman in the room – the spoken-for Miss Matilda Hayward and the English beauty, Miss Alice Doran excepted – Miss Astin would want to be with him.

'I have a suggestion,' Sydney said. 'Why don't we all go back to my house and have a private party. I have a well-stocked liquor cabinet and we can put on some music and relax.'

Alice clapped her hands with delight. 'That would be great fun, what do you think, Daniel?' she asked.

Percy spoke before Daniel had a chance to respond. 'What a great idea.'

'How kind, Mr Fenton,' Phoebe said, with a glance to her brother who gave a nod of agreement.

Percy organised the party. 'Why don't we go ahead now

and we shall see you there promptly? We can fit two more in your carriage, Sydney.'

'Indeed.' He looked to Miss Phoebe Astin. 'Would you and your guest care to ride with us?'

'We can do that,' Ambrose spoke up on behalf of himself and his sister, but with a glance and raised eyebrow to Gideon and Matilda as the date had been originally just the four young people.

Sydney wondered what Ambrose's relationship was to Miss Astin, he could not recall from the introductions when he was only half-listening. He would have to discover it on the journey over, but he had trumped Gideon Hayward in getting Miss Astin to himself for a brief time and Mr Gideon Hayward's expression showed he was displeased.

While Percy sought a couple of lady friends to make up numbers in the party, Sydney kept one ear to the conversation around him. He heard the young English woman and her beau, Daniel, discussing their plans with Matilda and the gallery owner, Gideon.

'Thomas will not like us attending,' Daniel said in a hushed voice. 'It may be relevant to the crime he is trying to solve.'

'I agree,' Gideon said, although Sydney suspected he had other motives for wanting to talk Miss Astin and Miss Hayward out of visiting. 'We could be putting the ladies in danger.'

'But there are enough of you men present to protect us, and I can't imagine what danger we would be in,' Alice said.

Sydney was not concerned; he had heard many wild

rumours about himself and his family home over the years from him being a creature of the night that only came out at dusk – one story he quite enjoyed – to him killing his lovers with passion, a story that had not hurt his reputation, especially since he rarely took on a lover and was completely devoted to her and her alone when he did.

'We can keep an eye out for anything strange,' Matilda said. 'That will satisfy Thomas, I'm sure.'

Sydney stood, amused by their suspicions and keen to have Miss Phoebe Astin in his carriage for the journey home. Turning to face them, he asked: 'Shall we then? We shall see you there soon,' Sydney said graciously to the remaining party, and departed with Percy, Ambrose and Phoebe Astin.

Chapter 34

The mansion on the hill was a sight to behold. A grand sandstone home, surrounded by manicured gardens, ponds and a tennis court. The hansom drove them through the open gates right up to the entranceway where a footman stood at the door, waiting to greet them and escort them in.

'Oh my,' Matilda said glancing at it through the open doorway of the hansom cab as Gideon impatiently waited to assist her out. She allowed him to do so. Seeing his frustration and ensuring Alice and Daniel did not overhear, Matilda said: 'You are worried he is interested in Phoebe. But are *you* enamoured with my beautiful new friend?'

He grimaced, not one, like most men, to voice his emotions. 'I have barely had a chance to make an impression or to get to know Miss Astin. But yes, I would like to do so.'

'I shall try to ensure Mr Fenton is distracted elsewhere then,' Matilda said. 'Do step up when you get the chance,' she coached him.

'Yes, ma'am,' he promised and she gave a small laugh.

Sydney Fenton appeared in the doorway and welcomed them in personally. 'Come through, Percy is mixing cocktails, Heaven help us!' he joked. Matilda noticed he was more confident in his home environment and a gracious host.

They passed through an enormous entranceway with a large timber staircase going up the centre before separating and dividing in the middle to a left and right-wing. Sydney stayed on the lower level and led them into a large room with an unlit fireplace, and a ceiling that was so high, Matilda had to step back to look upwards, almost knocking over Alice.

Phoebe smiled on seeing her and moved towards Matilda to take her hand. 'Come sit with me, Matilda and Alice,' she said, and Matilda noticed Gideon was most pleased with that development and that Phoebe wasn't off being given a private tour of the house or similar by Sydney Fenton. The men moved to the liquor cabinet to provide the ladies with beverages.

'This place is amazing,' Alice gushed. 'We have castles at home, but they are old, cold and in disrepair. This is truly beautiful.'

'It is,' Matilda agreed, with a glance around. 'Quite foreboding.'

'Mr Fenton said his mother lives in the other half of the house but they have separate entrances and barely see each other,' Phoebe said. 'Could you imagine rattling around in here by yourself all day and night?'

Matilda smiled. 'You and I are too used to noisy brothers, and Alice grew up with two sisters. It would be odd to have so much space and no one to share it with.' She looked behind to ensure the men were occupied and said: 'Do you think there is any truth in what the author said, that Sydney Fenton is a murderer?'

'It is a strange statement to make if it is unfounded,' Alice agreed.

Phoebe leant in closer. 'On the way here, Mr Fenton apologised for the outbreak and called it preposterous. He said Mr Turner would do anything for publicity for his book.'

'I suspect Mr Turner must deeply despise Mr Fenton to accuse him of such a thing and risk ruining his reputation,' Matilda said. 'But, then again, Mr Fenton was talking of love lost and never loving again. Who is this lost love?'

'Do you think he murdered his last love?' Alice whispered, wide-eyed. The ladies stopped talking as the men joined them.

'I shall put some dance music on, shall I, Sydney?' Percy proclaimed. 'Let's set the mood!'

'Absolutely, there is plenty of room to take a partner if anyone feels inclined,' he said with a glance to Miss Phoebe Astin.

'That was a beautiful poem, Mr Fenton, if you will permit me to say so,' Matilda said, diverting his attention as she promised Gideon. 'I am sorry that you have lost your love.'

He looked a little surprised and stumbled on his response.

'Forgive me, that was the topic was it not?' Matilda asked. 'I thought from the passion reflected in your poem, that it could only be something you experienced firsthand.'

'Oh, yes, thank you, Miss Hayward. It is or rather it was,' he said, with a small bow of the head to acknowledge her praise. 'I did indeed lose a love. Hence my question, do we only ever get one true love? How could it be that we are granted a second chance at love and could that too, be called true love?' Again, he glanced towards Phoebe Astin.

'Sydney does not love lightly,' Percy said, joining them and indulging his friend's melancholy.

Matilda noted the other gentlemen in their party did not look as if they were enjoying themselves. Percy was trying too hard to compensate for Sydney's quiet nature; Gideon was studying Phoebe to see if she was reacting to Sydney's attentions; Daniel looked like he would much rather have gone with Thomas than be stuck with several men whom he had very little in common with, and Matilda did not know Ambrose well enough to determine his views, but he was seeking Daniel's company so she suspected they would soon have a few drinks and suggest the party depart. She needed to find out more about Sydney Fenton before then, something that might assist Thomas.

'Would you like to dance, Miss Astin?' Sydney asked, and Matilda saw Gideon stiffen.

'If it is not too presumptuous, I would love a tour of your home,' she responded. 'The artworks are amazing.'

'That would be my pleasure.'

'Oh, me too,' Alice said, and Matilda agreed. If Sydney Fenton hoped to be alone with Phoebe, he would be sorely disappointed.

'Will you join us then, gentlemen?' Sydney asked, his manners overtaking his frustration in extending the invitation.

As Alice recognised the painting by a British artist on the wall, Matilda took the opportunity to speak with Phoebe, and gave Gideon a look that said 'step up!'

'Do you live near your office?' Matilda asked.

'Yes, only a ten-minute walk which is convenient, sometimes too convenient,' she said with a small laugh. 'We do keep odd hours.'

'I am well versed in that,' Matilda assured her. 'My hours are very normal, but Thomas is most unreliable, and Gideon – as the manager of the gallery – often has after-hour events.'

'You have a lovely gallery, I came to Marlon Dominey's first exhibition,' Phoebe said.

'Did you? I don't recall seeing you and I'm sure I would have remembered,' Gideon said.

'It was a Sunday and a very nice gentleman was working that day.'

'Ah Wilkie, that is Mr Wilkie Watkins, my weekend manager. He's quite a character,' Gideon agreed and Matilda drew away on the pretence of studying a lamp and leaving them to talk but staying near enough to overhear anything of interest. As they walked along, Sydney Fenton's voice drifting back providing explanations of the history of objects and artwork, Matilda could observe each room and note anything that might be of value to Thomas. She had no idea what that might be or what to look for, but that did not stop her from attempting to be useful.

As they came to a large room that looked like a laundry of sorts, with several large tables, shelves full of paint and bottles, and low hanging gas lamps, Sydney Fenton half closed the door and moved the group on.

'My craft room,' he said as a way of explanation. 'I've tried my hand at painting but I'm best suited to poetry.'

The group joined in his joke but Matilda's nose was on the job. She could smell an odour that she recognised from elsewhere... from Phoebe's studio. She dropped a little further back and waited until the group had turned the corner, and even though she wasn't feeling particularly brave, Matilda opened the door, dashed in and closed it behind her. Not before scolding herself for doing something so stupid, but she had done it now and here she was.

She hurried around the room, sniffing, reading labels, glancing underneath shelves covered in curtains and then, returning to the door, she opened it a sliver and listened. Nothing. No sooner had she opened the door she heard footsteps coming and raced out, half closing it as she found it, and went into the room the group had just departed. She raced to an enormous painting and stared up at it, realising then that the painting she was looking at was a portrait of the poet himself.

'Miss Hayward!'

Matilda wheeled around. 'Mr Fenton.' She glanced around dramatically. 'Forgive me, I've become separated from the tour, haven't I?'

He smiled, indulging her and she gave him the most charming look she could conjure – Matilda was not adept at flirting.

'I have been known to wander off course myself,' he assured her.

'It is a strikingly handsome and realistic portrait,' she said looking from the larger-than-life portrait of Sydney himself and back to the man in front of her.

'Thank you. The portrait of my father is also exceptionally good and life-like,' he said, with a nod to a painting on the other side of the room.

'I can see you in him,' Matilda said. 'Do forgive me for bringing you back. I promise to remain at the front of the tour from now on.'

'Then shall we?' he asked, offering his arm. Matilda could feel him studying her.

'We have met before, haven't we? One afternoon on the omnibus,' she said.

He smiled. 'We have indeed, I wondered if you would remember. I think I saw you another time as well near your work.'

'At the *Women's Journal*?'

'Yes, you are very hard to miss,' he said, and Matilda gave a delighted laugh.

'You are too kind.'

Is that why he was looking at me when he read the poem earlier, she wondered. He recognised me. They caught up with the group who were listening to Percy tell a story of how they acquired a particularly ugly statue in the corner of the room.

Matilda had what she needed. She saw for herself the embalming fluid and in her pocket was a lady's necklace with a pendant engraved with the letters S.A.W – could it belong to Sara-Anne Wilford and was she Sydney Fenton's lover?

Chapter 35

'But the night is so young,' Percy exclaimed as Ambrose made their apologies and the group prepared to depart. 'We've yet to dance,' he said, trying to persuade them to linger. 'There is an excellent port to be sampled.'

'Ah, you will have to go on without us,' Daniel added. 'Sadly, we all have occupations that require us to rise and be sensible in the morning.'

Phoebe pulled Matilda aside as they walked down the large hallway back to the entranceway where they would make their departure.

'I was worried something happened to you,' Phoebe said. 'I would have accompanied you elsewhere.'

'I was being an investigative journalist, or a detective, but don't tell Thomas that.' Matilda looked around and lowered her voice as she returned her attention to Phoebe. 'Do you remember the room that Mr Fenton said was his craft room?'

'Yes,' Phoebe said. 'Before he closed the door, I recognised the embalming fluid that I use on his shelf.'

'Ah-ha, I thought I could smell it,' Matilda said. 'Is it used for anything else? Is there a reason Mr Fenton might have it?'

'I can't imagine what else he would use it for, or why he would have it in the first place,' she said.

Matilda thanked her. Before they joined the men she added. 'I suspect Mr Fenton admires you and may pursue your hand.'

Phoebe gave a small shake of her head and smiled. 'While I am flattered and a great admirer of his talent, I work in a sober industry every day. I am not seeking melancholy and drama in a partner.'

Matilda lightened with relief. Now, she had a variety of information that would make Thomas and Gideon happy indeed.

Thanking Sydney for his hospitality, Daniel and Alice, Matilda and Gideon, Phoebe and Ambrose, walked down the long path through the estate and out to the road to hail hansom cabs. Matilda caught up with Daniel.

'I need to see Thomas tonight. I have information for him.'

Daniel frowned. 'It is well after midnight, but I imagine he is home by now and has left Linton Turner in the cells.'

'I can see myself home if you need to go,' Alice said.

'Definitely not —' Daniel started.

'We wouldn't dream of it,' Matilda finished, and smiled as Alice laughed at the pair of them.

'We shall see you home first, and then Matilda and I will continue to Thomas's home if you have no objections?' Daniel asked, and Matilda nodded her agreement.

'Of course, do what you must do. There is crime afoot,' Alice said most seriously.

*****

'There's someone here, a hansom has just pulled up,' Teddy announced with a glance through the window near where he sat on the couch in his Uncle Thomas's drawing-room. He was still awake and reading when his uncle returned from the watchhouse, and the men – both night-owls – shared an ale.

Thomas groaned. 'Is it a constable come to fetch me?'

'I can't see, it's too dark, but they're coming up the pathway and there are two of them by the looks of it.' Teddy rose. 'Stay there, I'll see to it.' Thomas thanked him and remained seated.

Teddy opened the door and grinned, and then realised he was not dressed for receiving a lady.

'Forgive our late arrival, Teddy,' Daniel said, but we saw a light was on in the window.

'No apology necessary at all, we are both up,' Teddy said.

'Hello, Teddy. So, Thomas is home?'

'Matilda, lovely to see you again. May I say you look most beautiful?'

'Thank you,' she said, with a smile of gratitude.

'And yes, Uncle Thomas just got home this half-hour past. Come on in,' he stood aside. 'Is everything okay?'

'Yes, indeed. I have some information and I would not sleep waiting to tell Thomas.'

Daniel rolled his eyes so that only Teddy could see and added: 'Heaven forbid, nothing changes.'

Teddy laughed and closed the door behind them. He indicated the drawing-room door just off the hallway where a small gas lamp was lit. The three entered and Thomas leapt to his feet on seeing Matilda.

'What's happened?'

'Nothing, everything is fine,' she assured him, and then her eyes moved to his shirt.

'Ah, forgive me,' he said, realising he was inappropriately dressed. He wore no waistcoat or necktie, the sleeves of his shirt were rolled up and his strong arms and his neck exposed. He glanced at Daniel with a frown for leading his sister in, as he rolled down his sleeves and straightened his shirt. He ran a hand through his hair.

'Don't worry about it,' Daniel said, and slipped off his own jacket. 'In a matter of weeks, Matilda will be seeing you wearing a lot less than that.'

'Daniel!' Matilda said and gasped.

He shrugged. 'We were all thinking it, I just said it.'

'Then I suggest you just think it too in the future,' his best friend, Thomas, ribbed him.

'Matilda, Daniel, will you have tea or a cool ale?' Teddy asked.

'Sorry, yes.' Thomas shook his head slightly as he remembered his manners. 'Or a seat.'

Matilda took the offered seat and accepted a glass of water while Daniel took an ale. 'We shan't be here long,' she said.

'So, what is going on?' Thomas asked, on Teddy's return with the drinks.

'Shall I leave?' Teddy asked.

'No, not at all,' Daniel assured him and they all made themselves comfortable.

'Did you find out if there was any truth in what Mr Turner said about Mr Fenton committing murder?' Matilda asked.

'Oh, sounds like it was an exciting night,' Teddy said. 'Is that why you left the club and went to the watchhouse?'

'Yes,' Thomas said. 'Just when I thought I was off for the night and in good company, the author starts yelling at the poet on stage and accusing him of murder. Add to this the pyjama girl Miss Sara-Anne Wilford's friend told Harry and me today that Miss Wilford was in love with a poet and might have had relations with an author.'

'And those two fit the bill, especially given the subject of Linton Turner's book,' Matilda added, getting Teddy up to speed.

Daniel looked from Teddy to Thomas and back. 'Don't you two talk about this stuff when you're together?'

Teddy shrugged. 'Not really. I tell Uncle Thomas about the characters in my day at the prison, and he tries to match it.'

Thomas grinned. 'It's not that hard given what we come across every day. You can knock off calling me Uncle, too.'

'Nope, I like it. Makes me feel younger,' Teddy joked.

'So?' Matilda asked again. 'Was there truth in his accusation?'

Thomas sighed and looked at her. 'Is that what you came here to find out?'

'No, I have information but I think you should start first,' she said, and Teddy and Daniel chuckled at Thomas's exasperated expression.

'I couldn't get much more out of him because he was inebriated, and when he sobered, he clammed up. Harry and I will talk to him again in the morning… which it is now,' he added. 'What did you find out?' He leaned forward placing his elbows on his knees, keen to watch Matilda excitedly deliver her news more than he was to hear the content.

'Well, we went back to Sydney Fenton's house and he gave us a tour. So I was looking out for anything that might be of interest.'

Thomas looked shocked. He put his hand up to stop her. 'You went to Sydney Fenton's house? A man who has just been accused of murder and was rattling off some poem about his love lost… you went to his house?' He stood, angry.

'Daniel?' he snapped, demanding an answer.

'Thom, sit, do not stress yourself, we were never in any danger,' Daniel assured him. 'Myself, Ambrose Astin, and Gideon were all present, along with that Percy fellow, the friend of Sydney Fenton.'

Thomas paced to the end of the couch and turned back to look at them. 'And what if the poet and Percy had drugged your drinks and harmed the ladies?' he shot back at them.

Daniel thought on this for a moment and had no good answer. The silence stretched out for several uncomfortable seconds while Thomas reined in his anger.

'You are upset with me, with us,' Matilda said soothingly.

'But it didn't happen, Thomas, so do not concern yourself with worrying about what might have eventuated,' she assured him and rose from the couch as well. She went to his side. 'See, we are all fine. So let me tell you what I found.'

'Forgive me, I didn't mean to raise my voice,' he said, his lips thinning in frustration as he looked down upon Matilda and gave a curt nod for her to continue. She moved away slightly to incorporate Daniel and Teddy in her delivery.

'Mr Fenton took us for a tour, and the artwork and architecture were amazing, weren't they, Daniel?'

'They were if that interests you,' he said casually. 'Myself, I prefer somewhere homely,' he said with a look around and Teddy laughed.

'And?' Thomas said, moving her along.

'There was nothing that appeared to be of interest until we got to a room that he called his "craft room", don't you agree, Daniel?'

Daniel frowned. 'I noticed nothing of interest,' he confessed.

'Then you were not thinking like a journalist or a detective, Daniel. What were you doing there?' Teddy teased him as he finished his ale.

'I was admiring Miss Alice Doran,' he confessed, 'it's my job.'

Teddy could see his uncle's serious countenance was getting more serious and invited Matilda to continue. 'My apologies for the interruption. Please, tell us why a poet needs a craft room.'

'Exactly, Teddy, thank you,' Matilda said, giving him an

appreciative look and returning to her seat, Thomas did the same. 'He said he was a better poet than a painter, but it wasn't a painter's room either. There were no easels or canvases, paints or brushes. There was, however, two large steel tables, and lots of bottle goods.'

Thomas nodded. 'That is very, very interesting. I will ensure Harry and I pay Mr Fenton a visit on Monday to see this for ourselves and ask him his thoughts about Mr Turner's accusation.' He sat back and relaxed.

'But that's not all,' Matilda said, and Thomas leaned forward again.

'I hesitate to ask, but go on,' he said, and Matilda gave him a slightly guilty look for what was to come.

'When the group moved away, I snuck back into the room...'

'You what!' Thomas exploded.

'Well, I needed to have a closer look.'

'Matilda! Daniel where were you and Gideon?' Thomas asked, throwing his hands up in the air.

'We were there with Sydney Fenton, Percy and the rest of the group. Matilda snuck back without us noticing,' Daniel said with a shrug as if it were no big deal.

'You must be very good at sneaking,' Teddy said, impressed.

'Years of practice,' Matilda agreed with a laugh. 'So I had a quick look around and I found embalming fluid. I thought I had smelt it earlier and I asked Phoebe and she said she saw it in the room as well and it was the product she used.'

Thomas stared in shock and disbelief at Matilda's audacity

and penchant for danger. He leaned back on the couch, put his hands over his face and muttered: 'For the love of God!'

'There's more, Thomas,' Matilda said and he groaned, withdrawing his hands from his face and sitting upright. She continued, and reaching into a small pocket in her dress skirt, Matilda retrieved the delicate chain with an engraved charm. 'I found this. It has the initial S-A-W engraved on it. What was the name of the pyjama girl?'

'Sara-Anne Wilford,' he said between gritted teeth.

'There you go then,' she said and handed it to him.

'You are amazing,' Teddy said impressed.

'You really are,' Daniel agreed. 'What do you think, Thom?'

Thomas spoke directly to Matilda. 'What if he came back and found you in there?'

'He did almost. But I was very quick and then I opened the door just a little to sneak out and heard footsteps so I ran into the next room and pretended to admire a huge painting – it was a portrait of him.'

'I saw that,' Daniel said, 'rather dramatic.'

'Is everyone missing the point here?' Thomas demanded. 'Matilda, you could be in the house of a murderer, and here you are alone in a room where he might have killed and embalmed a girl, and he is nearby. If he found you in there… I can't begin to think what might have happened.'

'Well, he didn't, Thomas, so don't carry on, and don't be so ungrateful for my findings,' she said petulantly.

'I don't need your findings,' he snapped. 'I want a fiancée who is alive and does not put herself in impossibly dangerous situations.'

'It is part of my job, Thomas, and I want to support you in your job.'

'It is *my* job, Matilda, not yours and you are not safe in that world.'

'Would you rather I stay home and prepare your house and evening meal?'

'That would make me very happy,' he said. 'Or stay in the office, do your writing without venturing into the home of potential murder suspects!'

'I'm thinking about getting a top-up,' Teddy said, with a glance to Daniel.

'Good idea, I could use one,' he said rising and the two men departed, the voices of Thomas and Matilda ringing in their ears.

Chapter 36

Aunt Audrey met the Hayward family at church on Sunday as was her usual habit and shared her carriage to the Hayward household for lunch afterwards with Matilda. She had received many comments on her sophisticated cream and lace dress and how refreshing it was to see her out of mourning black. She felt relieved to be in lighter colours but if honest with herself, Mrs Samuel Bloomfield felt some betrayal of her dear husband, as if admitting he was no longer top of mind to her, despite the many years since his passing.

'When will that young man of yours start attending church with us?' Aunt Audrey asked once settled and the ride had commenced.

'Perhaps never, Aunt Audrey. He always seems to have a work situation or call-out on Sunday morning.'

'Yes, I imagine he does,' she said suspiciously. 'How are your wedding preparations coming along?' Aunt Audrey raised an eyebrow at the expression on Matilda's face.

'What is that look reflecting, may I ask? Don't tell me you have concerns?'

Matilda sighed. 'Oh, Aunt Audrey, I do love Thomas but we had the biggest argument last evening about my work leading me into danger, and I can only imagine what it will be like when we are married and I displease him.'

'He has every right to be concerned,' Aunt Audrey proclaimed. 'An eminently sensible young man that. Whatever he said about not wanting you to take risks has my full support.'

Matilda grimaced and Aunt Audrey chuckled and patted her knee.

'My dear girl, it is inbred in our dear males to protect and cherish, and you do not want to ruin his manliness by not allowing him to take that role.'

'No, I guess not,' Matilda said, and relaxed further into her seat. 'But he knows me and knows what I do.'

'And you know him and what he does,' Aunt Audrey said. 'You don't want him to be in danger any more than he wants you to come to harm.'

'That is true,' she said looking out of the carriage window. 'Forgive me, Aunt Audrey. You are the closest person I have to a mother and I should have sought your counsel earlier.' She turned to face her aunt. 'What would you suggest I do?'

Her words touched, surprised, and pleased Aunt Audrey. She always believed Matilda to be headstrong and their relationship not as closed as she hoped. She answered: 'Do not tell him everything, my dear.'

Matilda looked shocked, her hand resting on her chest.

'That is one of the secrets of a good marriage. Just as you must keep some mystique to your personal grooming and preparation, do the same with anything you deem might upset Thomas.'

'But would I not be deceiving him?' Matilda asked, a little shocked at the advice.

'Only if he should ask you and you don't tell, then yes. But what he doesn't know, won't hurt him,' she said, and tapped her nose in a knowing gesture. 'Mind you, young lady, I am not supporting your reckless actions or placing yourself in danger.'

Matilda smiled. 'I understand and assure you, Aunt Audrey, I don't want to be harmed any more than I want Thomas harmed.'

'But remember, Thomas has a lot of responsibility and you don't wish for him to be distracted because you are causing him concern.'

'That is a very good point, Aunt Audrey, thank you,' Matilda said, happy she could justify some withholding of information with that excuse. She looked to her aunt with narrowed eyes. 'So, what have you kept secret from Uncle Samuel then, Aunt?'

Aunt Audrey laughed. 'Never you mind, but let's say we had a very happy marriage.'

*****

'Thank goodness Pa will soon finish upgrading the conservatory for Sunday lunch,' Amos said as he squeezed in next to his pregnant and larger wife, Minnie, at the end of the dining table and nearest to Aunt Audrey. He was her favourite, after all.

'By the end of the month we should be able to lunch in there,' Mr Hayward agreed, smiling at the large assembly around his table. 'It does my heart good to see so many happy faces here, and to see how well my children have chosen for their future happiness.'

'Indeed, brother, I could not agree more.' Aunt Audrey seconded him, 'and welcome Betty.'

Beside Mr Hayward sat Gideon, then Daniel with Alice, Minnie and Amos, and Aunt Audrey at the opposite head of the table. Next to her sat Elijah and Georgina, Matilda and Thomas, and Betty Purcell, recently inducted into the family, next to Mr Hayward.

'We just need to have your guest present, Aunt Audrey, and Gideon's flame,' Matilda teased.

Aunt Audrey offered no response other than a stern look in Matilda's direction, but Gideon smiled with pleasure.

'I did meet an intriguing young lady last evening, thanks to Matilda,' he offered and got everyone's attention.

'It appears that except for our lovely Minnie, we have the good fortune of most of the ladies around the table being introduced because of Matilda,' her father said with affection and gave Betty an appreciative glance.

Alice clapped her hands with glee. 'Oh Gideon, so you enjoyed the company of Miss Astin?'

'Very much so Alice, thank you, and from what Matilda tells me, she might enjoy my company too,' Gideon said.

'Of course she would,' Elijah his twin answered loyally. 'What is not to like?'

'Indeed, brother,' Gideon answered, 'we are the best of the Hayward's.' He grinned as the rest of the table guests deservedly teased and ribbed him.

'Now Aunt Audrey, Miss Astin is a little unconventional,' Matilda warned.

'That's what makes her so interesting,' Gideon agreed, straightening in his seat as if he was proud to have made such a discovery.

'What does that mean exactly?' Georgina asked Matilda. 'I too, am regarded as a little unconventional having come off the farm and missed a few lessons at beauty school,' she jested as Georgina often did at her own expense. 'One might compare me to a goose amongst the swans but yet you have all welcomed me to the table.'

'Nonsense,' Matilda said loyally.

'The pleasure is ours, Georgina,' Mr Hayward said.

'Especially mine,' Elijah said, taking her hand and kissing it. He too received a round of groans and ribbing for being romantic and Georgina laughed with pleasure.

Matilda looked to Thomas who was most formal beside her; the pair was still out of sorts after last evening's argument, but now Matilda knew how to handle it better in the future. She placed her hand on his leg under the table and he stiffened with surprise. As everyone joked with Georgina and Elijah, Matilda leant closer to Thomas and whispered. 'I am sorry about our fight, Thomas. I promise to be more careful and more considered in my actions in the future.'

She saw him visibly relax and his hand found hers under the table and held it, not that he was one for taking too many risks in the company of family or earning Aunt Audrey's displeasure so close to their wedding.

'I too am sorry and will try and be more...' he could not find any words. 'Well, I'll just try,' he finished and made her laugh.

Gideon held the floor. 'How is Miss Astin unconventional you ask, Georgina? Well, the very beautiful Miss Phoebe Astin not only dresses in a fashion that is not as formal as many of the ladies in society, but she is an embalmer and dresser at her family's mortuary.'

There were gasps around the table, and Aunt Audrey's hand went to her heart.

'Bless me, what next?' she proclaimed.

'I assure you, Aunt Audrey, Miss Astin is very much a lady,' Matilda hurried to add, 'and the business is very successful.'

'Just think on it, Aunt Audrey,' Gideon teased. 'Should Miss Astin and I become a pair, I will ensure when that sad and tragic day comes of your demise, that you will look better in death than you do in life if that is at all possible.'

There was laughter and looks around the table, as they waited for Aunt Audrey to return serve to her cheekiest and youngest nephew. But she sighed, shook her head and smiled.

'My boy, being the youngest as you are, I confess by the time I have come to getting you betrothed, I am somewhat exhausted. I shall happily settle for your happiness, no matter who the young lady is who chooses to manage you but I might just accept that offer.'

'Well said, Audrey.' Mr Hayward laughed, and clapped his son on the back. 'There you go, Son, permission to fall in love, not that you needed it, but it is always nice to have a blessing going forth.'

'Go forth I shall then,' he proclaimed.

'No doubt Miss Astin already realises what a good catch you are, Gideon,' Georgina teased.

'Well, my dear Georgina,' Gideon said, 'as I am almost identical to your beau, if her taste is as good as yours, we will both be happy.'

And the atmosphere was again at peace and happy around the Hayward table as Mary's Sunday roast was shared.

Chapter 37

Having been admitted through the large iron gates of Fenton Manor, on the highest point of Spring Hill, the two detectives stood back as the front door of Sydney Fenton's mansion opened and an enormous dog bound out towards them.

'Humphrey! Don't worry, he's friendly,' Sydney Fenton said, dismissing his footman and tying a robe around his body.

The large hound nearly bowled Thomas over, but straightening, Thomas patted the dog as they followed Fenton in.

'Did we wake you, Mr Fenton?' Harry asked.

'I wish you did, Detective,' Fenton said and ran a hand through his mop of dark hair. 'I would love to have the luxury of sleep, but some nights I only manage two or three hours. Have you breakfasted?'

'Yes, thank you,' Thomas said, noting it was nearing 10 o'clock. He followed Harry and Sydney Fenton in, the dog staying by his side and looking up at him.

'He's taken to you,' Sydney said, looking back at Thomas and Humphrey. 'He likes men with facial hair, don't ask me why.'

Harry chuckled and Thomas gave a small shrug, not unhappy to have earned a new canine friend. He was, after all, rather keen on dogs and would have one if he were ever at home. They followed Sydney into a large room with an enormous dining table where a small buffet of food had been set out for Sydney's breakfast.

'You will take tea though?' he asked.

'Best we get to the questions first, but thank you, Mr Fenton,' Harry said. 'You may need to show us to another area, before taking your breakfast.'

'Right then,' Sydney Fenton said, and stopped to look at them. 'What can I assist you with?'

'Mr Turner's outburst last night,' Thomas said, his hand still automatically patting the dog by his side that was of a size that did not require him to reach down to do so.

'Ah,' Sydney nodded, 'you heard about that then?'

'I was present,' Thomas said. 'Did you want to tell us your side of the story?'

Sydney sighed. 'If I must, but I at least need a cup of tea beforehand.' He helped himself, offered one to the detectives who declined and directed them to a smaller sitting area near the front window.

Once seated, he began. 'Linton Turner is delusional. I won the heart of a lovely lady, and Turner wanted her as well. She didn't want him, that is the story.' He gave a small shrug.

'And where is this young lady?' Harry asked.

'Dead.' Sydney turned to Thomas. 'As you would know if you heard my poem.'

'Is the lady in question Miss Sara-Anne Wilford, the pyjama girl?' Harry asked.

'Yes.'

'Why did you not come forward to report her missing or identify her from the posters?' Thomas asked, bewildered and frustrated.

'She wasn't missing. Sara came and went as she pleased even in death; she was a free spirit, that is what attracted me to her most.' His voice broke a little and he cleared his throat of emotion before continuing. 'You see detectives, I loved her and offered her my hand in marriage and she intended to accept once I had the blessing of my mother. It is only fair to involve Mother in such a big decision with the estate to consider.'

'And what did your mother say?' Harry asked.

'I didn't get a chance to ask her before Sara left this earth,' Sydney Fenton said dramatically.

'What about Miss Wilford's relationship with Linton Turner? He apparently loved her given his outpouring at the club,' Harry said, attempting to follow along.

'Sara was with Linton Turner for some time and he offered her marriage. They were engaged,' he said with a casual shrug. 'And then we met at the club. That was it. She loved me and me alone, Sara told me that many times.'

'Did Linton Turner ever threaten you or Miss Wilford?' Thomas asked.

'No. He's all talk, or should I say all words. But Sara and I, we were, what you might call passionate. Once we met, she could not return to him.'

'I confess to having a limited understanding of poetry, Mr Fenton,' Thomas began, 'but your poem at the club spoke of finding a new true love and if such a thing was possible.'

'Ah, Detective, you are unfair on yourself. You have great vision and saw into my soul,' Sydney Fenton said dramatically. 'I confess I was surprised to have the stirrings of love arising again.'

Thomas restrained from hurrying him along. He deemed the melodrama unnecessary, but it was clearly part of Sydney Fenton's performance art.

Fenton continued: 'I always believed Sara was my true love, my only love, and that I would never recover from her departure of this world.'

A butler entered and Sydney motioned for another cup of tea and asked the men if they had changed their mind. They declined again with their thanks.

'You were telling of the end of your relationship with Miss Sara-Anne Wilford?' Thomas tried to get him back on track.

'Not just the end, but the end of life,' Sydney said, and Thomas saw Harry restrain a smile. 'But as if the gods are smiling on me, in the last month I have met two incredible ladies.'

'Are they still alive?' Harry asked.

Sydney Fenton laughed. 'Goodness, I hope so, Detective. They were when I last saw them.'

'Who are the ladies in question?' Thomas asked, in case they did appear dead in the coming weeks and he would have the insider information.

'I believe you know them, Detective Ashdown,' he said, stopping long enough to sip his tea. 'I first saw this beautiful, intriguing lady at a bookstore and I soon found out she was a writer. What talent, what a clever girl. I studied her from afar for a while – on the omnibus, at her work, even arriving home.'

Thomas's eyes narrowed. 'Some might consider that quite threatening Mr Fenton.'

'Research and inspiration,' Sydney assured him. 'No different to an artist having a muse, or enjoying the company of ladies at a dance. But she wore an engagement ring. Still,' he pondered indulgently as if the detectives had all day to wait on his musings, 'engagements can be broken as was the case with Sara.' He smiled smugly. 'Her name is Miss Matilda Hayward.'

Thomas was startled into profanity. Flaring with anger, he burst from his seat, dropping back only when the firm hand of Harry on his shoulder re-seated him.

'My fiancée!' he proclaimed.

'Ah, you are the fiancé,' Sydney said studying him with renewed interest. 'She seemed to be out a lot without you.'

'Because I am required to maintain the law.'

'And the second lady?' Harry asked, moving Sydney Fenton along. Thomas sat rigidly, a spasm of a muscle working in his jaw.

'When I met Miss Phoebe Astin, I had to let Miss Hayward go.'

Thomas settled slightly. He imagined Matilda had no idea she was being followed by a man who had once loved a murdered woman. A man who could be the very murderer himself. Thomas's blood was boiling and he was sure Harry could hear the grinding of his teeth. Thomas could not decide if he wanted to throttle Sydney Fenton and every indulgent poet like him, or race to Matilda and give her a good dose of reality with the danger she placed herself in.

Sydney Fenton was still talking: 'Miss Phoebe Astin is intriguing – striking of appearance, a free spirit, not restrained by society in her dress or appeal, and single,' he said and sighed with pleasure.

'Let's return to the lady in question, Miss Sara-Anne Wilford,' Thomas said through gritted teeth. He wanted to hit the man and draw satisfaction from the impact.

'Yes, my first true love,' Sydney Fenton continued melodramatically.

'The last time you saw her... when was that?' Thomas asked.

'When I embalmed her,' he answered.

*****

The *Women's Journal*'s latest edition was due this morning, and as always, the office was abuzz with excitement waiting for it to arrive. Matilda and Georgina were particularly keen to see their final story and illustration of Miss Phoebe Astin and her unusual career in print, and to drop a copy around to her.

Morning tea was ready to be served when the edition arrived so the ladies could celebrate and review the contents, and no sooner had the last plate of jam and scones been placed on the table next to Ruth's speciality sponge cake, the wagon pulled up out the front and several men alighted carrying in copies.

'It's here!' Alice said, most excited as she gathered with her closest friends – Matilda and Georgina – and waited for the ties to be cut on the pile of papers.

'I always feel so nervous waiting to see it, even though I know how my final illustrations look,' Georgina said.

'As do I,' Matilda agreed. 'Thank goodness Betty and her team are so good at correcting my copy so at least I know it won't have errors in it… like it might if left to me!'

'A huge relief,' Alice agreed.

They eagerly accepted a copy and each flicked to the pages where their work was featured. There was much oohing and aahing and congratulating each other and all the ladies of the journal for their features.

'Oh Georgina, your illustration of Phoebe is so perfect, I can almost feel her stepping off the page,' Matilda said, very satisfied with how her story and the page appeared.

'You both did excellent work,' Mrs Lawson said stepping amongst them and surprising the young ladies. 'It was also a nice little scoop, Matilda, that your detective allowed you to write about Miss Astin assisting the police with the illustration of the pyjama girl.'

'Thank you, Mrs Lawson,' Matilda said. 'It is wonderful the pyjama girl has now been identified and, between us,' she said with a look around, 'we were a guest of Miss Astin and her brother at the Quill Club this past evening, whereby the author Mr Linton Turner, accused Mr Sydney Fenton, the poet, of murdering the pyjama girl.'

'Goodness me,' Mrs Lawson said. 'Well, this is going to be an interesting case. Do stay on the job, Matilda. Report what you can without impeding on the investigation or crossing the line.'

'I will, thank you, Mrs Lawson.'

Their editor moved away to speak with some of the other staff and Alice said to Georgina: 'We missed your company at the Quill Club, it was a shame you did not come.'

'I was surprised too,' Matilda said. 'Elijah and Gideon are usually in each other's company socially.'

Georgina smiled. 'I learnt something very interesting, but you did not hear it from me, ladies, as it might be a secret, but I can't imagine why…'

'Do tell,' Alice said eagerly and Matilda nodded with keen interest.

'Elijah told me that if either he or his twin, Gideon, was interested in the company of a young lady, the other would not appear with him initially until that relationship was secured. They have an agreement,' Georgina said.

'I did not know that,' Matilda said, 'but the twins have always had their own secrets.'

'Why is that, do you think?' Alice asked. 'Is seeing two of them at once too much?'

Matilda laughed. 'It is at home,' she said in jest.

'Perhaps they don't wish to impede on the other brother's

chance of winning the girl when they appear so similar,' Georgina said with a small shrug.

'Yet they are so different of nature,' Matilda said.

'So very different. It is most odd, but men are often quite baffling,' Georgina said summing it up, and both ladies laughed.

'I didn't get the chance to ask at Sunday lunch, but did you get in terrible trouble from Thomas for going to Mr Fenton's house?' Alice asked. 'Daniel said Thomas was most cranky when you paid him a visit late that evening.'

'He was rather ropeable,' Matilda agreed. 'But we have both cooled down since and agreed to be on our best behaviour.'

'Which means?' Alice asked.

'I shall be careful what I tell him in future!' Matilda said.

Women's Journal
Tuesday, 26 February 1889
Fortnightly edition Vol.1, No.35.
Price, 3d.

The artistic mortician

A new series featuring some of the most
fascinating careers being undertaken
by the women of our town. Report by
Matilda Hayward. Illustration by
Georgina Urry.

--oOo--

Miss Phoebe Astin has no fear of
ghosts or spirits as she sits working
with the dead most days. Nor is she
often surprised by clients' requests
including a clairvoyant who wanted
her deceased husband removed from
the house head first instead of feet
first, in the hope he would come back.
Miss Astin is a mortician and embalmer
at The Economic Undertaker in Tribune
Street, South Brisbane.
  Our lady readers will know from
experience the effort one must make to
look presentable before we venture out

to face the world each day. But this intriguing lady ensures we look our best when we meet our maker.

At aged three-and-twenty, Miss Astin has met many of our town's citizens, but they, in turn, have not had the pleasure.

'I have hosted many ladies, gentlemen and dear little children as they begin their eternal journey,' Miss Astin said, 'it has been my pleasure to have cared for them even for the briefest time.'

The Economic Undertaker is a family business born of necessity, Miss Astin explained.

'My parents met an untimely death and my grandparents took myself and my two elder brothers in,' she said. 'Imagine not only unexpectedly having three children to raise but the expense of burying your beloved?'

Miss Astin explained that her grandparents wanted a dignified farewell for her parents and felt distressed at the cost to achieve this.

'As a consequence, when my brother Julius came of age, he founded The Economic Undertaker and now the family works together to provide a dignified and affordable funeral, no matter your budget.'

Miss Astin's role is unique. As it is becoming more common for our deceased loved ones to rest in the mortuary rather than in our parlours, particularly with the heat and in some cases extended families living abroad and not able to be present to mourn, Miss Astin prepares the deceased for viewing, presenting them in the manner in which they were remembered in life.

The Economic Undertaker is also contracted to receive deceased Brisbane Hospital patients that do not have a family to undertake their funerals.

'It is a very large part of our business, so often we are the family for the deceased. That is how I consider my role. It may be a simple act like brushing their hair, shaving the men, or ensuring they are properly shrouded if viewed by acquaintances or well-wishers. Everyone deserves a dignified departure.'

Where the deceased has living relations but the family request her services, Miss Astin ensures that the departed look at peace for viewing on the day of their funeral.

'Make-up for the deceased is different from that of the living. It must add depth, where colour is gone. It might, in some case, have to hide wounds,' Miss Astin explained.

'Their countenance should be restful, their clothing representative of what they wore in life, and their hair and make-up, particularly in the case of the ladies, tasteful and presentable,' she said. 'They should appear as they are remembered.'

Miss Astin accepts that many might find her occupation unconventional.

'It is not for the fainthearted,' she said, attributing her interest to her love of drawing, particularly facial features.

'The body goes through some changes within hours after death and time is of the essence to preserve it,' she said.

As a qualified embalmer, Miss Astin does not find this element of her work in demand.

'Embalming is an option for preservation, although compared to

Great Britain, we do not embalm very often and prefer to bury quickly.'

Readers will know of the recent death of the lady referred to as the pyjama girl, found on the steps of St Mary's Catholic Church, South Brisbane. Miss Astin assisted police with an illustration of the deceased for identification purposes.

'She was a beautiful young lady and had quite striking features,' Miss Astin said. 'Sometimes my illustrations have been required to send around the country if the deceased might be part of a police missing person's investigation.'

When asked if she felt the presence of the pyjama girl or any of her deceased clients, Miss Astin replied: 'I always feel their presence and form a bond with my clients because for just a short while, I am the last person in their company before they are put to rest. I hope I have served them well.'

Chapter 38

The detectives both reeled at Sydney Fenton's admission. It wasn't every day that a person admitted to interfering with one of their victims. Most lied, shifted blame, and denied all knowledge.

'I'm sorry,' Harry clarified sitting forward on his seat, 'Did you say that you embalmed Miss Sara-Anne Wilford?'

'Yes. I am not qualified in the art of embalming, if one can be qualified in it,' Sydney Fenton mused. 'My father, when he was alive, was an excellent taxidermist. Mother still has several rooms full of his collections of birds. The Ornithological Society and bird clubs would always be asking for tours. But I didn't take on many of my father's lessons and I believe the skill is a little different. So, I referred to several books and I feel I did my true love justice.'

Thomas stood; it was all too much for him. 'So, you murdered Miss Wilford and then embalmed her?' he snapped.

'What? No, of course not, Detective. Goodness, no! I never said I murdered her,' Sydney Fenton rushed to appease him. 'Why on earth would you think that?'

'Because we have a murdered dead woman who was your lover and you have embalmed her,' Thomas stated the obvious.

Sydney Fenton pursed his lips. 'Yes, I can see how you would draw that conclusion.'

Thomas shook his head and looked out the window to momentarily gather himself from exploding.

'Mr Fenton, please explain from the beginning,' Harry said patiently. 'How did you come to be in possession of Miss Wilford's deceased body?'

'Sara and I had one of our passionate fights and she left for the evening. She always came back, but…' he gathered himself before continuing as he became emotional. 'This time she did not come back alive. My doorman rushed to wake me at some ungodly hour the next morning as he found her lying dead at our front gates.' He closed his eyes, placed his hand on his heart and drew a deep breath. 'I'm just grateful that Mother did not find her.'

'What state was the young lady in?' Harry asked delicately.

'Detective, she was very much dead,' he said. 'Someone dealt a savage blow to her head. She was ice cold and white.'

'Was she dressed in the blue silk pyjamas?' Thomas asked.

'No. She was wearing the dress she wore when she left me earlier – a beautiful red gown. She knew I liked it on her.'

'So, you had Miss Wilford brought inside and then you embalmed and dressed her?' Thomas asked incredulously. 'Why did you not call the police to report her death?'

Sydney Fenton looked at the two men with confusion.

'Detectives, imagine if you found your loved one on the doorstep, beaten and dumped like she had been discarded. I could not let her be seen like that. I love her, still, forever. She deserved her dignity. I bathed her, and then I investigated embalming and preserved Sara so she would be as beautiful in death as she was in life.' He lowered his voice as if Sara-Anne Wilford would be upset at the thought and added, 'it meant she could stay with me forever.'

Thomas rubbed his brow, exhausted by the logic of Sydney Fenton's mind.

'What about justice for her death?' he asked.

'How am I to know she did not fall or inflict her injuries herself?' Sydney Fenton asked. 'No, it is much better I give her a fitting farewell, she was the love of my life.'

'So how did she get on the church steps?' Harry asked.

'She was stolen from me. Why would anyone do that?' he asked.

'Why indeed,' Thomas said, suspiciously.

Sydney Fenton added: 'I rose one morning and went to visit her and she was gone. I always suspected Linton Turner stole her.'

'Is your doorman who found Miss Wilford's body at the gate, here at present?' Thomas asked.

'Yes,' Sydney said, and gave a wave to the door to imply he was outside there, somewhere.

Thomas looked at Harry and their look determined a course of action – they knew each other well enough to read it.

'Best you show me the embalming room and where you lay Miss Wilford, please Mr Fenton,' Thomas said, as Harry rose and went to find the doorman to see how much truth was in Mr Fenton's account of the death of Miss Sara-Anne Wilford.

*****

Matilda and Georgina, with permission from their superiors at the *Women's Journal*, took several copies of the latest edition of the magazine, and departed to visit Miss Phoebe Astin at *The Economic Undertaker* and Mr Linton Turner at his place of residence. Matilda had been remiss in dropping in the previous issue with Mr Turner's interview in it, partly because of Thomas's insistence she avoided the author, if possible, but with Georgina by her side, and the investigation not showing any evidence of Mr Turner's involvement, she could not see the harm.

'May I ask you something, Georgina, if it is not too intrusive?' Matilda enquired as they rode together on the omnibus.

'Of course,' Georgina said. 'I have few secrets, ask away.'

'Do you think my family is... peculiar?'

Georgina paused, surprised and then burst out laughing. 'Not at all. Why would you ask that?'

Matilda smiled as she grabbed the handrail tightly after going over a bump that almost dislodged her from her seat.

'At lunch on Sunday I was trying to see my family through the eyes of yourself, Alice and Betty, and given I introduced all of you to my family, I wondered how we faired with other families. Is that odd?'

Georgina smiled. 'Not at all, well not that I know, but I am hardly an expert on families. I am an only child, so I've always envied those with siblings. To be welcomed into a home with a large family is very exciting for me.'

'We haven't always got on,' Matilda admitted. 'We fought for most of our young lives… competing for what we wanted and attention but I think after my mother died, we all became a bit closer.'

'That also happened to my cousin's family, it is a shining light from great sorrow. It is interesting to watch you all interact, especially with Thomas who seems like one of your family.'

'That is true. He was always there when we were growing up, like another brother. But as adults, we are all much closer and I hope we remain that way.'

'Bringing in your choice of sisters-in-law might help,' Georgina teased.

Matilda laughed. 'It wasn't my plan but it is working out splendidly.'

They drove along in silence for a brief while.

'I know you are homesick; I hope you are a little less so since meeting Elijah,' Matilda said.

'You and Elijah, my work, the ladies, have all been a great comfort. But I confess I wish to head home.'

'With Elijah?' Matilda asked, and then hurriedly put her hand on Georgina's arm. 'Forgive me, that was impudent of me to ask. Please do not feel the need to answer.'

Georgina smiled. 'It is you and I – you can ask me anything. You know I am rather abrupt by nature.' She took a deep breath and thought before answering. 'If Elijah would have me, I would go wherever he wanted to go. But if he wanted to become a country doctor – and I think it would suit his temperament – I would be truly content should Elijah return home with me, in good time.'

'I believe it would suit him very well, and you would not be that far away if you returned to your town.'

'A day's trip… a lovely getaway for you and Thomas,' Georgina teased. A thought occurred to her. 'If I should have the honour of becoming Mrs Elijah Hayward, would you be more concerned that your family was peculiar with me in the fold?'

Matilda laughed. 'You might help us earn that title,' she teased.

'Except you would be Mrs Thomas Ashdown, so the burden of the peculiar Haywards would fall on me!' Georgina pointed out.

Matilda looked surprised. 'I had forgotten that. How strange that you would get my name and I will lose it. Maybe one day women will keep their own surnames even if they are married.'

'I cannot imagine it,' Georgina said.

'Nor I,' Matilda agreed, and they happily accepted the offered hands of gentlemen as they alighted at their stop.

Chapter 39

Thomas warned Sydney Fenton not to leave town while the case was ongoing, or he might find himself on the wrong side of the law.

'We'd have grounds for putting him away if you are worried he is going to skip out on us,' Harry said. 'Interfering with a corpse, wasting police time…'

'I think we'd be just wasting more police time bringing him to the station. Imagine the poetry that would come out of a night in a cell,' Thomas said and groaned.

Harry grinned. 'It would be so melancholy and dramatic. Righto then, let's go see what Mr Turner can tell us now that we have a little more information under our belt.'

The men arrived at the front door of the author's terrace house within fifteen minutes. Thomas turned on hearing his name called by a voice he had heard calling his name many times over the years. Matilda and Georgina approached, and Matilda gave him a wave, a look of pleasure on her face at seeing him. He would never tire of looking at that beautiful little face, even if she did frustrate him no end at least once a day.

'Matilda! Miss Urry,' Thomas said, greeting them. 'You are not coming to visit the author, I assume?' he asked, knowing full well that would be the most likely scenario and cutting straight to business.

'Hello Thomas, Detective Dart,' Matilda said with a warm smile and Georgina greeted the detectives with enthusiasm.

'We are very well, thank you, Thomas,' Matilda teased. 'Are you not, Georgina?'

'Exceptionally well, thank you, Detective Ashdown,' she said, joining in the joke.

'And may I say how lovely you both look on this warm day,' Detective Dart said and Thomas gave them all a wry look.

'Fine then. It is lovely to see you both and yes, you look lovely, ladies,' he retorted and removed his hat.

Matilda and Georgina laughed at his attempt to redeem himself.

'Oh, Detective Dart, you have your work cut out for you,' Matilda said and sighed. 'Now before you get all worked up, Thomas, I did not drop the last issue to Mr Turner as you feared his involvement in something nefarious. But since that time has passed and you have not made an arrest, I have a copy of the *Women's Journal* for him, and another to drop to Phoebe at *The Economic Undertaker*.'

'Oh wonderful,' Detective Dart said, 'she's an amazing young lady. Did you illustrate her Miss Urry?'

'I did indeed, Detective Dart. Allow me to show you,' she said, and rifled through a copy.

'Oh my,' he said admiring the work once the page was located. 'You have truly captured her likeness.'

As they discussed the interesting Miss Astin, Thomas engaged with Matilda.

'I have some concerns about the author and your visit, Tillie,' Thomas said quietly, with a glance to the windows of the terrace house. 'Please allow me to give your edition to him and you ladies be on your way.'

Matilda was about to protest and thought about their recent fight and her determination to do better. He held her gaze, his face masked with concern.

Matilda gave a small nod. 'If Georgina has no objections, then that would be fine, thank you, Thomas.'

Thomas nearly fell over in surprise; he straightened and accepted the issue from her.

'Oh, I rarely object to anything,' Georgina piped in and made Harry laugh. 'I found it serves me well.'

'A fine motto for life indeed,' Harry said, 'I may adopt it.'

'Did you want to take our copy to Phoebe at *The Economic Undertaker* as well or are we permitted to take it there ourselves?' Matilda teased him.

'I have no desire to do that and I'm sure you are safe there, for now,' Thomas said with a smile.

The front door swung open and the author, Linton Turner, came down the steps, dressed and presentable, and pushing a pair of spectacles back onto his head.

'A man is trying to write and I am distracted by the social life my steps appear to be having without me,' he said in good humour.

'Our apologies, Mr Turner,' Matilda said, with a small laugh. 'Georgina and I were just dropping you in a copy of your story in our newspaper, albeit late.' She nodded towards Thomas. 'Detective Ashdown has it for you as we must be off.'

'So soon?' he asked.

'Yes, our managers have us on the clock,' Georgina joked. 'But we'll leave the detectives with you.'

'Oh good,' he said, his voice dripping with disdain which the ladies also found amusing.

'Thank you,' Thomas said, taking Matilda's hand ever so briefly. She gave him a teasing smile.

'You are most welcome, Detective. I shall see you soon, hopefully.'

'My wife always hopes the same thing of me,' Detective Dart added, as they bid the ladies farewell.

'I think you might have found a young lady who regards you with affection, Detective,' Linton Turner said, and welcomed them in.

'My fiancée,' Thomas clarified.

'Indeed,' Turner said, and glanced back at Thomas with a raised eyebrow. 'You have done well for yourself. How does a detective meet a writer? Research for my book,' he explained his curiosity, closing the door behind them. 'Did she interview you at a crime scene?'

'That would be a likely scenario,' Harry agreed.

'No,' Thomas added. 'I am a childhood friend of her brother; we have known each other for most of our lives.'

'How convenient,' Mr Turner said.

Harry took the lead. 'Mr Turner we've come into some information that we would like you to clarify please.'

The detectives accepted a seat and declined a cup of tea. Thomas continued where Harry left off.

'The poet, Mr Fenton, whom you accused of murder the other evening, tells us you were once engaged to Miss Sara-Anne Wilford. That might have been worth mentioning to us, do you not think?'

Turner pursed his lips and nodded. 'Yes. I thought of doing so but then I thought about how that would not look good in my favour, especially given the topic of my book. I assure you, I did not kill Sara even if I was the jilted lover.'

'You as good as implied she was a prostitute,' Thomas reminded him.

'I was angry and harsh,' Turner admitted.

'Why did she leave you?' Harry asked.

'I imagine you know the answer, Detective.'

'Yes, but let's hear your version,' Harry said. 'Seems only fair.'

Turner sat back and looked like a beaten man. 'I loved Sara. Enough to marry her, enough for life and she assured me of the same returned sentiments. You are both betrothed men or soon to be,' he said, noting Harry's wedding ring and learning of Thomas's engagement. 'Imagine if your beloved called off your engagement because she met another man she preferred more.'

'Sydney Fenton?' Thomas asked.

'Exactly. That melodramatic fop,' Turner said with disgust.

Thomas couldn't disagree with him on that. He could understand that the Fenton's wealth might be attractive for a lady seeking security, but the man himself appeared so weak.

Turner continued: 'And then, Sara dares to return to me to ask me will I restore my offer when she is outcast by his family. Goodness, I may have loved her but I am not a cuckolded fool!'

Thomas sat forward, resting his elbows on his knees. 'Rejected by the family… we have not heard of this. Can you tell us what Sara said?'

'Of course. She accepted Fenton's hand in marriage but he wanted her to meet his mother.' Turner rolled his eyes. 'Sara said when Fenton departed to let his mother and Sara get better acquainted, Mrs Fenton told Sara that she would never marry her son, ever, and to not bother coming back. That is when she came to me and he did not pursue her. He didn't come to the club or visit her workplace, or ask after her. It devastated her.'

'Did she stay with you then?' Harry asked, and the author shook his head in the negative.

'She stayed a couple of days and then went back to insist on an audience with Fenton. I told her to have it out with him and tell him to stand up to his mother. That was the last time I saw her alive. She disappeared, so I thought she might be somewhere licking her wounds. I knew she wasn't with Fenton because he came to the club alone and was writing this woeful poetry about love lost and so on,' he said with a flourish of his hand. 'I assumed he did what his mother told him to do and called off his engagement with Sara.'

'Where were the blue pyjamas from?' Thomas asked.

'I gifted them to her, long before my book came out. When she left me, I changed the draft of my story to feature the victim in them.' He looked guilty. 'It was a nasty stab at her, I admit, but I was angry and spiteful.'

'But she would not have been wearing them when she left Mrs Fenton and called here?' Thomas asked. 'So she must have stayed somewhere and was wearing them when murdered.'

'All her clothes were at the Fenton mansion; she had been living with the poet. But I don't believe the mother knew that.'

'Thank you, Mr Turner,' Thomas said. 'I just wish you had told us this sometime back and saved us running around in circles.'

He gave a humble nod. 'I apologise detectives but I don't know what you don't know or might want to know.'

'Assume we want to know everything related to you, Miss Wilford and Mr Fenton's relationship,' Harry said. 'Is there anything else you can think to tell us?'

Linton Turner sat for a moment and thought. 'Only concerning the character of Fenton. Sara was his third fiancée in a matter of years and they were always great loves and great losses,' he said, rolling his eyes. 'His mother never remarried I believe, so she wants a suitable bride for him and an heir. He always brings home girls from the club who are actresses, singers, or dancers and Sara fell into that category. He is no intellectual giant, but one might think with his money, reputation and looks, he would cast his net wider.'

'Thank you, that is most interesting and helpful,' Harry said.

'Is it?' Linton Turner asked, surprised. 'Well, that's good then.'

'Thank you for your time, Mr Turner,' Thomas said, and the two men departed, deep in thought. Once the front door of the terrace house had closed with Linton Turner behind it, Thomas nudged Harry. 'I need to pursue an angle,' he said in a low voice as they hurried their step to catch an approaching omnibus.

'You want to speak with Mrs Fenton I imagine, but did not Sydney Fenton say she was away?' Harry asked.

'He did. But he also said his father practised as a taxidermist. What if his mother did too? What if she got rid of the young woman she did not think was suitable for her son and dumped her out the front where Sydney would find her. Were there more women who did not return home? Sara was, after all, the third fiancée.'

Harry narrowed his eyes as he thought. 'It's a desperate scenario. You are thinking that some of our town's missing women could have lost their lives at the hands of the lady of the house?' Harry avoided saying the family name on the very public mode of transport.

'Possibly. These ladies were no doubt deemed artists or loose women and their disappearance might not have been given the credence deserved.'

'That would be too bizarre,' Harry said, 'but we've dealt in similar.'

'We have,' Thomas agreed. 'Let's not rule it out. What if Sydney did not embalm her but is covering for his mother?'

'Or he assisted her perhaps,' Harry offered.

'It is beyond frustrating how neither Linton Turner nor Sydney Fenton offer anything more than what we ask. It is like being spoon-fed every time,' Thomas said with a sigh.

'To the Fenton's household now and we can speak with Mrs Fenton, if she has returned,' Harry said.

'First, a trip to the newspaper,' Thomas suggested. 'Let us go armed with the correct information before we visit the Fenton's household. If the author is telling us the truth that Sydney Fenton was engaged twice before his commitment to Miss Wilford, there must be public announcements of Fenton's other engagements and I want to know the names of the other two ladies and where they are today.'

'Excellent. Let's hope they too are not the subject of crime books or we will be well and truly chasing our tail,' Harry said with a sigh.

Chapter 40

Matilda and Georgina walked along Tribune Street reaching their destination and entered the premises of *The Economic Undertaker* with great trepidation. Should there be a grieving family in the foyer they vowed to quickly remove themselves and ask to speak with Mr Randolph Astin outside, but fortunately the foyer was empty.

Matilda physically relaxed and glanced behind at Georgina who reflected her thoughts as they entered.

'Ah, welcome. Miss Hayward and Miss Urry, is it not?' Randolph asked, and gave the ladies a small bow.

'Mr Astin, what a good memory you have,' Matilda said. 'Please forgive the intrusion.'

'The living is always a welcome sight at our funeral parlour, ladies,' he joked.

'As long as we leave in the same condition, we will be very happy,' Georgina said with a chuckle and Randolph laughed.

'Absolutely,' he assured Georgina. 'While we are happy

for the business, we are not actively seeking clients.' He gave her a wink and she laughed. 'Ah, publication day! I am very keen to see your story and illustration of my dear granddaughter,' he said with a nod to the newspaper in the ladies' hand.

'I hope we have done her justice,' Matilda said, and offered a copy to Randolph.

'Page ten, Mr Astin,' Georgina said, and both ladies waited while he flicked through the pages and stopped on seeing the illustration of Phoebe.

'Oh my. That is beautiful, you have done a wonderful job, Miss Urry, thank you,' he said, his finger tracing over the image. 'Shall I take you to Phoebe? I'll read your words while you visit, Miss Hayward.'

'Yes, please,' Matilda said, delighted with his praise of Georgina's work. 'Has she time for visitors?'

'Always. Her clients are most obliging, they never complain.' Randolph led the way even though the ladies had been there before, but he preferred to announce them formally allowing Phoebe time to cover the body on her table.

'Matilda, Georgina!' she exclaimed with delight as she looked up from her work. 'It is wonderful to see you.'

'I shall leave you to it, ladies,' Randolph said and departed with their thanks ringing in his ears.

'Your timing is perfect,' Phoebe said, and leaning to her work table, she picked up a letter on very thick and expensive paper and waved it at them. 'I received an invitation to join Mr Fenton and his mother for lunch today and to bring a guest, but I did not feel comfortable going. What say the three of us go, I'm sure they won't mind the intrusion and it could be fun to dine in such surrounds?'

'Ooh, we would love to, would we not, Georgina?' Matilda asked.

'Absolutely. But I cannot sadly. Ruth, my manager, has several jobs lined up for me this afternoon with clients who wish to advertise. These fingers know no rest,' Georgina said, and wiggled them with a small laugh. 'Whereas the editorial ladies, such as Matilda, usually have today at leisure to distribute their copies and prepare for tomorrow's meeting.'

'That is true,' Matilda said, 'but let us send a note to the office begging for you to be let off for an extended lunch break… we'll call it a goodwill exercise with one of the town's most affluent residents.'

Georgina looked impressed. 'That may work. I'm sure Mrs Lawson would not mind the patronage of Mrs Fenton or some advertising from her business interests, whatever they may be.'

'And I'm sure Ruth believes you deserve a lunch treat,' Matilda said. 'Our office is but two blocks from here.'

'Well, that is settled,' Phoebe said, and offered Matilda the writing instruments. 'Ambrose can take it and wait for a response, I'm sure he won't mind and he has no clients at the moment.'

Matilda and Georgina hurriedly penned the request and Phoebe rang a small bell bringing her grandfather to her workroom. He took the note and was happy to put Phoebe's brother to work.

'Do warn him, the building is full of women,' Georgina joked with Randolph.

'Goodness, I hope we get him back with a reply then,' Randolph said with a laugh and departed.

'Matilda was telling me about her Wednesday ladies' evenings that are starting soon,' Phoebe said to Georgina, 'We can all catch up regularly then. I confess I don't make time to engage in many social activities and Grandpa is always urging me to do so.'

'I am very much looking forward to it,' Georgina agreed. 'If Elijah is not working, I will be sure to send him to Thomas's place for the men's club evening so we are both gainfully occupied. Then later, I will find out from him what the men spoke about.'

Matilda laughed. 'Excellent! It will be fun.' Changing the subject, Matilda offered up the *Women's Journal*. 'We have brought our latest issue for you; I hope you will like it.'

'I have no doubt I will, thank you,' Phoebe accepted it with pleasure, and placed it on her desk, promising to read it cover to cover later and keep the feature page of herself forever. 'Grandpa will have it framed before you have left today!' she joked.

'May I ask who your guest is and what he died from?' Georgina said, studying the young man lying on Phoebe's table.

'He is most distinguished, is he not?' Phoebe said. 'I best cover him,' she said rising to put her material sheeting over the young man. 'Pneumonia has taken him too soon from this life, it still fells many.'

'Terrible,' Georgina said. 'It is not dissimilar on the land... pleura-pneumonia is taking the life of cattle, despite the best efforts of our scientists to halt it.'

'I forget how knowledgeable you are, Georgina,' Matilda said, admiring her. 'Not only are you a wonderful illustrator, but I imagine your parents miss you sorely on the farm.'

'I was very affordable labour,' she said with a laugh. 'Had he family?'

Phoebe nodded. 'He has left a widow and young son. It is unpredictable this journey of life we are on.'

Matilda agreed. 'It is a good reminder that we should cherish our loved ones and do as much as we can while we are here to do it.' She read the expression of sadness fleetingly on Georgina's face and Matilda anticipated an announcement sooner rather than later. She expected Elijah would propose to Georgina, and he would move away to practice life as a small-town doctor while Georgina assisted with the family farm. The world was changing, but the thought of lunch at the Fenton mansion and meeting Mrs Jane Fenton cheered her immeasurably.

In fifteen minutes, the very handsome Mr Ambrose Astin had promptly returned and called on the ladies. He entered and bowed. 'At your service, Miss Hayward and I assume, Miss Urry?' he asked with an engaging smile as he read the names on the note. 'It is good to see you again, Miss Hayward. I hope your brother and fiancé are both well.'

'They are, thank you kindly, Mr Astin,' Matilda offered the note to Georgina and formally introduced the pair.

'You escaped unscathed from the premises of the *Women's Journal* then, Mr Astin?' Georgina teased him.

'I have lived to tell,' he said in good humour, returning her smile.

Georgina opened the note and proclaimed: 'Oh I am free to join you with Ruth's blessing.'

'Excellent,' Matilda said.

'Best we start then,' Phoebe said. 'I was going to send word that I could not attend due to a last-minute appointment.' She looked a little sheepish. 'I did not think that was too rude given the lateness of the invitation, and all my work does tend to come rather spontaneously so it is a small untruth. But we have to be there in under forty minutes. Shall we?'

'Allow me to take you there in the hearse if you have no objections to travelling in a vehicle that also transports the dead?' Ambrose asked. 'I assure you I won't put the plumes on the horses.'

'Must we lay down and cross our arms over our chest or does it have seats?' Georgina joked, and the group laughed at her unique perspective.

'You may sit,' Ambrose said with a grin, 'you are going a lot less far than most of my regular passengers.' He glanced towards the heavens and the ladies laughed.

'Thank you, Ambrose,' Phoebe said. 'Ladies, let's lunch.'

Chapter 41

The detectives waited patiently in the reception area of the newspaper office as a senior lady with silver steel-framed glasses perched on her nose and hair the same colour as the frames, ran a finger down a ledger in front of her.

'Engagement Fenton,' she mumbled several times. 'Ah-ha, here is one entry, detectives!'

Thomas grabbed his notepad and pencil to take down the date and name. He waited patiently as the clerk read out the whole announcement. He felt Harry nudge him just as Thomas opened his mouth to ask for just the name only. Harry's look said to let her have her moment of helpfulness and importance.

The clerk read from *The Brisbane Courier*: 'The engagement is announced of Mr Sydney Fenton, only son of Mr Charles Fenton (deceased) and Mrs Jane Fenton of Spring Hill, and Miss Maud Mandon, third daughter of Mr & Mrs F. Mandon, of Sussex Street, West End. The marriage will take place in June.' She looked up at the gentlemen. 'That was three years ago – 1886.'

'Excellent, thank you. Only one more to find then, as we know one of the young lady's names,' Harry said.

'Let us see then,' she continued, turning each page and running her finger along the column that read male surname.

The detectives waited again. Thomas's foot began to tap, and Harry pressed his shoe on Thomas's and raised an eyebrow. Thomas gave him a wry look and moved his interest to observe customers at the counter placing advertisements.

'Here it is, if this is not the lady you have?' the clerk said, looking up at them with a raised eyebrow.

'Perhaps just tell us the lady's name and we will know right away,' Harry said, doing his best at being diplomatic.

She nodded. 'A Miss Sara-Anne Wilford?'

'We have her, thank you,' Thomas said, 'but she is the last one. So, there must be one before that engagement.'

'There's every chance they did not advertise,' the senior clerk said, 'but let me go back in case I've missed it. Some of the handwriting is most illegible.' She gave a short shake of her head as if the person who wrote it ought to be punished.

Thomas drew in a breath, waiting, and listening to the annoying hum the clerk made as she constantly repeated the name "Fenton". Then, she pronounced she had found it.

'Excellent,' Thomas said most enthusiastically and grimaced again as she read out the entire announcement.

'Mr and Mrs S. Dobin of Waterworks Road, Ashgrove, are pleased to announce the engagement of their daughter, Edith Mary, to Mr Sydney Fenton, son of Mr Charles Fenton (dec.) and Mrs Jane Fenton of Spring Hill. The marriage will take place in November.' The clerk looked up from reading. 'That's November 1887, last year, mind you.'

'Edith Mary Dobin,' Thomas wrote the name and then turned to Harry. 'We know that name.'

His partner nodded and thanked the clerk. 'You have been extremely helpful, thank you for your time and patience.'

'My pleasure detectives. My brother was a policeman, my father a soldier and my grandfather was very much into community service. I have a lot of respect for the work you do.'

'Thank you, that is gratifying,' Thomas said, doing his best to emulate his partner, and noting the impressed look on Harry's face. The two departed and no sooner were they out the door Thomas questioned Harry. 'Edith Dobin... where do we know that name from?'

'Your mates, Burton and Lou, that was their case – the missing woman buried recently.'

'Yes, you are right!' Thomas said. 'You have a great memory for names, Harry. Miss Edith Dobin was the lady found in the river; her mother could only identify Miss Dobin from a birthmark on her leg, if memory serves. So, she was Fenton's second fiancée.'

'I wonder if it really was Miss Dobin that her parents buried that day,' Harry said.

'Let's do a quick check of the name "Maud Mandon" to see if she is a missing person or has a street address,' Thomas said, 'and then I suggest we visit Sydney Fenton and his mother and see how competent they are at embalming and taxidermy.'

They hailed a hansom, climbed in and headed to the station. Thomas was deep in thought when Harry asked: 'Tell me what you are thinking in that complex mind of yours.'

Thomas smiled. 'I believe there is one more thing we should know before we call on the Fentons.'

Harry nodded for Thomas to continue.

'We need to know the basic steps for embalming. I want to put Sydney Fenton on the spot.'

'Ah, excellent idea, I see where you are going with your train of thought. If he does not know the basics, then he did not embalm the pyjama girl,' Harry said. 'Shall we drop over and ask Miss Astin?'

Thomas grimaced and Harry chuckled.

'Let's quickly ask the coroner then, I'm sure Patrick will know and he is nearby.'

'Much better idea,' Thomas agreed.

'Do you reckon we could fit in a quick bite for lunch before we visit the Fentons of Spring Hill?' Harry asked.

'If you eat quickly,' Thomas joked. 'Might be best we eat before we explore what is "stuffed" at the Fenton mansion.'

'Let's just hope none of it is human,' Harry shuddered.

Thomas felt in his gut that if Miss Maud Mandon was a missing person – and that seemed to be the case with Sydney Fenton's women that they were missing or short on family connections – she may well be resting at the Fenton mansion. He had not written off the thought either, that Miss Edith Dobin could be there as well and not the lady resting in a recently dug grave.

*****

Ambrose Astin offered his hand to each lady to assist them to alight from *The Economic Undertaker's* carriage.

'Delivered alive and kicking, as promised,' he joked with Georgina as he helped her down the step.

'Indeed, thank you, Mr Astin,' she said. 'I bet you don't say that too often to your clients.'

He laughed. 'There's truth in that. Well ladies, enjoy yourselves.' He looked up at the mansion.

'We will, thank you, Ambrose,' Phoebe said, placing a kiss on her brother's cheek.

'I suspect you shall dine well,' he added.

'It has been rumoured that the Haywards have the best cook in town,' Phoebe said with a shy glance at Matilda, 'so Mrs Fenton's cook may have to compete.'

'You must both come to tea or Sunday lunch soon, Phoebe and Mr Astin, and judge for yourself,' Matilda said. 'But don't attempt to poach Mary, she's had offers from the best!'

Phoebe laughed. 'Never.'

'I shall hold you to that invitation, Miss Hayward,' Ambrose said, and with a small bow, departed.

'My, it is quite fearsome, isn't it?' Georgina said, taking in the grandeur of the Fenton Mansion. 'One would need a map to ensure you didn't get lost.'

Matilda laughed at the idea. 'Mr Fenton mentioned he lives in the left-wing and Mrs Fenton in the right-wing. One huge wing each, imagine! I am sure I would miss Pa and my brothers.'

'As would I,' Phoebe agreed. 'I wonder why she invited me to lunch,' she mused as they walked up the path.

'I suspect Mr Fenton wants to court you and Mrs Fenton intends to study you today to see if you are a suitable future wife for her son,' Matilda said.

'Goodness me,' Phoebe exclaimed.

'Oh, forgive me, I thought you and Gideon had formed an attachment,' Georgina said, confused after the Sunday lunch declaration by Matilda's brother. 'Or should I not have said that aloud?'

Phoebe smiled with delight and Matilda laughed and looked equally as pleased.

'Not at all. My brother is very keen to declare his interest,' she said turning to Phoebe, 'if you were open to the idea?'

'I most certainly am,' Phoebe said unrestrained, and she exchanged a look of warmth and happiness with Matilda.

'You will have no brothers left to partner now,' Georgina said, 'I'm glad I got in early to get one,' she joked as they arrived at the door and an elderly manservant opened it.

'Here we go,' Phoebe said, taking a deep breath as if the luncheon was a challenge.

Matilda feared it might be.

Chapter 42

It delighted Mrs Jane Fenton to receive three young ladies for lunch. She assured Phoebe she was not at all concerned at the extra guest given the short notice of her own invitation.

'I am impulsive by nature,' she assured the ladies, 'am I not, Sydney?'

'You are, Mother, unlike me,' he agreed, and they exchanged a look that spoke of great affection.

Mrs Fenton continued in a softly spoken and refined voice: 'Sydney mentioned he had the pleasure of your company several evenings back, Miss Astin and Miss Hayward, and it is lovely now to meet your friend, Miss Urry.'

'The pleasure is ours,' Phoebe assured Mrs Fenton.

The party of five took lunch in a room with enormous glass floor to ceiling windows that looked out across the grounds. It was a stiff and rather formal affair, with Sydney looking his smouldering best and Mrs Jane Fenton at work, studying the young ladies present. She did not care if the ladies were or were not interested in her son, that was by the by and unthinkable that they might not be. Mrs Fenton wanted Sydney married and wanted an heir and grandchildren, and it was time he found someone appropriate, she had told him with firmness. He had mentioned meeting the ladies to give his mother hope. Immediately, she invited them to lunch.

'Miss Astin, your family works in the death industry, I believe?' she said almost disdainfully, dabbing a napkin to her lips.

'Yes, Mrs Fenton. After my parents passed away when I was younger, my brother vowed to create a business that ensured everyone was given a dignified funeral regardless of means. So, Julius began the business and myself, my brother Ambrose and grandfather, all work together.'

'Very admirable,' she said, but her expression did not reflect her voice. She did not see Phoebe as suitable with that terrible occupation and her less than conventional dress style, not to mention the informal way she wore her hair. Jane Fenton had already disregarded Georgina as a potential for her son – she was too ungainly for Sydney. He needed a pretty young lady who could be a loyal and dutiful wife of good standing. She must be across matters of business, able to host parties as required to move her son in the right circles, and able to produce an heir. Regardless, Jane Fenton politely asked after Georgina's heritage and interests. One could not forget their manners despite the haste to achieve the project at hand.

'Ah, yes, I have heard of your family's cattle station. It is one of the largest in the state is it not?' she asked, impressed but not enough to change her mind. She was not losing

Sydney to the country and they did not need the Urry's money; Jane Fenton's fortune was well managed.

'There are several very large stations in our area,' Georgina answered modestly and politely.

The luncheon was most informal and they nibbled on a selection of dainty sandwiches, cakes and biscuits, and sipped tea from the best China as the conversation progressed and Mrs Fenton turned her attention to Matilda.

'Would your father be Mr James Hayward of Highgate Hill, Miss Hayward?' she asked, not inviting the ladies to informally call her by her Christian name, and hence they were not free to do so in return.

'Indeed, that is him, Mrs Fenton. He recently retired from the law and my eldest brother, Amos, has taken over my father's practice.'

'Yes, I had heard that. I have not met your brother but your father is a very admirable man and highly respected. I had the pleasure of meeting him when I was pursuing matters in legal circles many years ago, and more recently at several charity events.'

'Ah, yes,' Matilda said and smiled. 'He is often requested to attend them by his sister, my aunt, Mrs Samuel Bloomfield.'

'Audrey!' Mrs Fenton exclaimed.

'Yes, she is a great campaigner and always busy as I am sure you know, with your own charity and community work.'

'Thank you, we all have to do our bit,' she acknowledged Matilda's generous words. 'Well, I didn't make the connection with Audrey and your father, that is wonderful,' she said and gave Sydney a look and a raised eyebrow.

Then and there she knew Miss Matilda Hayward was the girl for Sydney. Dainty, well-bred, well-connected in society, and charming. She would look beautiful on his arm and produce a fine-looking heir. Jane Fenton vowed to let Sydney know as soon as the luncheon was complete that she had made her choice and Miss Matilda Hayward was to be Mrs Sydney Fenton. The engagement ring sparking on Matilda's hand was completely overlooked.

*****

Returning from the Roma Street Police Station's dining room on the ground floor, Thomas and Harry checked with John at the reception desk on his findings in the missing person's register. John's expression as he saw Thomas and Harry coming down the hall, told them he had news.

'What have you, John? Any luck finding that Miss Mandon is missing?' Harry asked.

'Sadly, yes, Detective. Miss Maud Mandon is on our missing person's list and has been for the past three years.'

Thomas looked at Harry. 'The timing is about right. She got engaged to Sydney Fenton three years ago in 1886 according to the clerk.'

'And then she went missing,' Harry agreed. 'The other lady, Miss Edith Dobin got engaged in the year after, 1887, and Burton and Lou only just found her, if that was indeed Miss Dobin.'

'Will that be all, Detectives?' John asked, waiting to snap

the book closed. He learnt as a young constable never to comment on a case unless invited, despite the name Fenton causing him to raise an eyebrow.

'Yes, good on you John, much appreciated,' Harry said.

'Any time, Detectives,' John said, returning to relieve the constable on the front desk for his lunch break.

'To the coroner and then the home of the Fenton's,' Thomas said.

'This is not going to be an easy conversation to start with Sydney Fenton and his mother,' Harry said with a frown. 'Hello Mrs Fenton, might you have any embalmed young ladies in the mansion?'

Thomas couldn't help but chuckle as they donned their hats and walked out of the station and towards the coroner's building. Sometimes a laugh or two was a good relief break, even if the subject was in poor taste.

'Yes, on the drive over, we best come up with a way to start that discussion or we will find ourselves deposed outside the gates in no time,' Thomas agreed. 'I favour bluntness myself.'

'I know,' Harry said and sighed, before nudging his young protégée and giving a laugh. 'So, what do you suggest?'

Thomas thought for a moment. 'Let's just ask Sydney Fenton to show us his hobby room again. There was nothing peculiar there last time but it will give us grounds to request he steps through the embalming process.'

'Yes, that could work. Failing that, we can ask to see the late Mr Fenton's bird display and where he did his work. Let's put ourselves in the action,' Harry said.

'Sounds reasonable, Mr Fenton and his mother's reactions will tell us what we need to know, hopefully.'

The detectives entered the building of the coroner and made their way to Patrick's room.

'He's not here,' Harry said, frowning, his body half in the doorway as he glanced around.

'I'm here.'

They heard a voice call from the corner of the room behind the door. The detectives stepped into the room and found Patrick sitting at the small table in the corner.

'Catching up on paperwork,' he explained. 'I don't have any of your bodies, do I?'

'Not today, fortunately,' Harry said with a chuckle. 'Can we take ten minutes of your time to pick your brain?'

'Please,' the coroner said and indicated a seat. Harry accepted and Thomas paced.

'Patrick, can you tell us the first five steps or so, very basic steps, you would undertake if you were going to embalm a body?' Thomas asked.

'Hmm, that's a question no one has asked me before,' Patrick said, removing his spectacles and placing them on top of his paperwork. 'Well, let's see. Basic, huh?' he said, with a glance to Thomas who nodded.

'Right then, timing is important so if you or your subject is doing this process, it is a waiting game.'

'Good to know,' Harry said.

'Assuming that the family or mortician has washed the body, laid it out, put the limbs in the right position and packed the body openings, then you begin by cleaning out the circulatory system. This is done by flushing or injecting it with cold water until it runs reasonably clear from the body. This can take a while, from two to five hours.'

Thomas nodded his understanding. 'Clean out the circulatory system until it runs clear.'

'Then,' Patrick continued: 'You inject alcohol to extract as much water as possible. Allow about fifteen minutes for this, and then ether is injected. This can take between two to ten hours.'

'Clean out, inject alcohol, inject ether, so far this could take up to fifteen hours,' Harry nodded.

'Correct. Then inject a strong solution of tannin, allowing anywhere from two to ten hours, and finally, you dry the body with warm air passed over heated chloride of calcium, which can occupy you for a good couple of hours. That's it, you're embalmed!'

Thomas turned to Harry. 'Can't see the poet doing that, can you?'

'No, but you are right, let's put him to the test. Patrick, thank you. You are a wealth of knowledge.'

'Thank you and some of it is useful,' Patrick joked.

'To the Fenton's then,' Thomas announced.

'Good luck with your embalming, Detectives,' Patrick called after them as the men departed for the Fenton Mansion on the highest point of Spring Hill.

Chapter 43

After the luncheon was cleared, the ladies were about to take their leave when Mrs Jane Fenton suggested a tour of the home and grounds.

'After all,' she said with a glance at Matilda and then Sydney, 'the future Mrs Sydney Fenton will be the lady of the manor and will refurbish Sydney's wing to her tastes of course. When I depart this earth, she will need to manage the entire interior of the estate for Sydney's sons and the next generation.'

'Goodness what an enormous job that would be,' Georgina exclaimed and Matilda and Phoebe repressed a laugh, imagining that was not quite the response Mrs Fenton was hoping from them.

Phoebe offered it instead. 'It is already so tastefully decorated, Mrs Fenton, I can't imagine there would be much to do but add perhaps a few personal items in the bride's favourite colours.'

Sydney smiled at them. 'Mother is right though. While

I am writing, the lady of the manor must be comfortable in her surroundings, entertaining, raising our children.' He looked at Phoebe, while Mrs Fenton smiled at Matilda.

'Please, let's have a tour then,' Matilda said, finding the situation a little awkward. 'It would be wonderful to see your wing, Mrs Fenton. The paintings we saw in Sydney's wing are quite extraordinary.'

'Did you see the portrait of Sydney?' Mrs Fenton asked as she led the way.

'Yes, most striking,' Matilda said, and fell behind the party, hearing their voices rise and fall as she looked at the rooms and artwork pointed out. But in her head, Matilda's mind was racing and not concentrating on the tour at hand. She wondered if in fact there was something very odd about the Fenton family, and her own family were quite respectably normal by comparison. Mrs Fenton was looking at her as if she were a future daughter-in-law when she had Thomas's ring displayed upon her finger; Sydney was watching Phoebe as if he had lost his heart; and Georgina was by far acting the most normal, which was quite extraordinary.

Then Matilda's heart stopped as they entered a large room the size of a grand ballroom. It was filled with dead animals mounted in poses as if in life.

'Oh my,' Matilda gasped with shock. She stepped back bumping into Phoebe. It was terrible, a nightmare, she wanted to free every animal and leave it to roam or fly.

Phoebe touched her arm. 'Are you alright?'

Matilda slowly turned to her. 'No, I don't believe I am,' she whispered.

'It's very confronting, even for me, and I imagine for Georgina too, despite the fact we are no strangers to death or working with animals. Come, I will suggest to Mrs Fenton that we move to the garden.'

'Please,' Matilda nodded as she saw Mrs Fenton looking back eagerly, seeking their company as Sydney moved to the next room. But Matilda stood transfixed as the group walked ahead through the room. She didn't think she could move ahead and follow; it was too confronting. She looked behind; perhaps she could turn back and go get some fresh air. Yes, that would be best, she was feeling quite ill.

No. She could do this. Keeping her eyes straight ahead she hurried through the room, through the tortured animals around her, watching her trapped in their last moments of life. She entered the next room and breathed easier. It was a clinical white room akin to a hospital room.

'We are getting into the bowels of my home,' Mrs Fenton laughed. 'This is where my dear husband, Charles, did his work. Gone so many years now,' she said and sighed.

Sydney Fenton touched his mother's shoulder. 'Father liked everything to be meticulously laid out – he had an orderly mind.'

'He did,' Mrs Fenton said, smiling in memory. 'Poor Sydney never had a stomach for it. Goodness knows his father tried to show him how to do it many times but...'

'I abhor it,' Sydney agreed.

Matilda agreed with him. She leaned against the counter momentarily, hesitant to look around in case she saw any more animals. Oddly, she noted the chemical smell was still quite strong.

'Are you still practising taxidermy, Mrs Fenton?' she blurted out. 'It's just that the chemical smell remains.'

'Oh, I potter, but I do not have the talent my husband had. I guess we must donate all the animals one day, Sydney,' she said. 'Come, let us move out to the gardens.'

'Yes, let us,' Matilda agreed enthusiastically but not before something in the corner of the room caught her eye.

*****

The detectives arrived at the Fenton mansion close to 1.30pm and were greeted at the door by the imposing doorman.

'Mr Fenton and his mother are entertaining and unavailable,' he told the men.

'Well, that is unfortunate,' Harry said. 'We will just start with Mr Fenton then please, if you could fetch him. Tell him Detectives Dart and Ashdown wish to have a word.'

The doorman looked as if the request was outrageous and Harry clearly did not have an understanding of the English language.

'I'm afraid that is out of the question,' he replied.

Thomas cleared his throat, weary of being detained by a doorman. 'It is not a request. Please ask Mr Fenton to join us immediately, or we will enter and search for him.'

The doorman's eyes widened in surprise. He gave the detectives a disdainful look and left them standing on the doorstep as he departed to find Mr Fenton.

'For the love of God,' Thomas muttered, 'privilege always thinks it is above the law.'

'I've seen it a thousand times,' Harry agreed. He glanced around the beautiful grounds and squinted in the distance. Thomas turned to see what he was looking at behind his shoulder.

'Is that Miss Hayward, Miss Astin and Miss Urry? Surely not,' Harry said, straightening and blinking as if he was seeing things.

'It is! What the hell are they doing here? That must be Mrs Fenton with them,' Thomas said, noting the mature, small woman with them.

'Detectives, I understand you need to see me on a matter of some urgency?' Sydney Fenton said.

The two men snapped to look toward the doorway where Sydney Fenton addressed them.

'Mr Fenton,' Harry began. 'Our apologies for pulling you away from your guests, but we have a few questions and the timing is a matter of urgency.' Largely because both men were tired of chasing their tails and wanted the matter put to rest.

Sydney Fenton nodded his understanding and invited them in. Thomas glanced back at the gardens but he could no longer see the ladies. With a shake of his head in frustration, he followed Harry.

'We would like to go to the room where you embalmed Miss Sara-Anne Wilford, please,' Harry said.

Sydney Fenton looked surprised. 'If you wish, this way please.'

The detectives followed him down the hallway, into a stairwell and down to another level, to the room that Sydney took Thomas into last time. Thomas noted it looked unchanged.

Sydney stopped in the doorway and waved a hand around. 'This is it.'

The two detectives entered and Sydney Fenton followed them in. They placed themselves around the table where Miss Wilford was said to have been embalmed.

'Could you talk us through the embalming process please?' Thomas asked.

Sydney Fenton started with surprise, he shuffled uncomfortably and his usual look of confidence was missing, shaken.

'Why, may I ask?' he enquired, looking from Harry to Thomas. 'I would rather the experience stayed between myself and Sara-Anne. My last act for her.'

'Indulge us, please,' Thomas said, ignoring his feeble protest. 'The process you undertook to embalm Miss Wilford?'

Sydney walked around the table at the opposite end to the gentlemen. He cleared his throat, ran his hand over the end of the table and started: 'I washed Sara-Anne's body, and then, I filled her with a formula.'

'How did you do that, Mr Fenton?' Harry asked.

'I used a tube,' he said.

'I imagine you saw your father do similar when he was working on his hobby,' Thomas said. 'So, after washing Miss Wilford, what was the next step you took and how long did it take?'

Sydney stopped. 'I… you know I didn't embalm her, Detectives, let's stop this charade.'

'I did,' a female voice declared.

The detectives turned to find an attractive, well-groomed, middle-aged woman standing in the doorway.

'I embalmed Sara-Anne Wilford for my son. But then she was stolen from us and we know why and by whom.'

'We do?' Sydney asked, surprised.

'Mrs Fenton, I presume?' Thomas clarified, and she gave a brief nod.

'We are sorry to interrupt your party, Mrs Fenton,' Harry said, 'but police work does not abide by the clock.'

'I understand,' she said curtly.

'Can you please explain? You embalmed Miss Wilford?' Harry said, and exhaled with frustration while Thomas pinched his nose for a moment and closed his eyes to gather his thoughts. He had anticipated her involvement but could not quite fathom a lady could be involved. Opening his eyes, he said: 'Perhaps we could start at the beginning.'

'Yes, Mother, I'd like to know what you know as well,' Sydney said, his voice betraying his confusion. No doubt she told him to say nothing, Thomas imagined, and now she had declared her hand.

'The drawing room then,' Mrs Fenton said, and moved away. The men followed.

Chapter 44

The three ladies waited fifteen minutes in the garden keeping an eye on the entrance to the mansion and keen to depart now that lunch had been served and somewhat enjoyed, but no one returned for them.

'As much as I enjoy being outdoors, this is quite frustrating. I did wish to return to the office this afternoon,' Georgina said.

'As do I,' Phoebe agreed.

'And I too am ready to depart,' Matilda said.

'Do you think we should see ourselves out?' Georgina asked.

'It might be the best thing,' Phoebe said. 'But it seems terribly wrong to leave without offering our thanks.'

'I think we should go inside and bid them farewell or leave a message of thanks if they are unavailable,' Matilda said. 'I admit I do want to know what is going on.'

Phoebe laughed. 'Spoken like a true journalist.'

'I confess I do too,' Georgina said. 'Matilda is rubbing off on me. Let us go then.'

The ladies straightened their hats, gathered up their skirts and made their way to Mrs Jane Fenton's wing of the mansion.

'They are in the taxidermy rooms,' the doorman announced. 'Allow me to show you there.'

'Please do not trouble yourself, we know the way,' Matilda assured him, not at all happy that she would have to pass through that terrible hall again with all the animals on display.

'Why would they be back in there?' Phoebe said, as they hurried along. 'Perhaps we should not go in after all.'

'I was thinking the same thing,' Matilda said, 'but now that we are on our way.'

Georgina gave a small laugh.

'I am always leading you into trouble, Georgina, I'm sorry,' Matilda said with an affectionate smile to her dear friend.

'I wouldn't have it any other way,' Georgina assured her.

'Come this way,' Phoebe said with sensitivity. 'I think we can avoid the display room then.'

'Thank you, that would be appreciated,' Matilda said, and Phoebe was found to be correct. Moments later they arrived at the room in question.

'They are not here,' Phoebe exclaimed as she entered and the ladies followed her in.

'That is most odd,' Matilda agreed. As she studied the room, she asked Phoebe: 'Is this the sort of room where a person could be embalmed? Not just animals?'

'Absolutely,' Phoebe answered. 'This table is perfect for

the job, and the area is spotless and cool which is ideal for the body's preservation.'

'Where to next then ladies?' Georgina asked. 'We should have left a trail of breadcrumbs to find our way back. Although that might not be the best thing to say with all the poor dead birds next door,' she mused.

'Look at this. It is the product I use,' Phoebe said, reading some of the bottles on a shelf.

'I saw it earlier and intended to seek your input. I didn't know taxidermists used the same products as embalmers,' Matilda said with interest.

'They don't,' Phoebe assured her. 'When I embalm, it preserves the body intact, but a taxidermist uses the creature's own skin mounted on an anatomical form.' She glanced at Matilda. 'Sorry, that is a little hard to hear.'

'That is fine,' Matilda assured her. 'I am not usually distressed by the workings of things. But seeing that room with all those poor creatures...'

'So, if a taxidermist and embalmer use different products, it begs the question...' Georgina started and looked at Matilda with a raised eyebrow.

'It does indeed, Georgina, you are developing a good nose for a story,' Matilda said with a smile. 'If they are different techniques, why is there embalming fluid in here?'

Phoebe lowered her voice. 'You know, the pyjama girl was embalmed and not professionally. Please keep that to yourself.'

Matilda gasped. 'She was Mr Fenton's girlfriend. Oh dear, does everyone know that or have I let slip a police secret? Best keep that to yourself just in case.'

'I think we might be in a very dangerous place,' Georgina said, with a glance to the door. 'Let us get back to the entrance hallway now.'

Matilda heard Georgina's words but her curiosity took over. 'I wonder if Thomas and Detective Dart have been here? Thomas was not happy about us being in Mr Fenton's company the other evening. Now I understand why.' She looked under the table and opened some drawers.

'What are you looking for?' Phoebe asked, emulating her to help.

'Something, nothing, I don't know. A clue,' she said and gave a laugh as if they were on a great adventure.

And then she found it. Opening a large cabinet, Matilda screamed with fright and stepped back, bumping into Phoebe.

The eyes of a young woman stared straight at her.

Chapter 45

T homas leapt to his feet. 'That scream, where did it come from?' he rushed to the room's entranceway. 'Harry, it might be Matilda!'

'This way,' Sydney Fenton said, brushing past him, and hurriedly leading the way down the hallway with Thomas and Detective Dart in pursuit.

'Stay calm, Thom, keep your head,' Harry said, hastening along beside him.

The three men burst into the taxidermy room to find the ladies pale and shaken.

'Thomas!' Matilda exclaimed on seeing him. 'It is the most awful sight,' she said still standing in front of the cupboard just opened.

Thoughts of his nightmare rushed back to him as her words were eerily similar. He raced to her side and pulled her away, guiding Phoebe and Georgina in the same direction. She allowed him to lead her; everything about him said strength.

'Ladies, please,' he indicated the corner where nothing could be seen. 'Wait here for us and we will escort you out.'

He studied Matilda's face as he led her there. 'Are you alright?' She gave a nod but said nothing.

'Everything will be alright now,' he said, quietly, taking charge and waiting for her to nod her understanding. He glanced at the other two ladies who turned their attention to Sydney Fenton as the poet pushed past the group and went to peer in the cupboard. His reaction as he reeled back in horror told Thomas and Harry everything they needed to know. He did not know about the embalmed woman in the room's storage area.

'Maud!' he exclaimed. His hands went to his face as his mother appeared in the doorway.

'I left you in the garden,' she snapped at the three young ladies.

'But you left one of us in the cupboard,' Phoebe retorted.

'I thought Maud abandoned me. I never knew why when we made plans to marry,' Sydney was saying to Harry at his side. He reached out to touch her, still beautiful, frighteningly lifelike but snapped to look at his mother instead. 'Why?'

'You need to ask me that, Sydney?' she said, as cool as if she were entertaining guests and not about to be outed and punished for her crime.

'Edith… did you do this to Edith as well? Where is she?' Sydney asked, and then looked even more alarmed if it were possible. 'You told me you found Sara dead at the front gate and you would help preserve her for me forever. Did you kill her?' He stepped menacingly towards his mother until

Harry intervened, keeping them apart. It was the most passionate that Thomas had ever seen Sydney Fenton.

Mrs Jane Fenton put her chin up defiantly. 'You were intent on ruining this family and our future line with your actresses and showgirls. I did what any discerning parent would do.'

'Kill and embalm the suitors?' Thomas asked, astonished.

'My father threatened to feed a few of my suitors to the pigs, but it was only said in jest,' Georgina added from the corner.

Thomas saw Harry repress a smile, while Phoebe giggled. Matilda stood wide-eyed with a look Thomas recognised as shock. He wanted to run to her and assure her all would be well, but in a room full of people, with a case breaking, she was safe there while he managed the fallout around him.

'Call for one of your staff for me please,' Thomas ordered Sydney. Mrs Fenton who stood in the doorway overstepped and called out for her butler who arrived in seconds.

Thomas instructed him: 'Take a horse or the carriage and go straight to the Roma Street police station. Tell the Desk Sergeant that Detective Ashdown requests back-up urgently and give your address.' The butler looked to Mrs Fenton for approval.

'Just do it or you will find yourself in the lockup,' Harry snapped at the man.

Mrs Fenton gave a nod of approval and her man hurriedly left. Thomas fixed his gaze on Mrs Fenton as if anticipating she might do some further act of harm to the ladies present.

'Why?' A small voice asked.

Everyone turned to look at Matilda. It was a simple question and the reason behind it was the hardest to fathom.

'Why not just talk your son out of the engagements?' Matilda continued, her eyes affixed on Mrs Fenton. 'Why not allow him to marry whom he loves? Why did you embalm them? Why was Miss Wilford left on the church steps?'

Thomas's concern for her overran his frustration. They were the questions he most wanted to ask as well.

Mrs Fenton threw her hands up in the air as if in despair that nobody understood her actions.

'Because you got away with it,' Phoebe said, and Mrs Fenton gave a small smile as if she had outsmarted the world until now.

'But no longer,' Thomas added. 'And the author Mr Linton Turner's role in this?'

'Mr Turner, Mr Sutton and I had a deal,' she said, and Sydney gasped.

'My friend Percy? What… was he involved?'

'Yes. Given Mr Turner did not do his part, Mr Sutton delivered.'

'Delivered what?' Sydney snapped.

'Oh, Sydney,' his mother said with a sigh. 'You might be in the fortunate position of having all your needs met with your inheritance and your poetry, but Mr Sutton is not.'

'Percy could have told me if he needed money,' Sydney said, frowning with disbelief at the scenario opening around him.

'No man likes to beg for charity, Son. So, I gave him a handsome income to do a small job for me.'

'Kill three women?' Harry asked.

'No, not that. Claiming a debt.'

And with that, she said no more until the police arrived to take her away.

*****

Within two days of the dreadful discovery at the Fenton mansion, Mrs Jane Fenton, Mr Percy Sutton and Mr Linton Turner had been charged with various offences from murder to misleading an investigation.

Matilda, having secured an interview with Mr Sydney Fenton and hearing exclusively the full story from Thomas, including quotes from the two detectives, completed her story for the *Women's Journal*. Georgina's illustration of the pyjama girl on the steps, the embalmed corpse of Miss Maud Mandon and the arrest of Mrs Jane Fenton accompanied the story.

Mrs Lawson declared Matilda and Georgina had surpassed all expectations.

Women's Journal
Tuesday, 12 March 1889
Fortnightly   edition   Vol.1,   No.36.
Price, 3d.

Death of the unsuitable brides

FEATURE STORY: An exclusive interview
and a sad tale of love and loss that
started with the finding of a body on
the church steps of our town. Report
by Matilda Hayward. Illustrations by
Georgina Urry.

--oOo--

When an unfortunate young woman turned
up dead on the steps of St Mary's
Catholic   Church,   South   Brisbane,
dressed only in blue silk pyjamas, the
people of our town were aghast. Little
did we know that the young lady, later
to be identified as Miss Sara-Anne
Wilford, would be the first of three
women to be found dead and embalmed by
a mother intent on securing the right
bride for her son.

The people involved in this dastardly tale read like a cast from a stage play or a book. There is Mrs Jane Fenton of Spring Hill, known for her benevolent work for the community and charity groups. The Fenton name is well respected, their home is a landmark of our city, and her son, Sydney, a talented and renowned poet. Mr Sydney Fenton may also lay claim to being a victim of our story.

Also involved was Mr Linton Turner, an author, whose recent best-selling tale, 'The Pyjama Girl Mystery' is sold-out on its first print run. The author first met the deceased – the 'pyjama girl'– at the Quill Club where members of the Valley Literary Association gathered. Mr Sydney Fenton was also a member and frequented the club.

Amongst our cast is Mr Percy Sutton – the close companion of the poet, Mr Sydney Fenton, and himself a club associate and member of the Valley Literary Association.

Also in the names of players are three ladies, all formerly engaged to Mr Sydney Fenton – Miss Maud Mandon,

Miss Edith Dobin and Miss Sara-Anne Wilford, the latter who for a brief while, we knew as the pyjama girl.

Her friend, Miss Kate Chivers described Miss Wilford as a great beauty, kind and talented. What follows is shocking and not for the fainthearted reader. Steel yourself, readers, for what is to come.

Miss Wilford was once the beloved girlfriend and soon-to-be wife of the author, Mr Turner. But Miss Wilford jilted her successful beau when she claimed to have met her true love, poet Mr Sydney Fenton.

'Our love was all-consuming,' Mr Fenton, poet in residence at the Arts Centre, told the Women's Journal. Miss Wilford was his third fiancée over the period of three years. He believed the first fiancée, Miss Maud Mandon, had changed her mind and abandoned him. His second fiancée, Miss Edith Mary Dobin, also left him. Her family have been searching for her for several years but never believed Mr Fenton to be of blame.

'I was broken-hearted by Maud and Edith's deception,' Mr Fenton said, claiming it accelerated his melancholy belief he would never find love and was not worthy of it. Little did he know the women did not leave him but were murdered.

His despair was perpetuated when Miss Sara-Anne Wilford was found dead at the front gates of his mansion.

'She was brutally bashed and I could not bear to see her that way,' Mr Fenton said. 'I washed and prepared her for death so she might be as beautiful in the next life as she was in this life. It was all I could do for her.'

Well-respected detectives from the Roma Street Police Headquarters, Detectives Harry Dart and Thomas Ashdown, were bemused as to why Miss Sara-Anne Wilford's death was not reported when she was found dead at the gates of the Fenton mansion.

But Mr Fenton was convinced she had met an accident and when his mother, Mrs Jane Fenton, offered to embalm Miss Wilford using the room where Mr James Fenton (deceased) once practised his taxidermy work, Mr Sydney Fenton accepted so that his beloved could be with him forever. A strange request perhaps, but according to Mr Fenton 'not for a poet and her lover.' She was not however to remain with him forever as planned.

'My beloved Sara-Anne disappeared from where I laid her to rest in our family vault where I could talk with her at my leisure,' Mr Fenton said. 'When I read of a woman found in the pyjamas on the church step, I knew this to be the plot of Mr Turner's new book but I never thought it would be Sara-Anne.'

Detectives were unable to identify the pyjama girl and sought the assistance of Miss Phoebe Astin from The Economic Undertaker to create a lifelike image for distribution.

Author, Mr Linton Turner, assured the detectives it was not an event he had construed to promote his book and he would never stoop to such a dishonourable deed.

After extensive police work, Detectives Dart and Ashdown discovered all three fiancees were missing and one of the ladies, Miss Edith Dobin, had been incorrectly identified when a woman's body was found in the river and buried recently.

In a macabre and shocking twist, the detectives - having worked out Mrs Fenton's involvement - arrived to speak with her as yours truly, along with Miss Georgina Urry, Women's Journal illustrator, and Miss Phoebe Astin of The Economic Undertaker were attending a luncheon at the Fenton mansion.

In a moment of horror, we shockingly discovered the embalmed body of Miss Maud Mandon and the detectives with post-haste found the remains of Miss Edith Dobin in another storage area.

The question remains why these young women's lives were cut short. The answer is simple - their future mother-in-law did not deem them suitable. Mrs Jane Fenton invited each of the ladies around for morning tea and using poison most effectively, the ladies did not leave the premises alive.

The pyjama girl - Miss Sara-Anne Wilford was the exception. A fight ensued at morning tea when Miss Wilford wilfully refused to break off her engagement and in anger, Mrs Fenton struck a blow to Miss Wilford's head, killing her.

Detective Ashdown said of the

confession received from the lady of the house: 'Mrs Fenton did not believe the ladies suitable for her son and the future of the Fenton name and fortune. The ladies' remains will be returned to their families for burial.'

But there was another twist to this macabre tale - the involvement of author, Mr Linton Turner and Mr Sydney Fenton's close friend and associate, Mr Percy Sutton.

Mr Turner was not involved in the treacherous murders and hiding of the corpses, but we now know that working with Mrs Jane Fenton, he did indeed encourage some misadventure.

Detective Harry Dart said: 'Having heard from Mr Percy Sutton of her son's fondness for Miss Sara-Anne Wilford and the young lady's relationship with Mr Turner, Mrs Fenton paid the author a large sum of money which sustained him between books, to offer his hand in marriage to Miss Wilford, thus removing the lady from her son's life.'

Detective Ashdown added: 'Mr Turner happily agreed and fell in love with Miss Wilford. However, she left of her own free will and therefore Mr Turner did not believe he reneged on the deal nor should he return the sum paid.'

Mr Percy Sutton, unbeknown to his best friend, Sydney, was on Mrs Fenton's payroll. His role was to advise the poet's mother of unsuitable liaisons and on hearing of Mr Turner's refusal to pay back the money, he concocted a plan.

Well familiar with the plot of Mr Turner's new book from the reading at their club, Mr Percy Sutton suggested to Mrs Fenton that she could seek revenge by staging the scene from the book to incriminate Mr Turner. She willingly agreed.

It was Mr Percy Sutton who left the body of Miss Wilford on the church steps. However, detectives were not so quick to point the finger at the author, despite the attention the crime drew to Mr Turner's book. They were, as always, right.

And so there lies a sorry tale for three young ladies who did nothing more than fall in love with the wrong man, and a young man betrayed by his mother and best friend, and robbed of love deemed not suitable.

Chapter 46

On the very evening after Mrs Fenton was taken away and the bodies removed from the Fenton mansion, before the story ran, before the interviews were granted to Matilda, before Georgina completed her last illustration, and before the town and country learned of the heinous and duplicitous crime, Thomas was in agony. It was nearing eight o'clock that evening when he finally escaped his duties to check on his fiancée's state of health after the shock she received. The sun had set on a very warm February day and Thomas could see the lit lamps of the Hayward household glowing through the windows as he made his way up the path.

Arriving at the front door, he gave a light knock and entered, knowing that Harriet had most likely left for the day, along with Mary the cook. He had been told he did not need to knock, but until he was married to Matilda, he remained in the doorway until he heard footsteps coming from the drawing-room.

'It is just me, Elijah,' he said, pleased to see that of all the brothers present, the doctor was in the house.

'Thom, come in, don't stand on ceremony. Join us. Father and I are having a port,' Elijah said. 'Daniel is out with Alice.'

'I've come to check on Matilda,' Thomas said.

'Of course,' Elijah said and gave a small laugh. 'I forget sometimes that your focus has changed. I insisted she take to bed, come in and we'll talk.'

Thomas's brow furrowed with concern; he removed his hat and followed Elijah into the drawing-room, where he greeted Mr Hayward and accepted a glass of his fine port.

'Have you eaten, Son?' Mr Hayward asked. 'We'll rustle you up a meal.'

'Do not go to any trouble, Sir, thank you. Teddy will have a plate warm for me when I get home.'

'I believe congratulations are in order,' Mr Hayward continued. 'Another case solved, albeit a very tragic one.'

'Yes,' Thomas said, accepting a seat and impatient to see Matilda. He glanced to the doorway hoping she would hear his voice and appear, before returning his attention to the men. 'I must say, not much shocks me these days, but this one certainly did.'

'Perhaps that is a good thing,' Elijah said.

'I am worried about Matilda. What she saw...'

Elijah nodded. 'She was shocked, it was a terrible fright and Tillie doesn't shock easily.'

'And Georgina?' Thomas remembered to ask after Elijah's belle.

'I paid her a call and she is fine, thank you,' Elijah said.

'Georgina is a little hardier in matters of death and was forewarned before she saw the body. I called on Miss Astin at *The Economic Undertaker* too, and found her to be quite well.'

'Thank you. It is the unexpected that affects us,' Thomas agreed. 'We are trained to imagine the scene before arriving to lessen the shock.'

'Does that work for you most times, Thom?' Mr Hayward asked.

'Surprisingly it does, Sir. But for Tillie opening that cupboard and finding an embalmed lady looking at her...' He gave a small shake of his head and sighed. 'I hoped to see her.'

'I know,' Elijah said, 'but let me assure you she is fine. She showed no signs of distress or illness, but Harriet and I put her to bed with some of Cook's soup that heals all, and she agreed to rest.'

Thomas smiled. 'I remember that Irish broth. Heals bones too from memory.'

Mr Hayward and Elijah laughed, and Mr Hayward rose.

'Let me see if she is awake, Thom, since you are anxious.'

'I don't want to put you to any trouble,' Thomas said.

Mr Hayward gave him a wave of his hand to relax. 'I know you, Thom. You will fidget and be distressed until your mind is at rest. One moment if you please.'

'Thank you, Sir,' Thomas said, and exhaled with relief. He turned to find Elijah smiling at him.

'It is a wonderful thing that you and Tillie are together, and still a little strange,' Elijah said.

'It would be stranger not to be together,' Thomas said. 'I couldn't imagine coming to visit with Daniel and seeing Matilda with someone else.'

'Well now that you mention it, that would seem strange,' Elijah agreed.

'Thank you for looking after all three ladies,' Thomas added. 'Georgina is a good influence on Tillie and has such a good head on her shoulders.'

'She is very pragmatic, her most endearing quality,' Elijah said, and the men shared a laugh as Thomas recounted Georgina's comment under duress and warned Elijah to behave or he might be fed to the pigs by Mr Urry.

Mr Hayward entered and Thomas shot to his feet. 'Is she—'

'Awake and keen to see you, Thom. She will be down momentarily,' Mr Hayward said, and smiled at the look of relief on Thomas's face.

'Thank you, Sir. I am grateful to you but I see I displeased Elijah that I have stirred his patient.'

Elijah gave his future brother-in-law a wry look. 'I shall let you off on this occasion, but only because you are family,' he said in jest.

And then Matilda entered in a simple house dress, her hair loose around her shoulders. Thomas's eyes brightened when he saw the beautiful form of his beloved standing in the doorway and rushed to her side, unconcerned about the audience of two watching. He had been so worried for her all afternoon that he could barely focus on his work.

He took her hands. 'Tell me you are feeling well?' he said, his voice betraying a strong current of emotions.

'I am fine, you need not have been concerned,' she said, and narrowed her eyes at him. 'You know me.'

'Yes,' he said and kissed her hand. 'But seeing that terrible sight is far worse than anything you have seen before I am sure, even with four unattractive brothers,' he teased, and Matilda and Mr Hayward laughed as Elijah protested.

'Elijah, if you will,' Mr Hayward started, 'I need your help for ten minutes in my study?'

'Of course,' Elijah agreed.

Thomas nodded his thanks to Mr Hayward, and Elijah smiled, understanding the ruse. Thomas had ten minutes and he planned to use them well.

'I am so sorry I could not come to you sooner; I have been worried all afternoon.' Thomas looked down upon her face.

'I understand, Thomas. You had work to do and tomorrow I shall pursue the same.' She touched his face. 'I am hardier than you think... I did not enjoy a robust childhood to become a swooning woman now.'

'I know. But the first time one sees something of a horrendous nature can have an impact; by the second time we are a little more seasoned.'

'Do not forget I have seen several crime scenes and dead bodies at Phoebe's place of work.'

'But not one unexpectedly hiding in a cupboard,' he said wryly, and she smiled, conceding the point. 'I have but a few minutes with you and I don't wish to speak of bodies.'

'What did you want to speak of then?' she asked with interest.

'Nothing. Kiss me and I shall relax and sleep well for the rest of the evening.'

Matilda smiled. 'In a short while, I shall be resting beside you every evening.'

'I know,' he said, touching her hair and trailing his fingers over it. He inhaled her delicate scent and studied her face so achingly familiar and beautiful. 'Kiss me.'

Matilda glanced to the doorway and moving up on her toes, leaned forward and pressed her lips to Thomas's. He felt his body physically relax. It was not the first time he had stolen a kiss or two, but tonight he needed it more than ever.

As she pulled away, he moved closer, feeling her small frame through the fabric of her cotton dress. He lowered his head and sought her lips again, and then hearing footsteps, straightened and stepped back putting space between them, but still holding Matilda's hands.

'Thank you,' he said, and gave her a small smile which did nothing to convey the intense feelings swirling within him from the effort of pulling away.

'You always had a way of getting your own way,' she said, teasing him.

'That's not how I remember it,' he said.

'Remember what?' Elijah asked, re-entering the room with his father.

'Which one of us got our own way the most,' Thomas said.

'Definitely Tillie,' Mr Hayward said, and laughed on seeing Matilda's indignant expression. 'Well, it is true my dear. As our beloved only girl, and Gideon the youngest boy by twelve minutes,' he said with a glance at Gideon's twin, Elijah, 'you were both indulged, and I suspect nothing has changed.'

'I best be leaving then,' Thomas said. 'Thank you, Mr Hayward, Elijah, I shall rest easy now.'

'I shall see you out,' Matilda said.

'I don't think so,' Elijah said, noting her informal dress and pulling rank as the family doctor. 'You shall return to bed and I shall see Thomas out, not that he needs an escort given he is family, but we do like to make sure he leaves.'

Thomas laughed, surprised at how good it felt to laugh. He felt lighter now.

'Be warned. Soon I shall leave and I shall take your Tillie with me,' he joked.

'Is your house ready for me yet?' she asked, as they wandered into the hallway and she took to the steps. 'I am not coming if not.'

Thomas stopped and looked at her wide-eyed and concerned. There was still some work to be done.

Matilda laughed at his expression.

'I think she can still wind you up, Thom,' Mr Hayward said, and Thomas's shoulders dropped and he gave her a well-earned smirk.

'Goodnight, Matilda,' he said formally.

'Good night sweet prince,' Matilda teased him, quoting *Hamlet*, and laughed as she turned and went upstairs. When she disappeared from sight, he turned to find Elijah and Mr Hayward smiling at him. Thomas cleared his throat and wished them goodnight, departing with their gentle laughter following him from the house.

He smiled all the way home. *Sweet prince.* Next month, they would be home together.

THE END

This work is a book of fiction, but as always, I have tried to be as accurate as possible and reflect the history of the day. As this novel is set in 1889, I based the autopsy thoughts by Dr Patrick Nevins on the autopsies of Jack the Ripper's victims in 1888. It was surprising how thorough and advanced post-mortem findings were in that era, with quite thorough examinations. I also discovered from Trove (the Australian National Library) that toxicologists in this period were very competent and were often brought in to court to share their findings during cases where poison was the alleged cause of murder.

The Economic Undertaker really existed. My husband, journalist, Chris Adams, discovered their faded old sign on the side of a building in Camberwell, Melbourne, Victoria, and always loved the title. He thought it would make for a good book, so I 'borrowed' it from him.

I have found little evidence that female cosmetic morticians existed in that era, but I did find images shared online of goods removed from a funeral parlour in the 1880s and mortician kits from the late 19th century that consisted of vintage mortuary cosmetics, embalmer's makeup, and mortician's powder including Royal Bond's *Life-Glo Tint*, De-Ce-Co's *Tinting Blending Powder* and jars of *Kalon Pigment* cream in peach and tan. Thus, Phoebe is possibly ahead of her time.

Mourning was a very serious business in the 19th century and a burial process might take up to eight days. But the Australian climate, and in the colony of Queensland where this book was set, the hot spring and summer meant bodies were put into the ground within two days. Post-mortem photography was rarely practised in the 19th century because of this hasty burial.

Most funerals in the Victorian era were conducted at home, with the body washed, dressed and placed on display for mourning. It was not the undertaker's job to wash or prepare the corpse but there were exceptions. For example, in the mid-1880s when a bachelor died suddenly, the mortician charged the estate ten shillings for completing this duty in the absence of family.

As the services of undertakers or funeral professionals developed, they often held several jobs to sustain their earnings – they might be carpenters or builders, made coffins, or provided carriage service that doubled for hearses as needed. Priests performed the services in most instances. For the purposes of my story, I have moved the story forward a few years where the funeral directors, namely *The Economic Undertaker,* took a more active role in the burial, and bodies were not kept in the home but taken to the funeral home or mortuary.

The exception was the hospital burials. Many of the hospitals in the mid-to-late 19th century had contracts with funeral directors to prepare and bury patients that died in hospital and had no one to claim them. For some undertakers it made up over fifty per cent of their business, and I have claimed some of this business for *The Economic Undertaker*.

By the end of the 19th century, the undertakers had stepped up in duties, thus they began calling themselves funeral directors and morticians rather than undertakers. Their role expanded to include preparation of the corpse including shaving the men, combing their hair, and arranging ladies' hair to appear as they did in life. In the late 19th century, some of the funeral homes offered a room for the family to gather privately.

As mentioned in the earlier author's note, the term *mortician* came about in 1895 when *The Embalmers' Monthly* magazine suggested the industry needed a new name that was less confronting than undertaker. Hence mort plus physician became mortician. The word 'mort' meaning death had been around for centuries. Not long into the 20th century, the full-service funeral director/mortician became the normal model. It must have been a relief for relatives who preferred to have a funeral director undertake the work, due to heat and/or few family members in the 'new' country.

I found the information on how to embalm a body from an article on the Brunelli process for embalming in 1882.

There really was a pyjama girl mystery but not until much later in 1934, as crime buffs will remember. A poor young lady was murdered and remained unidentified for quite some time. She was embalmed and put on display to the public. Despite the young lady being eventually named as Linda Agostini, there is still contention to this day that the pyjama girl was not correctly identified and a lady lies in a wrongly marked grave.

The stories the ladies discussed at their work meeting such as the survey on what happened to women who divorced in that era, and the petition to prevent the hanging of Louisa Collins, were genuine news stories of the era.

"Whittington and his Cat" was playing at the Gaiety Theatre in January 1889 in Albert Street, Brisbane and Mr Watkins, as stated, was the manager of this fine establishment. Pleuro-pneumonia did take an awful toll on cattle in the year this book was set, not only in Australia but in other countries including the UK.

The poems I have reproduced were original pieces or poems I embellished from an 1889 Brisbane newspaper titled '*The Week*' and their '*Poets' Column*'. They were by various contributors who tried their hand at writing verse.

What a fascinating era!

My thanks:

I am in debt to the National Library of Australia – Trove. What would we do without this fine resource? I also came across some excellent resource material including the thesis of Hilda McLean listed below. For an entertaining and educational understating of the era, check out the video in the references below. *'Ask a Mortician'*– Kate Lynn is a genius.

My thanks to Penny Clarkson for her proofreading prowess!

Also in the *Miss Hayward and the Detective* series…

Murder at the Freak Show

Matilda Hayward is determined to have a career; after all, it is 1888! While reporting for the *Women's Journal* newspaper, Matilda is sent to cover the visiting 'Freak Show' and to interview Mrs Anna Tufton, a giantess. During the interview, the giantess slips a note to Matilda begging for her help to escape from the show she is forced to do by her husband. But when the giantess's husband is found murdered, the giantess is a likely suspect.

Matilda enlists her lawyer brother, Amos, to help prove the giantess is no killer and to free her from a life of exploitation. But a close family friend, Detective Thomas Ashdown – who has feelings for Matilda having known her since childhood – would prefer Matilda was nowhere near his murder case. There is mystery, danger, and love afoot!

The Artist's Missing Muse

Miss Matilda Hayward admits she is no art critic but when she meets artist, Mr Marlon Dominey, and his beautiful muse, Miss Sapphire Reubens, she can appreciate beauty on and off the canvas. Her brother and art gallery manager, Gideon, is to exhibit Mr Dominey's latest collection and Matilda and Miss Alice Doran – her fellow writer for the *Women's Journal* – get a preview of the inspired work featuring his muse illuminated and immersed in water.

But when muse, Miss Reubens, can't be found, and two artists are found murdered and posed in the manner of their paintings, Matilda and her new beau, Detective Thomas Ashdown, fear the artwork might be a death portrait. There is mystery, passion and love afoot!

Mystery at the Asylum

Miss Matilda Hayward has a nose for a story which serves her well as a writer for the *Women's Journal* newspaper. Her beau, Detective Thomas Ashdown, is not quite as enthusiastic about her role. When Matilda's brother, Elijah, takes up a doctor's position at the Asylum for the Insane, she volunteers, seeking more life experience to improve her writing. Joined by her illustrator friend, Miss Georgina Urry, the two ladies are thrust into the mystery of several strange asylum deaths as patients believe they can fly. When Thomas is sent to investigate, their worlds collide. Now the race is on to find the sinister threat dwelling inside the dark and gloomy walls of the asylum.

There is secrecy, danger, and love afoot!

Murder in Bridal Lane

Miss Matilda Hayward has a wedding to plan and while ordering her bridal bouquet in Bridal Lane, she finds a note in her sample bouquet requesting a liaison. Innocently believing the note to be a mix-up, Matilda engages her brother, Daniel, to attend the liaison with her, but the young paramour rushes off. He is later found beaten and bruised in an alley off Bridal Lane by Matilda's fiancé, Detective Thomas Ashdown, and his partner, Detective Harry Dart.

When a respected lacemaker is also found murdered in the same laneway, the note takes on a new significance. Matilda is assigned to write the obituary for the Women's Journal with her illustrator friend, Miss Georgina Urry, and soon finds herself embroiled in danger in the middle of a murder case, much to her fiancé's displeasure. There is mystery, danger, and love afoot before Matilda makes it to the altar!

Coming next... The Lady Mortician's Visions series:

The Missing Brides
Miss Phoebe Astin and her brothers, Julius and Ambrose, lead an unconventional life working in the family funeral business – The Economic Undertaker. But Phoebe is not just a talented mortician, she is a medium for the spirit world, and often enjoys the company of her clients before they move on to the next world. When one gentleman begs her to investigate his murder, Phoebe contacts her brother's friend, Detective Harland Stone, and soon she finds there are several missing brides, feared murdered. For the Astin family, being dead is no excuse for letting crime go unpunished!

The Fake Child
The Doll House Collector.

You might also enjoy by this author...

The Forgotten House (historical fiction):

"If you've ever been truly in love, you'll identify with Lexie and James." Judy Alter, Story Circle Book Reviews.

Once the grandest of homes, now deserted and ramshackle; Autumn Manor lies in ruins. But when Carrie Howell asks her granddaughter, Rachael, to stop awhile in front of the old mansion, Rachel decides to investigate the house's history. Behind the facade, she finds a love story interrupted by war. Who were these people her grandmother was remembering, and what was her connection?

Jesse Clarke series (cosy mysteries):

Death by Sugar:

"If you are a fan of Kathryn Ledson or Janet Evanovich you will love unravelling the mysteries in the Jesse Clarke series." Carol, Reading, Writing and Riesling.

Private investigator, Jesse Clarke, thought sugar was such a friendly substance, until it appeared in two of her cases for all the wrong reasons. Traces of sugar were connected to a bomb that blew up her client's Mercedes. Was the bomb meant to kill or was it just a warning of what was to come? And could sugar have duped the immune system of a client's mother over thirty years ago, resulting in death? Juggling the two cases—one in the present and one in the past—Jesse finds herself talking to the living and the dead to get results.

Death by Disguise:

"A fantastic read that had me laughing; it thoroughly surprised me!" Christine – Goodreads

The dead are walking and it is not even Halloween! Sassy private investigator Jesse Clarke knew it would not be a normal week when two dead people are spotted alive but their death certificates say otherwise, Spiderman steals a collection of costumes made for the next Comic-Con, and Batman drops in to warn her that all is not as it seems. Supported by her own man of steel—the tall, dark and handsome Dominic; business partner Ed; police contact Officer Jason who has more than a professional interest in Jesse; and, best friend Melanie, Jesse finds herself talking to witches, superheroes and morticians to solve her two cases and looking behind the disguises for answers!

Death by Reunion:

Jesse Clarke's 10-year school reunion boasted a few shocks – and that didn't include Jesse running a publicity and private investigator business. Rather, the talk of the reunion was

Alex Bryson, the overweight kid who transformed himself thanks to winning a place on the TV reality program, Lose it! But a week after the reunion, Alex is dead. That's not the only reunion that's taking up Jesse's time. At a family reunion and 80th birthday celebration for a family matriarch, a very expensive Titanic relic goes missing – a Titanic Mourning Bear. And now T-Bear, as he is known, is showing up all over the country! With support from her boyfriend, Dominic, along with her grumpy business partner Ed, Police Officer Jason, and Jesse's enthusiastic best friend, Melanie, Jesse is back solving mysteries while juggling publicity clients include Mona and her choir, again.

About the Author:

After studying English Literature and Communications at universities in Queensland, Australia, and obtaining a Counselling Diploma, Helen Goltz has worked as a journalist, producer and marketer in print, TV, radio and public relations. She was born in Toowoomba and has made her home in Brisbane.

Visit Helen's website at: www.helengoltz.com

Or Facebook at: www.facebook.com/HelenGoltz.Author

Follow on Twitter at: https://twitter.com/HelenGwriter

To hear of new releases and discount books, please follow Helen on **BookBub.**

References:

Ask a Mortician, *We Recreated a Victorian Funeral*. https://youtu.be/0OlF-EtoGBo

Maclean, Hilda Erica, *Funerary consumption in the second half of the 19th century in Brisbane, Queensland*. A thesis submitted for the degree of Doctor of Philosophy at The University of Queensland in 2015.

Okrent, Akira, How Morticians Reinvented Their Job Title, *The Mag*, 5 January, 2016. Retrieved 29 December 2021 from URL: https://www.mentalfloss.com/article/68177/how-morticians-reinvented-their-job-title

Remsberg, Virginia Russell, *From coffin-making to undertaking: The rise of the funeral directing industry in the 1880s*. A thesis submitted to the Faculty of the University of Delaware, August 1992.

Is Divorce a Failure? (1889, Jan 1). *The Brisbane Courier* (Qld.: 1864 - 1933), p. 7. Retrieved 24 Nov 2021, from http://nla.gov.au/nla.news-article3490633

Karyo Magellan, *The Victorian Medico-Legal Autopsy*, Part I: Dissection in Pursuit of the Cause of Death. This article originally appeared in Ripperologist No. 71, September 2006. Retrieved 29 November 2021 from URL: https://www.casebook.org/dissertations/rip-victorian-autopsy.html

Part II: The Whitechapel Murders - Autopsies and Surgeons – https://www.casebook.org/dissertations/rip-victorian-autopsy-2.html

Poets' Column. (1889, Mar 23). *The Week* (Bris, Qld.: 1876 - 1934), p. 28. Retrieved Nov 11, 2021, from http://nla.gov.au/nla.news-article186195079

Second chance poem inspiration from two sources: Poets' Column. (1887, September 17). *The Week (Brisbane, Qld.: 1876 - 1934)*, p. 34. Retrieved December 7, 2021, from http://nla.gov.au/nla.news-article182629205 and Poets' Column. (1887, August 20). *The Week (Brisbane, Qld.: 1876 - 1934)*, p. 5. Retrieved December 7, 2021, from http://nla.gov.au/nla.news-article182628423

Science. (1882, July 27). *The Shoalhaven Telegraph (NSW: 1881 - 1937)*, p. 2 (Our Literary Supplement.). Retrieved December 22, 2021, from http://nla.gov.au/nla.news-article128604254